the
RODEO
ROAD

the RODEO ROAD

Johny Weber

Hildebrand Books

an imprint of W. Brand Publishing

NASHVILLE, TENNESSEE

This is a work of fiction. However, the author has interspersed throughout this fictional story actual events and people whom she knew from the early 1970s when she traveled with her husband on the rodeo road. Ride along with her in this fictional story and see if you can find the actual events as she remembers them. Check out the Author Note at the end of the story to see if you are correct.

Hildebrand Books an imprint of W. Brand Publishing
j.brand@wbrandpub.com
www.wbrandpub.com

Cover design by JuLee Brand : designchik

The Rodeo Road / Johny Weber — 1st Edition

Available in Paperback, Kindle, and eBook formats.
Paperback ISBN: **979-8-89503-000-4**
eBook ISBN: **979-8-89503-001-1**
Library of Congress Control Number: 2024922005

CONTENTS

To my favorite horsewomen who are always there for me, Judy, Renee, Adele, and Teri, and to the men and women of Korkow Rodeos who welcomed me into their world of rodeo so very long ago.

It was the scream that woke her. She roused in a cold sweat, trying to push the sleep and confusion from her mind. It was pitch black, and she was disoriented. Then she realized the scream came from her. It was her own scream that woke her.

She heard the dog whimper and then her mind cleared. She was in her pickup camper and the old dog was on the floor beneath her over-the-cab bed. The dog heard her scream and was worried about her. She moved to the bottom of the bed, feeling her way in the dark to the edge, then finding the foot holds on the counter, then the storage box, and then the floor. She sank to the floor and let the dog crowd in on her, climbing into her lap. She held her, trying to slow her own breathing, trying to relax.

The damn nightmare came back to haunt her again. Just when she thought the nightmares would quit, another one came. In it, she screamed when the car went over the embankment and started to roll. She wondered if she had screamed when the accident happened. She didn't remember, only remembered the car, rolling and tumbling before coming to a stop. Then just the stillness, the blood, and the fear.

Groping for a flashlight, she flicked it on and found an old denim shirt, pulling it on over her T-shirt and shorts.

"Come on, Little Girl," she said to the old dog. "Let's check the horses."

She climbed out into the coolness of the June night, helping the old dog down the big step from the back of the camper to the ground. Using the flashlight, she found the horses tied to the trailer. *Where was she?* She shook her head, trying to get the brain waves going. *She was somewhere in Nebraska, pulled over in a fairground. What was the town? Rockford, no. . . Pickford, no. . .Thedford. That was it. She was in Thedford, Nebraska.*

She got to Thedford about an hour before dark and saw the fairground's gate standing wide open. She was tired, so she pulled in and let the horses graze on hobbles for an hour, and then had their hay bags and water ready at the trailer for them. She was lucky that the water hydrants were turned on for the summer. The horses had plenty to drink.

No one came and asked her what she was doing or told her to leave. That was the beauty of western towns. They welcomed visitors. The gates were open; "Come right in." So, she had driven her shiny red 1972 Ford one-ton pickup through the gates, found a level spot, and parked. Her parents had gotten her the new pickup with camper and trailer for a combination high school graduation, birthday, and Christmas present before she left for college last fall. She loved it, but never thought it would be her home. How times and circumstances change.

She checked the horses' hay bags and water buckets. They still had plenty of feed and water. That was good. She would have to leave early to make St. Onge in time for the rodeo. She wanted the horses full of feed and water when she loaded them. She should have checked her watch before she left the camper. It might be close to morning now. Maybe she should just get dressed and head out. She didn't think she would sleep again. She would be afraid of the dream coming back. It did that once, came back right after she laid back down.

She took a big breath, leaning against her gelding. He bent his neck, his muzzle searching for a treat.

"No treats in my sleeping T-shirt," she whispered, giving him a scratch under the chin. "I'll get you oats before we leave in the morning."

Satisfied, the gelding pulled a whisp of hay from the hanging bag and chomped on it, the sound relaxing the girl. She reached up and gave the gelding a stroke on his neck, then did the same to the mare. Calling the dog, she went to the camper. She had to help the old dog up the step to get inside. Then climbing into the camper herself, she pulled a quilt off the bed and curled up with the dog in the corner on the floor. Maybe she could doze. Maybe she could sleep. But she would do that with the comfort of a living thing with her. She hugged the dog close to her. Maybe Little Girl would help keep the nightmare at bay.

CHAPTER 1

SOUTH DAKOTA

The mid-morning sun baked the earth while faint cool breezes brought relief. Early summer had come to South Dakota and had brought with it warm, sunny days and clear, cool nights. Within sight of the Black Hills, the rolling terrain and grassy plains were green with summer growth.

The rodeo grounds were a mixture of bustling activity and lazy tranquility. In the arena and sorting pens, stock was being sorted and penned for the afternoon performance. The stock that wouldn't be used that day were turned out in an adjoining pasture, while the horses and bulls to be used were held in pens, ready for the upcoming performance.

Beyond the activity of the arena and above the hill that was the natural grandstand of this rodeo grounds, lay the temporary home of many. A jumbled mass of campers, pickups, cars, trucks, and trailers folded themselves along the grassy plains around the top of the hill. These were all contestants. The vehicles for the audience would come in a different gate and park adjacent to the arena. Here, on the flat above the arena, the contestants drove up and parked, insulating themselves from the crowds that would soon come and find a place to throw down a blanket or open up a chair on the hillside to watch the rodeo.

Among the mix of vehicles, horses stood tied to trailers, contentedly munching hay or dozing in the warm sun. An amusing test of skill was being displayed by some young ropers as they tried to see who could rope a bale of hay the fastest. Beside a small blue and white camper trailer, a table sat in the sun and was the scene of a lazy game of "cowboy pitch." There was laughter at the table as the hand finished. Cole Sanders rose and stretched, facing the remaining four players.

"Have to go to work now, boys," he said seriously, but the crinkles along his weathered eyes belied his tone. "You cleaned me clear out of nickels and dimes."

He turned to go, then hesitated, his gaze following a late model red one-ton Ford pickup pulling a sixteen-foot bumper stock trailer. The pickup carried a bulky over-the-cab camper and moved slowly as it made its way up the hill and over the potholed trail.

"Who pulls a fancy rig like that?" he questioned as he watched the outfit wind through the maze of vehicles, looking for a place to pull in and park. "I don't think I've seen it before."

The card game hesitated a moment as all heads followed Sanders' gaze.

"Never seen it before," answered Ted Langley, a short, lithe cowboy who rode barebacks and bulls. "License plate is from Colorado, though."

"You've got good eyes," drawled Sanders as he strolled away, and the card game resumed.

Cole headed toward his vehicle, a three-quarter ton pickup pulling a small bumper stock trailer. He wondered if Ben had watered the horses. He didn't usually have to second-guess Ben, but Ben's girl was visiting this weekend from the nearby college where she was taking summer classes. Sometimes, a young man forgets everything when his girl turns up. Cole glanced around and didn't see Ben or Josie. They probably went down to the concession stand.

Cole was a saddle bronc and bull rider and was well-built for these events. He had powerful shoulders and forearms, big strong hands, and carried not a speck of extra weight. He was not tall, standing five feet, nine inches in stocking feet. He was starting to look at all these young cowboys coming up and seeing them as kids, a sure sign he was getting old. But then he had been on the circuit for closing in on twelve years. At thirty-two, Cole was a decade older than most of these young cowboys. He knew he was in the twilight of his rodeo career, but as long as he was healthy and riding well, he might as well try to make the finals again. It would be something to make it for the ninth time. Not many can do that. While Cole had never come out as number one for the year, he had finished second twice, and the go-round buckles on his shelves at home gathering dust showed he had not gone unnoticed. But now, instead of traveling with old partners, long since retired, he had a new traveling partner and a steer wrestler to boot. Ben Two Horse hauled the horses, although Cole owned them. Cole could leave extra clothes in their rig, hop in with other cowboys, and make double the rodeos Ben could make hauling the horses. Still, when Cole's schedule hit the rodeos Ben was at, clean clothes were waiting, and if there were no motels nearby, there was a somewhat comfortable bed in the back. It worked for both of them.

As Cole neared his outfit, he saw that the newly arrived rig had pulled into place next to his rig. He watched as a slight, brown-haired girl climbed from the cab and walked toward the rear of the trailer. At her heels trotted a good-looking blue heeler dog. Cole slowed, curious to see the type of horse this girl, obviously a barrel racer, would bring out of the trailer. He saw that even though the trailer initially looked big enough for four horses, the two horses the girl had stood in the middle of the trailer over the axles. That was when he realized that there was a roomy walk-in saddle compartment in the nose of the trailer.

The horses were loose in the trailer with halters and ropes flung over their withers. They had turned around and rode backward in the trailer. This was how Cole's horses liked to ride and why he pulled a small bumper stock trailer instead of a regular two-horse straight-load. He liked the room a stock trailer gave his horses, allowing them to move around and find the most comfortable way to ride. He tried a two-horse straight load trailer once, but didn't keep it very long. On the ranch, he and his parents only had stock trailers so why not get what the horses liked and were used to? Of course, Cole had a big gooseneck trailer on the ranch, but for the rodeo road, he liked having the topper on his pickup, which meant he could only pull a bumper trailer.

It took but a minute for the girl to unlatch the back gate and open it. Cole noticed the horses stood quietly until the girl had their lead ropes in hand and asked them to unload. They came out in tandem. The near horse was a big roan gelding, well-muscled and maybe a bit homely-headed, but a cowboy's horse, for sure. *That roan should be roping steers*, Cole thought. The other horse was hidden behind the gelding until the pair turned with the girl as she turned back to shut the trailer door. Cole could see then that the second horse was much smaller. It was a little bay mare, as compact a horse as it could be. She had a big heart girth and a pretty head, but was not showy. Both animals were responsive and well-mannered. They showed strength and no doubt had speed, and they were in top condition. The girl tied them to the trailer, and then noticed Cole opening the back of his camper topper.

"Sir," she called out, "could you tell me where I could get some water?"

Damn, thought Cole, *I must be getting old when a young babe like this called me "sir." Maybe it was time he thought about quitting.* He smiled inwardly at his thoughts. Cole turned and pointed toward the arena.

"There is a hose and faucet this side of the arena that they are using for the stock," he answered. "I am going to untie my two and head down with them if you want to walk along with me," Cole gestured toward the sorting chutes behind the arena.

Cole gathered his two geldings and grabbed a bucket, and they started toward the arena. The girl walked quietly beside him. Her horses took no notice of his two, which indicated to Cole they were used to being hauled and seeing other horses. It took horses a while to know they wouldn't get attacked by strange horses. It took being well-mannered too.

"Nice dog there," Cole smiled at the girl, breaking the silence. He noticed the heeler never left the side of the girl.

"She's is special," the girl smiled. "But she is getting old. She's losing her sight and her hearing. Hard to see them fail like this, but guess it is part of life." The girl smiled fondly at the old dog. "But she is still a hell of a cow dog; she just doesn't have a lot of endurance anymore. So basically, she is retired."

Silence settled around them again. She isn't much of a talker, Cole thought. Seems kind of shy, but polite.

He found himself studying her as they walked. She was young. He guessed college-age. She had long brown hair with flecks of gold in it. She was slim, but shapely. You didn't miss that she was cute, but he could also tell she was reserved.

"Where you from?" he asked. "Can't say I remember seeing you before."

"I'm from Colorado," she replied, adding, "a small town in the mountains west of Denver a couple hours. I never traveled much before, always too busy around the place to get to more than a few shows and nearby rodeos."

"What brings you to South Dakota, then? You decide the place could make it without you?" he teased. They had reached the water, and they both set their buckets down. Cole began filling the girl's pail first.

The girl stood watching the bucket fill, keeping her horses back until it was done. It seemed as if she were oblivious to the question until the horses, both lowering their heads to drink together out of the pail, finally answered.

"Well, sir," she said softly, "there isn't any place any-more, so I had to move on." She didn't look at him. Cole fell silent with that. He wasn't quite sure what she meant by that comment. Had she lost a job or a home or a boyfriend? Whatever it was, there was a ring of sadness around the answer, and when he thought about it, maybe there was an aura of melancholy around this girl. Perhaps, it was that rather than being reserved that kept her so quiet.

"Sir," she spoke again, "where is the rodeo office? I have to pay my fees next."

"Girl, you got to quit this 'sir' stuff. You are making me feel like I'm old," Cole grinned at her. "My name is Cole Sanders." He stuck his hand out to her.

"I know that name," the girl replied, startled, shaking his hand. "You've been to the finals a bunch. Bulls and broncs." She looked at his horses. "I thought maybe you were a roper or dogger with these horses."

Cole laughed at her surprise, "Well, these are my horses, but I'm not a dogger. I don't have the size for it. Did that in high school where they usually used smaller steers, but bulls and broncs suit me better. I have a young neighbor who hauls these. He's the dogger. Long story, but his girlfriend is here this weekend, and I think the horses are not a priority at the moment."

Cole glanced toward the crow's nest. "I think the secretary should be up in the crow's nest now. The rodeo office is down the road in a gas station and grocery store combination, but as close as it is getting to the performance, she should be moved out here about now. I'd check up in the crow's nest after you get done with your horses." Cole pointed toward the back of the chutes, where there was a contestant walk-through gate. "Go up the stairs there."

"Thank you," the girl said. She picked up the water pail and dumped the remaining water from it. "I appreciate your help." She turned to go but then hesitated and turned back. "I'm Kasey Jacobs," she added solemnly. "It was nice to meet you." Then, leading her horses, she headed back to her trailer.

Cole watched her walk away for a minute. His horses needed the bucket refilled. When he looked up again, the girl and her horses had moved behind vehicles and were lost to sight. Cute gal, he thought, but sad. Or pretty as she was, maybe she was just one of those quiet, wallflower types. He watched his horses drink, and when they finished, he gathered up the pail and started back to his trailer. It was time to start thinking about the rodeo.

***

Kasey Ann Jacobs was just barely twenty years old, but usually taken for closer to eighteen. A small girl, only five feet three, she had big brown eyes and a slim figure. She was proud of her horses-her children, as she often called them. Her big red roan, aptly named Roan, was a past team roping horse. Somewhere along his road, he had been abused. When Kasey got him almost two years before, he could hardly be approached by a man. He was better now, but was what her dad's foreman, Walt, had called "watchy." The horse was always watching for some monster to jump out at him. Walt had helped her with the horse last summer until Roan began to understand that every man wouldn't beat him. For a long time, Kasey worked with the horse slowly and gently until he finally began to relax and trust her. He was used to crowds, though, and rodeo arenas. Commotion didn't scare him. A ten-year-old, Roan had been started on barrels when she got him. He hadn't competed but ran a good pattern in the home arena. Kasey had used him the last year of high school rodeo for barrels and breakaway roping. She wasn't good at roping, but she had caught her calves and at least made a good showing of it. She had fared only slightly better with the barrels and goat tying. They finished "up there" in the standings, just not up there enough to move on to the nationals. Still, if high school rodeo did nothing else for Kasey, it showed her what she wanted to do. She wanted to rodeo.

Kasey's second horse was the one she had known all seven years of the little mare's life. JC, the initials of the original owner of the mare, had been boarded with Kasey's family when they lived in Illinois. Kasey had been the first to handle the little filly as a newborn foal. It was Kasey who halter broke JC, and was first to put a saddle on the little mare. For that matter, she was the only one to saddle the mare and to ride her. So, when Kasey's father bought the Colorado ranch four years ago, Kasey had talked the little mare's owner into letting her buy the horse. Now, at seven, JC was well started on the barrels too. Her training was one hundred percent Kasey's doing. JC was quick and ran true every time. She still had to get her timing down on the fast runs, but little JC would run her heart out. Kasey was convinced the small size of the mare would not impede her times, except maybe in the largest of arenas where the run home was long. For those arenas, she could use the Roan.

Kasey tied the horses to the trailer, giving them a small amount of hay before going to her camper. The over-the-cab camper was a beauty, she thought. Dad had bought the whole outfit last fall for her to take to her first year of college. The plan was that Kasey and her mother would hit the rodeo trail with these two horses this summer. She felt Roan was ready, and JC was almost there. So, she and Mom would travel the rodeo road and see how it went. But Mom and Dad weren't alive now to see this first summer of rodeos. It was just her.

This was her fourth rodeo of the summer. She had placed with Roan in only one. She had been in the last hole of the payout, which had barely paid her back the entry fee and put some gas in the outfit. She needed to win something soon, or she might have to stop and get a job. Kasey grabbed her purse off the dinette seat in the camper and looked inside. She had enough for her fees. She might as well go and pay them, she thought.

Leaving the camper, Kasey looked fondly at the dog at her heels. Little Girl, what a friend you are to me. So silent, but always with me. Kasey knew the dog missed the rest of the family too. So, the dog was her shadow, not letting Kasey out of her sight if she could help it. There was something comforting about having the little dog with her. But, to walk to the crow's nest, it was best to leave the dog behind, so Kasey locked her in the camper. As Kasey walked toward the arena, she took in her surroundings. This rodeo was in a stand-alone arena, not part of a town or fairgrounds. The arena was flanked by a gentle hill that was a natural grandstand. Already, townspeople were laying out blankets, reserving a spot. The nearby town, St. Onge, was just a little hole-in-the-wall town, and this was the one big rodeo they put on each year. The whole rodeo grounds were spread out around the arena with one large area for parking for the contestants and another for the spectators. Behind the contestant parking was a holding pasture where bucking stock that were not being used this afternoon were grazing. There were no lights at this arena, so both the Saturday and Sunday performances were during the afternoons.

The crow's nest was cool and roomy with windows opened to the arena below. Kasey saw the man who had helped her with the water, Cole Sanders, standing in the back, visiting with a man wearing a dress shirt and holding the microphone. The well-dressed man she assumed was the announcer. Two younger cowboys were studying the typed lists taped on the wall while a couple of cowboys were talking to a woman whom Kasey took as the secretary. She moved to stand behind them and wait her turn.

When it was her turn, Kasey stated her name and waited for the secretary to locate her on the entry sheets. She carefully counted the money needed to pay her fees and waited for the secretary to find her contestant number in the pile of prepared numbers. Kasey picked up a couple of safety pins from the pile on the desk and turned to go when she heard a familiar voice.

"Kasey Jacobs," a tall lanky youth called out as he came in the door with two more men. "What the hell are you doing here?"

"Hello, Marc," Kasey smiled warmly up at him, "I'm trying my luck on the rodeo road, seeing if I can chase the cans."

Marc laughed and replied, "Say, you really disappointed me this spring by dropping out of school. I had my heart set on you getting on the girls' rodeo team so us guys could ride in that fancy outfit of yours."

Kasey's smile faded, "I'm sorry, Marc, I really am, but I couldn't come back."

"Hey, Kasey," Marc stepped closer, lowering his voice, "you didn't have grade trouble?"

Kasey looked up into his concerned face, "No, not grades. I was a bit short of money."

"Kasey Jacobs without money?" he laughed. "Come on, you must be kidding. They say your dad is stacked."

Kasey fingered her contestant number in her hands before she spoke. "My dad is dead, Marc," she spoke quietly as if trying to convince herself as well. "Dad, Mom, my brother, all dead, and our place is gone. So, the poor little rich girl isn't rich anymore," she hesitated before adding, "just poor." She gave a sad smile to offset the touch of bitterness in her voice and started to step around Marc, heading for the door.

"Damn, Kasey," Marc said softly as she went by him, "I'm sorry. . ." He didn't know what to say.

Kasey looked back at him, "I know you are, Marc. Thanks." And she disappeared out the door. She knew her eyes were filling with tears, and she was appalled that she might be caught crying if she didn't get out of there. She hadn't noticed that their conversation was overheard by the other cowboys in the crow's nest, including Cole Sanders.

***

Without lights, the performances started at two p.m. so the rodeo would be done well before dark. By the time Kasey got back to her outfit, horses were being saddled, and she could see riders going in to warm up when Kasey looked back towards the arena. She opened her saddle compartment and got her brushes. Kasey would ride Roan again. He was more seasoned than the mare. JC needed more training runs, so she was banking on Roan to do better. Kasey threw the saddle on and called to Little Girl. She didn't want the dog to follow, so she helped the old dog into the camper and secured the door.

As she rode down to the arena, Kasey saw the hillside was filling up with the crowd. Banners were being unfurled above the bucking chutes and the announcer was testing the PA system. Guiding her horse through the vehicles, Kasey made for the arena and joined the other riders. Roan moved into a nervous running walk as he entered, merging with the other riders.

Kasey reflected on her situation as she navigated through the crowd of horses and riders. She was virtually alone in the world. She had two horses, a dog, a pickup, a camper, and a horse trailer, free and clear. She had thirty dollars in a checking account and enough cash in her pocket to pay entry fees and fuel for a week. Her tiny camper refrigerator had enough meat and vegetables for her supper tomorrow. Other than that, it was pretty empty. *What a way to start a summer,* Kasey thought, kicking the roan into an easy lope. She noticed Roan's head lowering as his nervousness left him, and he settled down to work. *That's good,* she thought, *we don't have money enough to get used to the rodeo road slowly. I need to start winning soon or stop and get a job. When that thirty is gone, it's all over.* Kasey dropped the horse back down to a walk and changed directions.

Kasey left the arena when the announcer called for it to be cleared and waited outside for the Grand Entry to start. One minute, there was no one around, and the next minute the colors were riding in, and riders materialized to follow them. Kasey liked the Grand Entry at rodeos because it gave her nervous horse a feel for the arena, the crowd, and the noise. Weaving around the pivot horses and following the line seemed to give Roan some confidence.

After the Grand Entry, Kasey rode Roan back to her trailer. She dismounted, loosened the girth, and dropped the bridle from his head. Putting his halter on, Kasey tied him to the trailer. It was still a while to wait for her event, so she made her way to the top of the hill to watch the rodeo.

As Kasey watched the bronc riding and calf roping, she didn't recognize any contestants except one. She was watching the first event, bareback riding, when she recognized a young cowboy from her college. She remembered seeing him at rodeo club meetings. Kasey was pretty sure he was a freshman like she had been, and he went by the nickname Vermont. She didn't recognize him until he was walking back to the chutes after getting bucked off. Other than Vermont, she recognized a few names of nationally known cowboys, but she didn't know any of them. Kasey didn't expect to know anyone, though. She had rodeoed a little from home, some amateur rodeos, one year of high school rodeo, and one semester of college rodeos, but otherwise, she was new to the sport. Growing up in Illinois, there weren't many rodeos around. She mainly had gone to quarter horse or local horse shows for years, but once she started on rodeos, she had no desire to return to showing.

Kasey watched the beginning of the saddle bronc riding, seeing Cole Sanders ride a good bronc to the whistle. She knew his name from reading the *Rodeo Sports News*, the official professional rodeo magazine. Cole was a top bronc and bull rider and he showed it this day. He was sitting in the lead by a good margin when Kasey turned away to go and get her horse ready.

Kasey snugged up the girth on Roan and went to the saddle compartment to get skid boots and a bat. Returning to the horse, she pushed the bat handle into the gullet of the saddle. She didn't need the bat and seldom used it. But someone had, and Roan knew what it was for. She usually just scratched his neck with it before a run and he knew if he slacked off, it was there. But Roan seldom slacked off. He had a lot of try, always giving Kasey his best effort. Stooping to Roan's hind legs, Kasey secured the skid boots on his pasterns. Lastly, she took his bridle from the saddle horn, carefully putting it on the gelding. Quickly, she checked him to see if she had forgotten anything before swinging on.

There was an open space, devoid of vehicles, opposite the arena gate where contestants could warm up their horses, and Kasey made for that. The steer wrestling was starting in the arena. Kasey knew there was a clown act after the dogging, and then it was showtime for her. She could feel the butterflies begin in her stomach. *She had to get her nerves in control,* she thought. She was making little mistakes in the arena, and it was getting crucial that she started to win some money.

It didn't take Roan long to settle down now. He had the edge taken off him earlier, and he was ready to listen and work for her. She worked him in both directions, trotting and loping before pulling him down to a walk. The dogging was almost over, and it was time to pay attention to the announcer. Kasey pulled her program from her rear pocket and studied it one more time. She was third to run in a field of fourteen girls. Just right, she thought, not first but early. Maybe she could hold her nerves in check that long.

Kasey looked toward the arena to see the last two steer wrestlers getting ready. That was when she recognized the two horses Cole Sanders had been watering. The dogger settled his horse, intent on watching the steer in the chute. The cowboy dogging was a big man, young and with a dark complexion. Cole was riding the hazing horse. The steer broke out from the box with the horse and rider coming out fast behind him. Kasey could see the horses knew their job and put the young man in a good position, but it took him an extra stride before he got down on the steer, losing him precious seconds. He got the steer thrown in good time, though, and when the announcer came back with his time, he was still in the top four. Kasey hoped she could do as well.

Kasey moved away again, warming up her horse. She heard the announcer talking to the clown during the clown act, but she tried to concentrate on her upcoming run. She practiced the pattern in her mind, when to check and when to look toward the next barrel. She was running out of money. She needed to start running at a rodeo like she was running in her home arena when no one was around to watch. Kasey knew it was her nerves that were breaking her concentration.

The first girl to run made a good, steady run, but not necessarily fast. The time was 19.1 seconds and Kasey judged the course to be around 17.5, give or take. That first time would not hold up, she thought. The second girl was mounted on a tall, rangy sorrel. She went for the first barrel fast, but the big horse, on reaching the barrel, couldn't collect enough to make a tight turn. She swung wide coming out of the barrel. The next two barrels she took well, but her time, while better than the first girl, was not blistering fast.

Kasey heard the announcer call her name, but she was already approaching the gate, watching the gateman to wave her in. She nudged her gelding when she got the wave, and the horse picked up speed. She leaned forward and asked Roan for more, and when she went through the gate, she was flying.

They approached the first barrel, aiming for the pocket. A horse needed to go into the barrel just a little way from it so that these big animals could make a tight turn and not hit a barrel. This was called a pocket. Roan was heading for the pocket and running fast. As they approached the barrel, Kasey picked up the reins and cued him for collection. He had to slow down just enough to slide around the barrel without going wide. But Kasey instantly knew she had asked Roan to shut down too soon. She felt him collect and get ready for the turn, but it was too soon. Inwardly, she cussed herself. She urged the horse forward so that he didn't turn too soon and hit the barrel, but while they didn't hit the barrel, his turn was jerky. Like the girl who ran before her, her second and third barrels were good, but the damage was done. Her time was 18.6. She was sure it would not hold up.

Outside the arena, she dismounted and loosened the girth. She heard the announcer saying, "A good run for Kasey Jacobs, putting her in the lead."

Well, Kasey thought, she wouldn't stay there, and she was right. Kasey watched the rest of the girls run while she walked the roan around to cool him off. Of the next nine girls to run, she judged that four were really good. She knew those names by seeing them listed in the Women's Professional Rodeo Association standings. One of the four had a really good run, but hit a barrel, which gave her a five second penalty. The other three edged Kasey's time by at least a half-second. Then, a couple of local girls had great runs and placed ahead of Kasey. As these next girls laid down their runs, she dropped from first to second, then third and when the dust all settled, she was sitting fifth. The payout would be for the first four places.

Kasey led her horse back to the trailer, feeling better knowing she was close and that, without her mistake, would probably have placed. She was so sure that her horse was capable. The question was, could she get her nerves under control to help her horse. This was a two-go rodeo for the girls' barrel race, so tomorrow, she would do it all over again.

***

St. Onge was located in the rolling hills of western South Dakota. While not actually part of the Black Hills, the mountains could be seen from here. The stark prairie had given way to rolling slopes, with trees scattered more liberally than the prairie. It was pretty country, good cattle country. St. Onge itself was a tiny town with a post office, small general store, and little else except boarded-up old sandstone buildings from bygone years when the town flourished. But like all little towns still surviving in these western regions, the townspeople and the country folk who called it home had their traditions and institutions. This late June rodeo was both.

Cole had always liked this rodeo. It was a small professional rodeo that was well-run and drew a good crowd. The area and climate in June were usually pleasant, and the people who put on this rodeo went to great lengths to do a western weekend that everyone would like. Cole had hit this one every year since he struck out in the professional ranks. It was less than two hundred miles from his home, so it was an easy to make. He had entered Grover, Colorado on this same weekend, but the stock he'd drawn there wasn't worth getting on, so he turned out. It was cheaper to pay the turnout fee than to drive all that way for a low score. He didn't like to turnout stock, and usually by being in two events, he would be lucky enough to have a good draw in at least one event. But in Grover, he had one of those unlucky weekends where both the saddle bronc and bull he drew were not good. It would pay him to stay in St. Onge with Ben and the dogging horses and mount some cowboys out on them. They could all rest up for the three-rodeo run they would make this coming week. Ben was sparking his girl, who went to college in the nearby Black Hills State College. Josie was taking summer classes and Ben hadn't seen her since spring break, so he was hot to stay. Cole didn't mind. He liked St. Onge.

The town had a big tent set up on Main Street. Concessions and beer ran out of the tent, and this Saturday night, there was a band and a rodeo dance that was well underway by dark. Cole had driven down to eat and sat around visiting with some officials and the stock contractor who were sitting around at one end of the tent. *It must be a sign of his age that at eleven p.m., he was ready to head for his motel and the music was just so damned loud anymore,* he thought. He knew Ben would be with Josie, so he had the motel room to himself.

Cole left the tent and started down the road. He had parked his pickup along the road instead of coming into the town to find a parking place. It was too easy to get hemmed in if you parked in a small town like this. He didn't mind the walk anyway. It was a pleasant South Dakota night with no wind and cooling temperature.

He was almost to the end of the line of vehicles parked on both sides of the narrow road that came in off the highway when he was startled by the yip of a dog. He stopped and looked around. He recognized the fancy pickup and camper of that new barrel racer he met today. She had a dog. He wondered if the dog was tied to the side of the camper. Walking between the back of the girl's outfit and the hood of a car parked behind it, Cole emerged onto the shoulder and was surprised to see the girl sitting on the ground, leaning against the pickup wheel. The lights from town cast eerie shadows on the girl and her dog as they sat.

"Sorry," the girl said, looking up. "Did my dog startle you?"

"Not a problem," Cole smiled. "But I wasn't expecting it." Cole looked around. The music was easily heard from here, and with the tent sides up, the crowds could be seen inside. "You know, that is open to the public," he said. "There's dancing and beer in the tent."

"Well, I kind of figured that," Kasey commented. "I just thought it would be nice to sit out here and listen."

Cole moved to the side of the car behind Kasey's outfit and sat down, leaning against the front bumper. "Must be my age, but I can't stand all that loud music anymore. Think it is easier to listen to out here. But you must still be a teenager, so it can't be the music that is forcing you to sit out here."

"I just turned twenty, so I'm not a teenager," Kasey replied. "But I just thought I would sit out here. I don't know anyone in there anyway and I am sure there is a cover charge to get in."

"I saw you talking to Marc in the crow's nest. You know him. He's in there."

"I don't know him that well. I just met him fall semester at college," Kasey thought a minute before continuing. "I'm not much for crowds at the moment anyway."

Cole thought about that, remembering what he overheard in the crow's nest that afternoon. "I overheard you saying that you lost your folks recently," he said gently. "My condolences."

Kasey never moved her gaze from watching the tent, but after a moment, she said, "Thanks," and hesitated. "My folks and my older brother. Right after Christmas. We were taking my brother to the airport. He was in the Air Force and was home on leave. It was cold, and

Dad hit some black ice. We went through a side rail and down a pretty steep slope."

Cole let that sit between them for a few minutes. "If he were alive, I'd thank your brother for his service," Cole told the girl. "Had he served in Vietnam?"

"Just got back from a tour there," Kasey replied. "Ironic that he was flying missions over there, and he ends up getting killed in a car crash. Doesn't seem right."

They sat in companionable silence for a while, listening to the music. Finally, Kasey asked, "Did you have to go to Vietnam?"

"I went a few years out of high school. I was in some of the first divisions of ground troops sent over," Cole reflected on that before going on. "Grunts on the ground, we were. I went, I served, I came back. That is as good as it gets, I suppose. It broke up my rodeo years, but the bulls don't look near as dangerous after that."

"Vietnam veterans don't get a lot of thanks, but I thank you," Kasey said. "Maybe because Bob was there, I have a better perspective. The news sounds like maybe we will get out of there. Not sure what is right or wrong, but if it saves American lives, I can't be against it."

They sat, each in their own thoughts for a while. Kasey broke the silence first. "You were sitting first in the broncs today, but I missed the bulls. Did you ride?"

"I did. I'm sitting first there too. I hope it holds, but some good guys are up tomorrow."

"You heading somewhere else tomorrow?"

"I was up at Grover tomorrow, but I got a rotten draw in both events. Guess I'll stick here and help Ben with the horses," Cole grinned at that. "Basically, with Josie here, that means I'll take care of the horses. I have no idea if Ben will even turn up tomorrow."

Cole stood up. He was tired. He'd ridden in two events that day. "Was nice talking to you. Still think you should go dancing, but as for me, I am off to bed. Maybe see you at the arena tomorrow."

The girl nodded to him as he left. A sad girl, he thought as he walked away. Sitting alone on the shoulder of the road, thinking whatever thoughts she had while she listens to the rowdy music from the tent. Well, he guessed he might be sad too, if five months earlier, he'd lost his family.

***

Sunday opened to a beautiful June day. The notorious South Dakota wind was absent, and in its place was just a gentle breeze. The day was sunny but not hot. It was a great day for a rodeo. The crowd began to arrive by noon and the rodeo grounds came alive with activity.

Kasey decided to ride JC today. Roan had run in all of her previous rodeos, and she felt she needed to give him a rest. As much as she needed to win money, she also knew she needed to give the little mare a chance. When the mare was seasoned, Kasey had confidence she would be as good as Roan. Maybe better. If Kasey didn't win money soon, she knew she was about a week away from leaving rodeo behind and getting a job. Her nerves couldn't be any worse riding the little mare.

Kasey warmed up JC in the arena, winding between other riders and horses. JC wasn't used to all the noise and confusion. She shied at the flags, stared at the people along the fence like they were monsters, and jumped when the announcer barked out reminders to contestants to come and register. But she was responsive to Kasey's hand and leg cues, listening to Kasey's commands. As she circled the arena again and again, the little mare began to settle, and by the time the announcer called for the arena to be cleared, the mare was relaxed. Kasey hoped they could both stay relaxed. When it was time for the barrel race, Kasey was ready. Unlike Roan's run the day before, Kasey kept control of her nerves and checked JC at just the right spot. The first barrel usually sets the stage for a good barrel run, and JC slid around the barrel just perfectly. Kasey could feel it as they came out, heading toward the second barrel. For the first barrel, the little mare had to be on the right lead for the right turn. Kasey was holding the reins with her right hand. Midway between the first and second barrel, Kasey switched hands on the reins, preparing for the next two barrels, both left turns. She checked, and JC collected, sliding around the second barrel. Just as the pair came out of the barrel, Kasey felt her fingers catch in the horse's mane. JC had such a thick mane that Kasey couldn't free her fingers. Apparently, there was a snag in the mare's thick mane and Kasey was just unlucky enough to catch it with her fingers. Kasey had never had that happen before. She jerked hard to get her hand free from the mane. But she jerked too hard, and when her hand came free, she also touched the little mare's mouth with the reins. When JC felt the tension on the bit, she did what she thought Kasey had asked. She continued her turn. A barrel run can sometimes be won or lost in split seconds. This one was lost. As the mare overturned the barrel, she knocked it over with her hip. Kasey's heart sank. As they went on to the third barrel, she knew she had already lost. A five second penalty would not only knock her out of the go-round but also dash any chance of slipping in on the average payout. Another weekend rodeo shot to hell.

***

The activity at the rodeo grounds was winding down by the time Cole walked back up the hill to his outfit. He had walked his two horses down to an empty sorting corral behind the arena where they could stay for the night. The stock contractor was almost finished loading the stock, so the pens would be empty tonight. His horses could have the freedom of the corrals for a night before he moved on. Ben wanted to stay until morning so he could spend one more night with Josie. Cole had a room in a nearby motel, so once his horses were settled for the night, he could head out for supper before going back to the motel. He'd hook up the trailer in the morning and be ready to head out when Ben turned up.

As Cole was trudging up the hill, he saw Ted Langley's car winding through the maze of vehicles. Ted had a carload of cowboys with him, and they were ready to roll. But Ted pulled up beside Cole and rolled down his window.

"You've been talking to that new girl some, haven't you?" Ted asked. "I thought I saw you talking to her yesterday."

"I have," Cole replied. "She seems like a nice kid. Why?"

"Her dog just got hit, killed," Ted told him. "Carload of bull riders backed out in a hurry and the old dog just sort of stood there."

"Kasey said the old dog was getting blind and deaf," Cole replied. "Did they stop?"

"Nah, I don't think they even knew they hit the dog. It never even yelped," Ted went on. "I tried to wave them down, but they were gone."

"Where is the dog now?"

"I went over and knocked on her camper door and told her," Ted said. "She hadn't heard it either. Just thought I would mention it to you since you are parked next to her outfit."

"Thanks, Ted," Cole answered, thinking. "I'll look into it. That gal has had a shitload of trouble. This isn't what she needed right now."

Ted put the car in gear and then looked back at Cole. "I saw her heading out towards the back of the rodeo grounds. I'm guessing she is looking for a burying spot. I was going to ask her if she needed help, but these guys," Ted gestured at the cowboys with him, "are hot to trot."

When Cole reached his outfit, he could see the girl's figure at the far end of the rodeo grounds. There were a couple trees out there. He could see that she wasn't standing up, but other than that, he couldn't see what she was doing. He didn't hesitate but got in his pickup and headed toward her. If she was burying the dog, he guessed she did not have a shovel. But if you live in the mountains of Montana, your pickup always has a shovel in it. He never took it out, summer or winter.

When he got close, he saw Kasey kneeling and the dog was lying beside her. She sat back on her haunches as he drove up, and although her back was toward him, it looked as if she wiped her eyes before she turned to face him. Cole got out and pulled the seat forward. There was a shovel behind the seat, and he took it out.

"I heard," he said softly. "Let me help you."

She just nodded, sitting back to give him room. It was then he noticed what she was using. She had a little hatchet that she was using to break up the soil, then a bowl to drag the loose soil out. *Well,* he thought, *that would work, but not as well as a shovel.* He went to digging.

In the early summer, the ground was still moist and soft. It wasn't strenuous shoveling and didn't take long for the hole to be big enough.

"You think that is big enough?" Cole asked her. She hadn't spoken a word.

"I think so," Kasey answered. She had a sheet with her, and she started to wrap the old dog in the material. Cole knelt beside her and helped lift the dog so she could get the sheet under and around the little animal. Together, they lowered the dog into the hole.

"You want to go back before I fill the hole?" he asked.

"No, that's OK," she replied. "I need to see this through."

Cole nodded and began filling the hole. When it was filled, he smoothed down the mound and looked over at the girl.

"Ride back with me," he said. "Don't stay out here alone."

Kasey nodded and followed him back to his pickup. Cole replaced the shovel behind the seat. Climbing in, he put the pickup in gear and pulled away before he spoke.

"I heard how it happened. At least the old dog didn't suffer."

"I keep telling myself that," Kasey replied. "It is just so sudden. I had hoped I wouldn't have to lose anything else for a while." Kasey looked out the window.

They rode the rest of the way in silence. Just as they neared the trailers, Kasey turned to Cole. "Thank you for helping me. I'd still be out there with my little ax trying to get a hole big enough."

"Actually, I thought it was pretty clever to think of a hatchet and a bowl. Better than a kitchen knife," he smiled at her.

He was rewarded for his teasing with a small smile. "Dad had a toolbox, and it had this small hatchet in there. I figured it never hurt to have a toolbox, so I put it in my saddle compartment. I guess that paid off."

"So, are you pulling out tonight yet?" Cole asked.

"No, I'm going to stay here."

Cole didn't pursue that at the moment. They had reached their trailers, and he pulled in and parked beside Kasey's camper. Her camper door stood open with only the screen shut. Cole smelled her supper, probably waiting on her inside.

"Smells like you are cooking tonight," he commented.

"I made a stew today. I thought I could share some with Little Girl," she replied. Then, turning toward him, she spoke again. "Hey, would you want to stay and eat? I have enough for two, and it would kind of be nice to have something to. . . well to keep my mind off the dog," she finished lamely. "Well, I mean, if you are not heading out."

"We're heading out in the morning. Ben's girl has classes all day during the week. Apparently, summer school has long days to get the hours in. So, Josie will bring Ben to meet me in the morning, and then we will head out. So, yeah, it smells good. Beats another café meal."

"Well, it should be ready. I turned it off when . . . but it couldn't have cooled too much. Come on in. It shouldn't take long to reheat." Kasey opened the screen door and led the way into the camper.

Cole stepped inside and slid into the dinette while Kasey went to the stove. Cole looked around the compact space. A small dinette would seat two, and across from it there was a small stove and counter. Under the counter was a small refrigerator. There was a cupboard above the stove and a portable plastic sink on the counter.

"What do you have to drink?" Cole reached across the narrow aisle and opened the fridge.

"Actually, all I have is water," Kasey replied, not turning toward him. "Sorry."

"Hey, I'm going to run to my outfit for a beer." Cole closed the fridge. "Want a beer?"

"Thanks, no," Kasey answered. "I guess I haven't acquired a taste for that stuff yet."

Cole slid out of the seat and headed out. He was thinking of what he had seen, or rather what he had not seen. There was no food in the refrigerator. None. There was a ketchup bottle, almost empty and a mayonnaise jar, also almost empty. That was it. As he got up, he saw Kasey open the top cupboard and take out salt and pepper. There was no food in the cupboard either. No boxes of things. He thought about that. Maybe she just didn't carry much with her, he thought. Or perhaps she didn't have any money. She had commented the night before about the tent having a cover charge.

Reaching his pickup, Cole went to the cooler in the back. He and Ben always hauled a cooler stocked with beer and soft drinks. Often, they had a pack of bologna floating in the ice and a loaf of bread in a box. His dad always said a ring of red and a loaf of bread would keep the stomach filled. Cole and Ben had eaten the sandwich meat, but four slices of the bread were left. He took the bread and went to a box of food that needed no refrigeration. When traveling through the night, one never knew where the next meal would be if nothing was open. If a cowboy was hungry, a cold can of beans was always available. Cole looked into the food box. He grabbed a can of pork and beans and a big bag of potato chips. He took the food along with his beer and a can of Coke.

"You like these?" he asked, holding up the beans. "You like them cold or hot?"

"Hey, nice," Kasey said, smiling. "I'll heat them if you like them that way."

"Sounds good. I like them hot, but sometimes that isn't possible on the road."

When the food was ready, Kasey poured two bowls of stew and set the pork and beans pan on a hot pad on the table beside two small plates. Cole noticed that there was only enough stew to make two bowls, and she gave him the larger share. Cole took the bread out of the package, laid it out, and opened the bag of chips.

"You like Coke?" he asked. "I think it's Ben's, but he can get more."

Kasey nodded and popped the top. She set small plates out for the beans, and they dug in. The stew was good, with carrots and potatoes, and Cole enjoyed it. But he was glad he had brought some food with him too. He only took a half slice of bread. He figured he'd leave whatever was left over with her. If he left hungry, he could get more food in town. But he suspected this meal was meant to last more than one day.

They ate in companionable quiet for a bit. The breeze came in through the windows, and the little camper was comfortable. The bed was over the cab of the truck, but that was about the extent of the camper. There was no room for a bathroom. There was a tiny closet just inside the door.

"So where is home when you aren't in this?" Cole asked finally.

Kasey looked around. "Well, I guess this is all the home I have right now. I suppose I can find a place to park it if I have to."

"So, where did you live before?"

Kasey thought about that. "We moved every three to five years when I was a kid. My last home was in the mountains near a little town in Colorado. We had a ranch up there."

"So, your dad was a rancher?"

"No, not even close," Kasey laughed softly at that. "My dad was a real estate investor and speculator. He created things. Resorts, subdivisions, and the last was a ski resort area. We moved whenever he got a big project to work on, so he didn't have to commute hundreds of miles to be home. Most of his work was in Illinois, where I mostly grew up, but this last project was a big ski resort near Steamboat Springs, Colorado. He had investors, and he bought up a lot of land, and they were building condos, a ski lift, and a lake, complete with boat docks and boat houses. It was the biggest of his projects. When he was out buying the land, he saw a little ranch for sale not too far away, and he bought it, and we moved onto it. There was a foreman there already, so Dad didn't have to find anyone to run the ranch. We just lived there," Kasey stopped and took another handful of chips. "Of all my homes, it was my favorite place.

"The whole project was going to take at least five years," Kasey continued, "but a couple of the condos were finished, and they already had 40% of them sold, so it was going to be pretty lucrative. The ski hill equipment was delivered but not installed. The ski hills still needed landscaping work. The lake wasn't started yet.

Then Dad died and his investment partners panicked when there was no one to take the reins, and they pulled out. They got their money out, but the debts already incurred fell to Dad's estate, and there went the ranch. I got out with this pickup, trailer, and my horses because they legally were in my name. My sister got out with her little house and car because Dad had put them in her name. Everything else went to pay the debt."

"Your sister?" Cole asked, surprised. He hadn't caught that Kasey had more family in their previous conversations.

"I have a twin sister," Kasey said. "She and I both survived the crash. She's the only other family I have."

"So, where does she live?"

"Last summer, before we went to school, Dad got me this outfit, and he bought Kelly a little bungalow in the Ft. Collins area where we both went to school. He put the little house in Kelly's name, and she also got a car. It's just a little two-bedroom house, but we both lived there during the fall semester. Kelly still lives there."

"So, is that home then when you aren't traveling?"

"Well, I can always park my camper there, but Kelly got married last month, so she and her husband live there now. And to help make ends meet, they rented out the second bedroom." Kasey reflected on that for a minute and then added, "Kelly and I are close. We are twins, after all, but we don't have the same interests. And she's married and settled. That is two things I'm not. Settled or married. But worst-case scenario, yes, I can go there if I have to."

Kasey looked at Cole and changed the subject, "So where are you from? I suppose I should know since they write a lot of articles about you, but I guess I never paid attention."

"I come from a ranch in southern Montana. Unlike you, I have been in that one place my whole life," Cole smiled at that. "My grandparents settled there. My folks are there now, and someday, when I quit rambling, that is where I will settle. It's a nice ranch in the Wolf Mountains on the Crow reservation. We have deeded acres and an Indian lease too. We run over a lot of acres, meadows and mountain slopes. We raise both cattle and horses. When I finally quit rodeoing, I think we will increase the horse production, but for now, what we have is enough to keep my dad and one hired man busy. I help out whenever I am home. And I have invested my winnings in the ranch, improving bloodlines and getting better equipment."

"Sounds nice," Kasey commented. "What are your mountains like? Are they part of the Big Horns?"

"The Wolf Mountains are an old mountain range. They are pretty much like these Black Hills of South Dakota, only the Black Hills are rockier than my mountains." Cole looked out the window at the distant Black Hills. "It is good horse and cattle country. Not so rugged that it is hard to get around, but good climate and lots of water and grass."

"I bet they are pretty," Kasey told him. "I like what I have seen of these Black Hills. My folks, my sister, and I took a trip out here a couple of years ago. Took in the Deadwood Rodeo. That was fun."

"Deadwood is one of my favorites," Cole agreed. "There is something about Deadwood that everyone likes."

"So, where are you heading from here?" Kasey asked.

"Ben's taking me to the Rapid airport tomorrow, and I am flying to Reno. It's a big rodeo, and they don't take permits, so Ben is heading to North Platte. Then I'll catch a ride to Grand Junction. I'm up on Wednesday night there and then back to Reno for the second go on Thursday. I'll meet back with Ben and my outfit at North Platte on Friday. I drew up both Friday and Saturday at North Platte. If I make the Reno finals, I will fly out on Saturday night. It's going to be a full week. Where are you headed from here?"

"I'm going to stick here until Wednesday morning. I talked to a guy on the committee, and they aren't charging me to stay here. The water will stay on, so I am set. Then, on Wednesday morning, I am heading for Kingfisher, Oklahoma. I'm in the slack on Thursday night. I was surprised that Kingfisher is only one go. They must have a passel of barrel racers down that way to have enough overflow to have slack. Then I'm up in North Platte on Friday night, so I will have to push to get there in time. I'm up in North Platte on Saturday too."

"I thought you might be going to Grand Junction since you are from Colorado," Cole said.

"No way do I want to haul through those mountains if I don't have to," Kasey laughed. "I would if there were no other rodeos, but I'll stick to the plains."

Cole noticed the fading sun, gone from the horizon beyond the wooded hills. He slid out of the dinette and stood up.

"That was one good meal," he said, smiling down at the girl. "I thank you for that. But I have to get some hay down to my horses, and then I had better make tracks. I think a shower is calling my name."

"No, I have to thank you," Kasey responded. "I really didn't want to be alone for a bit there. And I thank you again for helping me bury my dog. That was nice of you."

"Wasn't a problem," Cole said gently. "It's hard saying good-bye."

"I know," Kasey murmured. "But she was only a dog." However, Kasey's eyes had filled, betraying her words.

Cole looked down at her, seeing her struggle suddenly for composure. "They are never just a dog when they move into your heart. It's not a weakness to grieve for something that is important to you." He patted her shoulder awkwardly and then turned and left the camper.

CHAPTER 2

WINDS OF CHANGE

Kasey spent two relaxing days alone at the St. Onge rodeo grounds. After everyone pulled out, the committee wanted the gates leading into the grounds shut. That suited Kasey just fine. During the day, she could let her horses loose to graze. The grass along the edges of the grounds wasn't cut before the rodeo, and this her horses could eat, saving her two days of hay. She didn't have room to haul more than a few hay bales, so whenever she saw free grass, she was happy to use it.

On Tuesday, Kasey dug through her purse, pulling out all the money she had. She had cashed a check and gotten cash from the rodeo secretary, and this is what she studied now. Kasey divided it into piles for gas money, entry fees, food, and hay. She had enough hay to last until Sunday since she hadn't fed any hay these two days at St. Onge. Kasey had divided the two slices of bread, the leftover chips, and the half can of pork and beans into meals for two days and made them last until she pulled out on Wednesday morning. She would stop at a grocery store somewhere on her way to Kingfisher and get whatever she could for the two dollars she had designated for food. Studying maps, Kasey had calculated the miles she'd drive and set aside money for the gas. She set her entry fee money aside. That and her gas money could not be touched for anything. She had thirty dollars and some change in her checking account. She'd hold off on using that until it was absolutely necessary. That was her reserve.

Kasey was at the end of the road if she didn't win something this week. She'd have to go back to Kelly in Ft. Collins. A job was always waiting for her in the Ft. Collins area so she wouldn't starve. She would just have to make it there first. That could be the next problem. She wasn't sure the money in her checking was enough. But she would cross that bridge if the week was a bust. For now, she had just enough to get her down the road through Sunday.

On Wednesday morning, Kasey loaded her two horses about mid-morning. She wanted them to graze before she left. She wasn't sure where she would stop that night, but there might not be a chance to graze anywhere, so she was conserving the hay while she could.

Kasey was about 10 miles from McCook, Nebraska, when disaster struck. She heard the tire blow before the pickup started to wobble. She hit the brakes, and as gently as possible, Kasey brought the outfit to a halt. Pulling off as far as she dared on the two-lane highway, she put on her flashers. Damn, damn, damn, she thought. Kasey knew it was a tire.

It was a back tire with a big hole blown out of the side of it. Kasey shook her head in disgust. These tires were less than one year old and didn't have that many miles on them. They should not be blowing out. They had good rubber on them. She took a breath; the tires were under warranty. All she had to do was get somewhere and replace it. But first, she had to change the darn thing.

The spare was under the truck bed, which was the first problem. Kasey went to her saddle compartment and dug out a jack, tire iron, and gloves. She knew this would take some time, so she unloaded the horses and tied them to the fence line along the road ditch. They could catch a snack while they waited. Kasey had just scooted under the pickup bed when she heard a vehicle approaching slowly from the rear. She listened to the tires crunching in the gravel on the side of the road and knew that someone was stopping. She hoped it was someone bigger than she was who knew how to change a tire and was willing and able to do just that. At the moment, Kasey couldn't even get the darn spare unhooked from underneath the pickup.

Kasey saw cowboy boots appear by the rear wheel of her tire and stop. Next, a grizzled face, topped by a cowboy hat, appeared under the pickup starting at her.

"Ma'am, you need any help?" the face asked.

Kasey scooted out from under the pickup and smiled up at the man. She guessed he was her father's age and had a kind look to him.

"My dad always made sure we girls knew how to change a tire," Kasey said, "but he didn't realize you guys put things on so tightly that we can't get the nuts undone! I can't even get the spare off. I would appreciate some help."

The man just smiled and took Kasey's place under the pickup. He had the spare out in no time and was jacking up the pickup.

"Where you heading with those fine-looking horses?" the man asked.

"I'm up tomorrow night in the slack in Kingfisher, Oklahoma. I was hoping to get somewhere into Kansas before I quit for the day," Kasey continued. "But with this, I better find a place to either fix it or get another spare tire."

"I've been to Kingfisher. Went down there to buy some cattle last summer. You can make it by midafternoon tomorrow if you head out at daylight." The man grunted some but got the lug nuts loosened on the tire. "You aren't far from McCook," the rancher told her. "This tire can't be fixed. You will have to replace it." He had the tire off now and fitted the spare onto the pickup with the lug nuts.

"When you get to the edge of town, a sign will be pointing east to the fairgrounds. Don't turn there. Keep going until you come to a stop and take a left. There is a tire place along the main drag. Bensons Tire, it's called. If you don't mind driving 70, you should get there just before they close. I'm about five minutes from home. I'll call them and let them know you are coming. You can drop the tire off today and pick it up first thing in the morning. I think they open at seven in the morning."

"That would be great," Kasey stated. "I don't mind driving 70, but does this road get patrolled? I don't really have the money for a speeding ticket right now."

The rancher tightened the lug nuts. "Getting about shift change, so don't think you will be bothered, but if you do get pulled over, the highway patrol officer is Benny. He's old Benson's youngest son. Just tell him I told you to speed to get to his dad's place to fix the tire. He'll probably bring you to town with lights flashing," the old man grinned. "I'm Raymond Edmonds. He knows me. Then, after you drop the tire off, just find the next street to take to the north again, and you will come right out at our fairgrounds. We have a pretty nice fairground, and no one will mind if you stay overnight. Not sure if there are electric hookups, but there is water by the arena. Do you need electric?" Raymond eyed the camper.

"No, I don't need electricity. And that would be great to stay close." Kasey spoke over her shoulder as she rolled the damaged tire around the trailer to put it in the tack compartment. "I can't thank you enough," Kasey went on. "Can I pay you for your trouble?" She hoped he wouldn't say yes. She'd have to take some money from her gas stash, which was dangerously low already.

"Hell, no," the man laughed. "I've enjoyed visiting with you. I ranch a few miles west of here and have nothing at home except chores to do. It has been my pleasure. But if you want, you could enter the rodeo at McCook later this summer."

"If I haven't gone broke by then, I'll do it," Kasey smiled. "And if I do enter, you better come and say hi."

The rancher helped her put away the tools and then stood and visited while she went to get her horses. Opening the back gate, she threw the lead ropes over their necks, and they jumped into the trailer.

"Hard to load, aren't they?" the rancher teased. "I got some at home that aren't quite that easy to haul."

Kasey smiled at the man. "They don't give me any trouble." She turned toward the man and extended her hand. "Thank you, Mr. Edmonds. I'd still be under there, probably cussing a blue streak. You are a lifesaver."

***

Kasey pulled into Benson's Tire two minutes after closing, and the owner was waiting for her. She left the tire, promising to pick up a replacement by 7:30 in the morning as she left town. She had no trouble finding the fairgrounds, and it was spacious and quiet. Kasey put her horses out for a while on hobbles to further save her hay.

At 7:15 sharp the following morning, she pulled up to Benson's to bad news.

"Ma'am," Mr. Benson said regretfully, "I hate to tell you this, but that warranty isn't worth the paper it was printed on. They have a clause in there that says it will not pay for road hazards, and they will swear it was a road hazard that caused this blowout. I have dealt with this company before, and they never pay."

"What is a road hazard?" Kasey asked.

"They will tell you that you must have hit a big rock or a pothole, and that caused the tire to fail."

"I know I never hit either of those, or anything else for that matter," Kasey asserted.

"I agree with you, missy, but here is the long and short of it. The company won't honor that warranty."

Kasey sighed, "So, I need a tire. What is a tire going to cost?"

"I can set you up with a good tire to match the others for $28."

Kasey thought about that. She had $30 in her checking account. She could write a check and hope her checkbook was balanced correctly. She nodded. "How long will it take to mount a new tire?" she asked.

"I'll have you out of here by 8 a.m."

***

Kasey pulled into Kingfisher with a couple of hours to spare. She had written a check to Benson's Tire for $29.50 and asked Mr. Benson for the $1.50 change. She could use that to buy some food. Kasey was sure she was right that her checking account had $30 and change, but she dared not write a check for more. She had to win something this week or go home. But where was home? She knew if she didn't win something this week, she'd have to call her sister and have some money wired. Then she'd have to go to Kelly's and get a job. Kelly's was as much home as she had right now. This would probably be the shortest rodeo season for anyone.

Perhaps it was the quietness of the rodeo grounds during slack or the absence of a crowd in the grandstand because despite having to get a good run down, Kasey found herself more relaxed. Maybe she was resigned to whatever was to come. In any case, she and Roan worked some circles before the barrel race started, and they felt good together.

When Kasey paid her fees, she checked the list to see when she was running. She was in the last slot of fourteen girls. That was the worst place to be, of course. First, she had thirteen runs before her to watch and get increasingly nervous. Second, the ground would be furrowed around the barrels by the time she ran. In some jackpot barrel races, the girls got their way, and the ground was worked up every seven or eight runs, but in the rodeo arena, that wasn't happening. The last slot was always the slowest and sometimes the most dangerous footing.

One by one, the first thirteen runs went down. Kasey expected to feel the same tightening of her muscles that she usually felt as she grew steadily more nervous, but on this night, she was surprised that she stayed relaxed. It had to be the atmosphere. With no crowds and no excitement, everything seemed low-key.

Kasey was ready when her name was called. Roan was alert, feeling her urge him forward. By the time they reached the entry gate, Roan was in full stride. He bore down on the first barrel, and just at the right moment, Kasey asked him to collect. They seemed to be on autopilot for the rest of the run. Every hoofbeat was in the right place. As a team, they ran the pattern, Kasey looking for the next barrel before even completing a turn. She knew as they dashed over the finish line that they had had a good run. Breathless, Kasey eased Roan to a slow lope and then a walk outside the arena as she waited for the announcer to tell her time.

"Now, that was a good run by this Colorado girl," the announcer said. "She ran a 17.5, a full second faster to end the slack in first place."

Kasey heard the time. The barrels were set at a standard pattern, so that was a very good time. Now, would it hold up during the next two performances? She hoped so, but at least now she had a chance. She had to call the rodeo office on Sunday to see if she had placed. If she did, the check would be mailed to Kelly's address, and Kelly would deposit it in her checking account. But now, she needed to get her horses fed and bedded down for the night. They had to leave early in the morning. She was in the evening performance in North Platte the next night. And North Platte was a big rodeo with a big payout.

***

The number of pickup and trailer outfits at the rodeo grounds in North Platte was intimidating. This was the largest rodeo Kasey had competed in. As she pulled in, she saw the outfit Ben and Cole traveled in parked on the outskirts of the rest. Ben had been in the slack at Kingfisher too, and Kasey had visited with him a little as they both were warming up their horses. Cole was off to Reno for the big rodeo there. Reno didn't take permits, so Ben, still a permit holder, opted for Kingfisher. Cole also entered in Grand Junction, Colorado, so, he would meet Ben at North Platte today for the Friday night performance. The barrel race was two go-rounds at North Platte. Kasey would run this evening and again on Saturday night. Ben was up tonight as the steer wrestling only had one go-round. Ben told her Cole was in the bulls at North Platte on Friday night and the saddle broncs on Saturday. Reno was another big rodeo and had finals on Sunday. If Cole placed in the top ten in either event in Reno, he'd have to beat it back to Nevada for the finals on Sunday. It was a busy week.

Kasey pulled into a space beside Ben. She knew no one else, so it was comforting to be beside some guys she knew and trusted. After Kasey had the horses settled, she went through her finances again. It was dismal. There had been a headwind coming north from Oklahoma to Nebraska, and it had affected her gas mileage. She had to make an extra stop for gas, which took her remaining money. She had just enough money to grab a hamburger at the concession stand but decided to wait until after her run. Kasey had had a little breakfast of her last egg and a piece of toast this morning, so she would just hold off until later to eat. She had no idea what to do about food tomorrow, but she was formulating a plan. First, she had to make her competition runs, and she wanted them to be good.

Because Roan had run so well at Kingfisher, Kasey had a boost of confidence. She decided to run him again during the first go at North Platte and switch to JC for the second go. As she warmed up her gelding, she heard the music, the announcer, and the crowd noises. It all seemed to roar after the quiet of Kingfisher, but Roan appeared just as calm this evening as the night before. Kasey willed herself to stay calm as well. She was seventh out of fifteen girls this evening, a much better spot than the night before. Again, it was a run-in gate, and Roan hit the opening at a dead run. They seemed on autopilot, working together as a team. When Kasey guided her horse over the finish line and out the gate, she knew they had made another good run. She waited for her time.

"The time for Kasey Jacobs is 17.4, putting her in first place so far," the announcer declared.

Kasey was elated. They were not at the end of the first go-round until these fifteen girls ran, but the girls who had already run in the earlier performances had not fared any better. If Kasey's time held, she would have a paycheck when this rodeo ended. And there was still the second go that Kasey would run on Saturday.

The remaining girls ran one by one, and when the last girl left the arena, Kasey held on to the lead. She was still broke until the rodeo was over, and the secretary wrote the checks, but she had money coming. She could stay on the road for a bit longer now.

After cooling Roan and making him comfortable at the trailer, Kasey headed to the concession stand. She had just enough money for a big, juicy hamburger. The one hamburger would fill her up for now, and Kasey would worry about tomorrow's food later. She wandered over to the arena fence and watched the remainder of the bull riding. She saw Cole come out on a rank, spinning horned bull, and he rode the brute to the whistle. He was sitting first when the score went up to the announcer. But the bull riding was only one go-round, so Cole would have Saturday and Sunday to wonder if his score would place. Still, it was a magnificent ride, so it sure looked like he would take a check home from North Platte.

Saturday dawned sunny and hot. The rodeo grounds woke slowly. Most of the activity consisted of livestock being fed and cared for. Some outfits hitched up and pulled out, and others started arriving after the noon hour. Kasey spent most of the day just lazing around. She walked her two horses out to a far corner of the grounds where they could find a bit of grass to graze on, but there were slim pickings for them, so eventually, she brought them back to the trailer and fed them hay. Kasey saddled Roan and ponied JC around to get them some exercise. She was going to run the mare for the Saturday night performance. Kasey wanted her gelding to have a chance to rest. He wasn't used to running so many times a week, and she didn't want to overuse him.

By the time the Saturday evening performance began, Kasey was getting very hungry. She drank lots of water to ease her hunger pangs, but that only helped temporarily. She hadn't eaten since the evening before, but she had a plan for that. First, Kasey had to get this run put down. She had one check coming for winning the first go. She wouldn't hear how she fared at Kingfisher until Sunday night, if then. Now, she was hungry for more than just food. Kasey was hungry for another win. She had seen both Cole and Ben in passing, nodding greetings. She had seen Cole's saddle bronc ride from a distance, and it looked like a good ride, but she missed the score. She assumed if Cole had made the finals in Reno, he would be heading to Nevada as soon as he was off his bronc.

Kasey was eleventh in the barrels. It wasn't the best draw, but not the worst. Fifteen girls were running in this performance. As Kasey warmed up JC in the area outside the entry gate, she felt herself beginning to get into what she was coming to think of as her competition state. She was not relaxed, but she was starting to feel focused. Kasey thought through the upcoming run, remembering what she needed to do to cue the mare at each turn, when to look to the next barrel, and how to watch for the flagger and not let the mare slow down too soon. She felt the jitters, but not in excess. Kasey had meticulously combed the mare's thick mane out before mounting so there would be no chance of getting her fingers caught. She had prepared well and knew she was as ready as possible.

JC had a faster starting speed than the big Roan. So, when the gate opened for Kasey's run, she kept the mare under wraps until she was just at the arena gate, and then she turned her loose. JC was ready, and like a bullet, she aimed at the barrel and accelerated. Kasey felt the mare's speed as she approached the barrel. Kasey almost pulled JC up too soon, feeling they would overrun the barrel, but in the last split second, she trusted the mare, cueing her at just the right spot to collect and turn. The little mare slid around the barrel and charged toward the second. Kasey switched hands on the reins and felt her confidence in JC grow. The second and third barrel turns were also perfect, and as Kasey crossed the finish line, she knew they had run a good pattern.

The announcer confirmed that when he announced Kasey's time. She was leading the second go-round. Kasey sat up, easing the mare down to a lope and, finally, to a walk. Now she had to cool JC out and feed the horses. Then, she had to clean up and go about getting supper. It was time to put her next plan to work.

***

Kasey eased her big pickup into a parking spot on the side of the street. This space was a couple of blocks from two cowboy bars. She grabbed her guitar case and started up the street. She had never panhandled for her supper before, but there was a first time for everything. Maybe she could get a few coins tossed in her guitar case near the bars if she caught any attention.

She heard noise from one bar before she rounded the last corner. Music was blaring out of the open door, and a crowd of cowboys and cowgirls lounged outside the already-filled bar. Kasey surveyed the scene. The music was loud; she couldn't compete with that noise, so she needed to be farther away. She looked down the street. There was the sign for the second bar across the street and down half a block, but while the door was open, no people were outside lounging around. Kasey went to investigate.

Looking in the open door of the tavern, she saw a band playing gallantly on the stage and a few tables filled. This pub served food as well as liquor, so most patrons were eating and drinking. The band was good, but there were no singers. Three men were playing assorted instruments. There was a piano player, a drummer, and a guitar player. It was good music, but without any vocals, it was not pulling in the crowds. Kasey glanced back at the busy bar across the street and back inside as she got another idea. Maybe, she thought, she could do better than panhandling.

Going inside, Kasey approached the bartender, who was wiping down the far corner of the bar. Kasey had torn the pickup apart before coming and had found seventeen cents under the seats. She took the last stool at the bar and waited for the bartender to approach.

"What can I get you, miss?" the middle-aged man, white apron stretched across his middle, asked.

Kasey dropped the seventeen cents on the bar and asked, "This is all I have. Could I get seventeen cents worth of orange juice?"

The bartender gave her a quizzical look but turned and opened the refrigerator behind him, taking out the orange juice container. Pulling out a small glass, he filled it up, bringing it to Kasey. He did not pick up her coins.

"Your band is good," Kasey commented, "but they lack singers. Are the singers taking a break?"

"I wish," the man replied. "It was a husband and wife that sings with the band, and they got in a car accident a half hour before they were to go on tonight. They are both in the hospital."

"That's not good," Kasey commented. "Were they hurt badly?'

"They are being kept for observation but should get out tomorrow. So that is the good news. But it was also so sudden that I couldn't get a replacement," the bartender continued. "The rest of the band said they would still come and play, but it isn't quite the same. Most of my regulars, as well as most of the towns' visitors, are across the street tonight."

Kasey thought about that for a moment before she spoke again. "Hey, mister, I have a deal for you. I haven't eaten since last night. I'd go up there if the band was willing and sing a few songs if you'd give me some supper after the first set. If you don't think I'm worth it, I'd take a grilled cheese and go my way. But if you think I'm worth it, a steak, medium rare would be great."

The barman gave her a calculating look and then smiled. "Miss, you're on."

Kasey leaned down and unsnapped her guitar case. Taking out her guitar, she left the case on the last seat, reserving the stool for her return. She drained her orange juice and surveyed the room. She saw a table on the side with the college cowboys she knew from Colorado. They had food in front of them and were busy eating. Kasey went up to the one nicknamed Vermont.

"Hey, Vermont," she said softly, "would you do me a favor?"

The shy young man looked up at her and nodded.

"If you think I'm worth it, would you go across the street and spread the word that they might want to try this place? Maybe tell them that it is looking up in here? See if you can get some to come over?" Kasey gave him a smile. "It would help me out if I could get more of a crowd in here."

Again, the young cowboy nodded, unsure of her request but pleased she had come to him. Kasey turned to watch the band, and as they came to the end of a song, she approached the stage and went up the steps. She walked up to the guitarist and stuck out her hand to him.

**

Seated at one of the tables along the dance floor, Cole, Ben, and Ted Langley were finishing steaks. They had opted for the quieter bar as they were more interested in eating than carousing. Ted and Cole were headed back to Reno for the finals the next day, so they intended to get a good night's sleep. It was Ted who noticed Kasey mount the stage.

"Isn't that the girl whose dog died last weekend?" he asked, nudging Cole.

Cole looked up, and recognizing Kasey, he nodded. Kasey was talking to the band, and after a pause, they pulled out another microphone and a stand from the back. With her guitar slung over her shoulder, it appeared that Kasey would join the band. Positioning the microphone, Kasey stepped up to it and began to speak.

"Hey everybody," she said into the mic. "I think we need to liven this place up a bit. This is a song that just came out. Hope you like it."

Without the band playing a note, Kasey sang the opening lines of "Delta Dawn" that Tanya Tucker was currently singing. "*Delta Dawn, what's that flower you have on?*" Kasey's voice sang the words to the first line slowly, strong, and clear, drawing out the notes. She closed her eyes, seeming to sing from the heart as she continued, "*and did I hear you say . . .*"

At this point, Kasey turned to the band and nodded. They came in strong, picking up the pace. She continued with the song, and by this time, everyone in the bar was staring at the stage. Off to the side, the young cowboy called Vermont jumped up and exited the bar, but before Kasey finished the song's last note, he was back, and behind him came a stream of people.

Ted looked at Cole, "You know she could do that?"

Cole stared at the girl on the stage, "No idea."

From the bar, the bartender called into the kitchen, "Throw on the best steak we have. Make it medium rare."

The song ended, and Kasey turned to consult with the band. Turning back to the microphone, she pulled the slack out of the cord and coiled it in her hand, seeing how much slack there was. Then she turned back to the crowd.

"Here's one that Loretta Lynn sings called, 'I'm a Honky Tonk Girl.' It is a good song to dance to," she said, and the band picked up the tune. It was a song with a good dance beat, but no one had begun to dance. Kasey hopped off the stage, bringing the mic with her. She approached a table of young cowboys, and picking one, she crooked her finger to him as she crooned, *"Ever since you left me, I've done nothing but wrong; many a night I've laid awake and cried."* She pulled the cowboy up, and they two-stepped away from the table, the young man grinning down at the girl. Dancing with him as she sang, Kasey moved him across the floor until she reached a table of girls. Reaching over, she pulled a giggling girl up and left her dancing with the young man. Other couples began to join them, and the dance floor began to fill. Kasey returned to the stage and finished the song.

"Where the hell did she come from?" Ted asked no one in particular.

"No idea," Cole repeated.

Ben mumbled, "Colorado?"

Kasey again consulted the band and turned back to the crowd. "This is a rodeo dance. I think we need to pick it up a notch. Here is a song by Jeanie C. Riley called 'Harper Valley PTA'. Hope you like it."

It wasn't just that her voice was strong and clear and that every note was right on; it was Kasey's presence on the stage as well. She radiated the songs. She became the character of the music and drew the audience in. She moved around the stage, making eye contact with people in the audience, smiling, laughing, and sashaying as she sang. The crowd loved it. After about twenty minutes, Kasey told the crowd that the band would take a break, and she headed to the bar.

***

The bartender came over to Kasey as she ate her steak. "Lady, if you stay, I'll pay you for the night."

"You're on," Kasey smiled. "And I will need a to-go box for part of this. I can't eat it all in one sitting. But leave the salad, and I will nibble on it after the next set."

"You really haven't eaten since yesterday?" the barman asked.

"It's been a bad week," Kasey replied, cutting another bite of steak. "But it is starting to look up."

***

Kasey rolled out the songs after that. She sang rousing Johnny Horton songs, "Sink the Bismarck" and "North to Alaska," then slowed it down with Patsy Cline's "Crazy" and "Walking After Midnight." The bar became so crowded that there was standing room only, and still, people were trying to crowd in.

Ben looked at Cole and Ted. "If you guys want to go back to the motel," he said, "I'll catch a ride back with someone. I want to listen to this."

Cole looked at Ben, "I'll stay a while. She's good."

"I'd like to know what the hell she's doing chasing cans when she can sing like that?" Ted commented.

After the second set, when the music started again, Cole got up and went to the bar for a refill. He signaled the bartender over and ordered a Bud. When the barman brought him the bottle, Cole asked, "Where'd you get your singer from?"

"Hell, if I know," he replied. "She came in here with seventeen cents and wanted as much orange juice as she could get with that." The bartender indicated the change, still sitting on the counter by her plate. "Said she hadn't eaten since Friday night. Said she'd sing for some food, and I was desperate enough to give her a try. It was my lucky day."

Cole looked back at the crowded bar. "I would have to agree with you on that," he said thoughtfully.

Only once during the whole night did Kasey falter. When a voice called out for her to sing the Donna Fargo hit, "Happiest Girl in the Whole USA," Kasey looked momentarily stunned, and then recovering her composure, she smiled and told the crowd that was a song she hadn't learned yet so she couldn't sing it. She moved on quickly to something else.

When the bartender announced the last call for drinks just before one a.m., the band launched into one last song, "I Fall to Pieces," another of Patsy Cline's. As Kasey sang, the bar quieted, listening to the mournful sounds. When she finished, the guitarist spoke into his microphone thanking everyone for coming. The band turned to start tearing down their equipment.

Kasey turned around to the band. "Hey guys, can I use the mic for one more?" she asked. When they nodded, she turned back to the crowd, where many of the people were already starting to stand up and move toward the door. Kasey spoke again into the microphone.

"Since it is technically Sunday morning, here is one last song to get you into the Lord's Day."

Kasey pulled the stool from the piano and sat down. Closing her eyes, she began to sing. She sang like she had when she started the evening, without musical accompaniment, in a strong, clear voice, "*Amazing Grace, how sweet the sound that saved a wretch like me,*" her voice was strong, drawing out the words. "*I once was lost, but now I'm found, was blind, but now I see.*" At the end of these lines, she began to strum her guitar softly as she continued.

The bar went absolutely still. People stopped moving, and some who had been leaving dropped back into their chairs. Her voice and that song were mesmerizing. She was almost finished with the second verse when the rest of the band joined her with background music. Kasey flashed them a smile and continued. When she reached the song's end, she repeated the first verse once more, telling the crowd to sing along with her. Hearing the familiar words again, many of the crowd joined in.

"I think I just went to church," Ted mumbled.

The bar was still when the song came to an end. It was like they were all under a spell, and no one knew what to do. Then suddenly, from somewhere in the back, a drunken voice rang out, "You shing 'em, shishter." The crowd began to laugh, and the spell was broken. From the stage, Kasey smiled and said into the mic, "Vaya con Dios, my friends." She shook hands with the band members and stepped off the stage, heading for her guitar case and her to-go box of steak.

Cole watched Kasey head to the bar and downed the last of his beer. Looking at Ted, he commented mildly, "Guess we didn't get that extra sleep we planned on. But Ben and I will still pick you up at 6:15 a.m. You going to roust the others?"

"I'll be up and get them moving. Can we make the airport in time?"

"Should be able to. Won't be much traffic that early. Ben will drop us off and go back to bed." Cole looked at the people streaming out of the bar. "See you in the morning then." He and Ben headed out to their pickup.

They were parked just a short distance from the bar, and Cole tossed Ben the keys and climbed in the passenger seat. There was something nice about having the young man with him to do a lot of the driving. Cole slumped in the seat and thought about the night. They had planned to just get a bite to eat and head to the motel. So much for plans.

Ben turned the corner and drove slowly, missing walkers heading to vehicles. Cole noticed a figure on the side of the street that looked familiar. It was Kasey, and she was surveying the front of her pickup. Cole punched Ben lightly and indicated the girl ahead.

"Stop a minute. Must be something wrong," Cole said. He rolled down his window. "Trouble?" he inquired.

Kasey looked up, and recognizing the two men, she smiled. "Well, not exactly trouble, but I am so hemmed in I can't get out. I don't think there is a foot on either end of this pickup. I guess I have to wait for whoever owns one of these vehicles to come out and move one."

Cole looked at Kasey's pickup, then back at Ben. "Take this back to the motel. I'll get her out and have her drop me off. Those outfits could have drunks going home with someone else and not be coming back for their cars until morning."

Cole climbed out of the pickup. "Give me your keys," he said. "These other cars might not move tonight. I can get you out."

Kasey was quick to take him up on the offer. She dug the keys out of her pocket and headed to the passenger side. She climbed in with the guitar case. "You are coming to my rescue again," she said. "Pretty soon, I will have to put you on a payroll."

Cole grinned at her. "This is no big deal, and you can drop me off at my motel on the way to the fairgrounds. It's on the way." While he talked, Cole had the pickup started and began inching backward, then forward, then back again, each time getting the big rig turned a little more toward the street. He drove with complete confidence, seeming to know just before touching the vehicle in front or behind. In a short time, the pickup could finally pull out on the street.

"I really didn't think that was possible," Kasey commented. "But I'm glad it was. I wasn't sure what to do. I didn't want to sleep in it in town."

"Young lady," Cole laughed, "I have driven too many miles to let a hemmed-in pickup get me. It's no big deal. But since I'm talking to you, I have to ask you a question that Ted asked me earlier, and I couldn't answer," Cole glanced over at the girl. "He asked what the hell are you doing running barrels at rodeos when you can sing so well."

Kasey smiled. "There is much more to the music business than just having a good voice. The really famous ones write a lot of their music. I don't do any of that. A career in music means agents and contracts and traveling, but without horses. I think it takes a special person to want to do that. I'm not that special person. Rodeoing has been my dream."

Cole nodded. They pulled up to a red light, and Cole looked at Kasey and asked, "So, who are you?"

Kasey was puzzled by the question. She looked back at him. "What do you mean?"

"So, who are you?" he repeated. "Are you the sad-eyed, serious girl I met last weekend or the vibrant, assured entertainer I saw tonight? You were animated on that stage. It was like you came alive up there."

"Oh," Kasey smiled, leaning back in her seat. "I guess in a way I am both, but the main me is last weekend's girl. When I get up on a stage, I become the music, the characters in the music. The music flows through me, and I can leave everything else behind for a little bit. Maybe that is another reason I don't want a music career. When I do perform, the music literally pulsates through me. It's like I can feel it in my veins. If I had a music career, I am afraid I would lose that feeling. For me, it's like having a high or something."

"But you couldn't sing the Donna Fargo hit," Cole commented. "You do know that one, don't you?"

Kasey nodded, looking out the window. "Singing that song right now would be a total lie. I couldn't do that. I couldn't do justice to that song. It's a joyful song. Maybe next year I can sing it, but not now."

Cole put the blinker on and turned into the Mo Rest Motel. The parking lot was crowded, so he went to the end and turned the pickup so that it was heading out before he put it in neutral. He opened the door and slid out while Kasey kicked her legs over the gear shift and slid into the driver's seat. Cole turned to her before shutting the door.

"I never want to hear that you don't have money for food again," he said gravely. "That is why you have friends. You come to friends if you need something."

"I knew I could raise food money tonight," Kasey defended herself. "It was no big deal. I wasn't going to starve in a day."

"I'm just saying, I don't want to hear of you going without food again," Cole gave her a severe look. "You get in a bind; you come to me next time," he hesitated, then added sternly, "I mean it."

Cole closed the door, but Kasey rolled down the window. "Okay, but hopefully, I won't ever be this low again. I'm finally having a good week." Just before Cole turned away, Kasey added, "Hey, you must not have made the finals at Reno if you are still here."

"Well, actually, I did," Cole smiled. "Four of us are chartering a plane to fly there in the morning. The plan was to stay in town for a good night's sleep. That plan got scrapped the minute you stood up there on that stage and opened your mouth."

"I'm glad you made the finals," Kasey said, "but sorry that you didn't get your sleep."

Cole smiled at her, "Don't be," he said, "I'm not." He slapped her door and turned away, heading toward the motel.

CHAPTER 3

DOWN TIME

On Sunday morning, the rodeo grounds in North Platte were quiet. However, Kasey noticed a difference right away. She hadn't gotten halfway to the hydrant with her horses and bucket, before several people greeted her. Suddenly, she was noticed.

"Hey, Kasey, that was a great show last night," came from one young woman stepping out of a camper. Then a couple of young guys roping a hay bale stopped to smile at her and comment, "You're the singer, aren't you? Great time last night." By the time Kasey reached the water, she was almost self-conscious as she saw some people nudging others and pointing. On the way back to her rig, one cowboy even fell in beside her and started talking to her. Kasey got the horses fed and escaped to the camper for some privacy. She wasn't expecting the attention.

At about nine a.m., there was a knock at her door. Opening it, Kasey was face-to-face with a middle-aged cowboy. "Ma'am," he said, "I heard you did a pretty good job last night with "Amazing Grace." We are going to have a cowboy church over by the grandstand at ten, and I was wondering if you would want to come and sing for us. People are saying that you are really good."

Kasey was surprised, but also pleased. It was a nice compliment, after all. She smiled, "I'll be over. Just let me know what you want me to sing, and I'll see if I know it."

"I'm pretty sure we'd want "Amazing Grace" again," the man said. "I don't run this shindig, but I speak at it occasionally. It is pretty informal."

Kasey wandered over to the grandstand just before ten, carrying her guitar. If anything, she got even more attention, and when she looked behind her, she felt like the Pied Piper with a line of people following her. She hadn't gotten far when Ben fell in beside her.

"You made quite a stir, you know," he commented.

Kasey smiled at him. "I didn't intend to do that." She replied. "I was just trying to make a couple of bucks."

"Yeah, Cole said you were out of money and hadn't eaten. He was pretty pissed about that."

"It wasn't that big a deal," Kasey defended herself. "I knew I could make enough to eat on. Cole shouldn't feel like he has to take care of me just because he caught me crying over a dog."

"Cole is a good guy," Ben went on. "He's taken me under his wing for several years now, or I sure wouldn't be here competing. I owe him all of this."

Kasey gave Ben a quizzical look at that, but they had reached the grandstand, and there was no time to pursue it.

The cowboy church was pretty informal. One cowboy Kasey recognized as a calf roper was the informal emcee, reading from the Bible and leading them in prayer. The man who had come to ask her to sing spoke casually about the cowboy way of life and related it to scripture. When he finished, he mentioned hearing from others that Kasey had sung "Amazing Grace" the night before and that she would sing again this morning.

Kasey strummed the guitar and began the song. In the cool, clear morning air, her voice carried well. As she had done in the bar, she invited the crowd to sing along as she repeated the first lines a second time. When the song ended, a voice called out, asking her to sing something else. Kasey thought a minute and began to sing, "Nearer My God to Thee," and after that, she finished with "God Be With You Til We Meet Again." In the silence that followed, someone started to clap, and the rest followed suit. Embarrassed, Kasey could only smile. She left that gathering with a whole assortment of new best friends, most of whom she didn't even know their names.

The Sunday performance started at 8 p.m., so it was a long day of waiting. But unlike the rodeos she had previously attended, she was seldom alone. People stopped to visit and then moved on. A handsome young bull rider saw Kasey at the concession stand and bought her a barbeque. When she took her horses out for exercise, people smiled and nodded. Kasey found herself invited to small groups as they visited outside.

But eventually, it was time to start thinking of the evening performance, and people became busy. Kasey was riding Roan again, so she saddled him and took him to the arena to warm him up with the other contestants already there. She brought him back to the trailer when they called for the arena to be cleared. Kasey took off his bridle, loosened his saddle, and gathered together the skid boots she would put on him before she mounted up again. Kasey didn't want to forget anything at the last minute. The rodeo started, and Kasey watched the bareback riders and then wandered back to her trailer. Waiting was the hardest part.

Finally, it was time for the barrels, and Kasey was ready. While her luck seemed to be changing with winning the first go, it hadn't changed in her draws. She was again at the bottom of the ground. There were a dozen girls in this performance, and she was last. But as her run approached, Kasey kept herself focused and relaxed. It paid off. She and Roan ran a flawless pattern again, only having a bobble coming around the third barrel when Roan had a slight slip on the churned-up ground. As they exited the arena, the time wouldn't place them first, but second place was theirs. So, Kasey would get a check for each go-round as well as the average check. This was a big payout for her. Between this win and her money from singing, Kasey was set for now. And there was a good chance she might be getting a check from Kingfisher. She had talked to a girl who had just come from Kingfisher the night before, and Kasey was still leading it there. Kasey could call her sister and have her watch for a possible check from that rodeo. Now, it was time to think about the Fourth of July rodeos.

***

Monday morning dawned with few outfits still at the North Platte rodeo grounds. For Kasey, it was a lazy morning. She would have to pull out this day, but she needed somewhere to go until the Greeley rodeo, which started on Thursday. It was an easy day of driving to get to Greeley, and there was no guarantee that the rodeo grounds would be open early. She thought she would go in that direction and find a little rodeo grounds or arena somewhere along the way where she could stop. So, before hooking up her pickup to the trailer, Kasey hit the grocery store and stocked up on supplies, took her propane tanks to get filled, and found a feed store that she could stop at on her way out of town with her trailer and replenish her hay supply. When she returned to the rodeo grounds, even fewer outfits were still there, but she saw that Ben was hooked up but hadn't left. He met her as she backed her truck up to the trailer and helped direct her to the hitch.

"Where are you heading from here?" Ben asked when she got out of the pickup and went to secure the hitch.

"Well, I am up in Greeley on Thursday and Friday nights," Kasey answered, "But that is three days away. I thought I'd just head that way and see if I could find a place to stop. Otherwise, I guess I'll go all the way and see if I can get into the grounds early. I stocked up on food, propane, and hay, so if I can find a place to park and unload, I'd prefer to let the horses relax. What about you?"

"I'm up in Greeley on Friday night, and Cole's meeting me there. He's up Friday night and then headed to Dickinson. I'll meet him again at either Belle or Mobridge. I forget which. He and Ted and some other guys are trying to hit as many as they can. Cowboy Christmas gets pretty wild sometimes."

"I've heard that. When I entered, I wasn't sure how I'd make more than the ones I entered. I go from Greeley to Belle Fouche and then Mobridge," Kasey continued. "I'm just learning the ropes here. But before that, I have three days to find somewhere to stay."

"Why don't you follow me?" Ben offered. "There is a roping arena around the Sterling, Colorado area I have overnighted before. No one cares. I am going there today, and Josie is getting dropped off there tomorrow night. She's on the Fourth of July break between summer sessions. She's going to travel with me, and I'll drop her back off at school after the Fourth."

"That would be great," Kasey answered, but added, "if you are sure it won't cause any problems between you and Josie."

Ben grinned, catching her meaning. "Josie knows me. Guess she has me hogtied, or maybe I'm just a one-woman man. We're going to get married you know. As soon as she graduates from college."

"I didn't know that," Kasey smiled back. "And if you are okay with it, I'd like to follow you. Just nice to know I am not camping somewhere strange all by myself."

So, it was decided. The two outfits pulled out of North Platte just before noon, and it was midafternoon when Ben pulled into an arena a couple of miles out of a Sterling. It was owned by a roping club. Kasey could see the arena had been used recently, probably for a week-end roping. But Ben told her he had stayed here before, and either no one turned up, or if they did, it was just an area rancher who stopped to visit.

Kasey thought the place was perfect. It was completely fenced with several acres around the arena that had plenty of grass. Kasey and Ben turned their horses loose to graze on different sides of the arena, and the horses did not attempt to wander toward each other. They were just glad to be free and able to graze and roll. They were too seasoned to worry about fighting with each other.

"I'm going to grill hamburgers," Ben told Kasey. "I got plenty. You want me to throw a couple on for you?"

"Hey, that sounds good," Kasey replied. "I'll throw together stuff for the rest of the meal. I meant it when I said I stocked up on food."

***

The meal was over, and with the sun setting, Ben and Kasey sat in lawn chairs around the campfire that Ben had built to grill over. The heat went out of the air as the sun went down, and the small fire crackled merrily.

"Thank you for suggesting this," Kasey started. "I'm not afraid to be alone, but it is nice to know I'm not."

"No problem," Ben answered, "Cole told me to check on you before I left and see if you had plans. Glad he thought of it."

Kasey gave Ben a long look. "I hope Cole doesn't think he has to take care of me just because he has a couple of times already. I don't want to be a bother."

Ben grinned. "It's just Cole. He thinks about others. He's a good guy."

They sat for several minutes watching the fire die down, and suddenly, Ben started talking again.

"I was 14 years old when I first met Cole," he said reflectively. "Cole had just gone to his first National Finals Rodeo and done well. In our part of the country, he was suddenly every kid's hero. Our tribal leaders got Cole to put on a weeklong rodeo clinic for Native boys. I jumped at the chance to go. There were maybe a dozen boys signed up, and a couple elders took us out each day. We went through all the rough stock and timed events," Ben stopped and took a sip of his beer, thinking. "The other boys had fun, but some didn't go all of the days. But I was there waiting for the van to take us out long before it was time to go in the mornings.

"There was something about getting out of town and being on Cole's ranch that I loved. I had ridden horses a lot, mostly bareback. There were always loose horses running around our village, and we boys would ride them a lot, but I hadn't really been on a ranch. Cole and his dad were awesome. His dad rodeoed when he was younger, so they were our coaches. When the week was over, I was lost just staying in town again."

Ben got up and threw another log on the fire. "I spent all day Sunday thinking about it. I was living with my grandmother then. I had been in and out of foster care when my grandmother was ill, but right then, I was back with her. I told her I had a job at the ranch, and I met the mail truck at the post office on Monday morning. It came in by 6:30 in the morning, dropped the mail bags, and left before seven. I talked the mail carrier into letting me hitch a ride to the turn-off to the Sanders' ranch, about nine miles south of town. They had a seven-mile gravel road going into their place. I hoofed it all the way but didn't get there until well after eight.

"Cole and his dad were already off riding on some cows somewhere. Cole's mom saw me with the horses and came out to talk to me. She recognized me from the week before. She's a neat lady. She was a barrel racer when Pete, Cole's dad, met her. She and Pete met while rodeoing when they were younger. Anyway, Anne asked me if I wanted to ride with her. She was going out to meet the guys as they came in. They were bringing some yearlings into the ranch headquarters. So, I rode out with her, and she told me how to hold my reins, where to place my feet in the stirrups, stuff like that. All I wanted then was to learn the right way to do things. I wanted to be just like Cole. I stayed out there all day, and they all just sort of acted like I was supposed to be there.

"When it got to be late afternoon, I figured I better head back. I was going to walk back out to the highway and thumb a ride. But Pete said no, they would take me back to town. Pete asked me if I wanted to come back, and of course I did. So, he said he wanted to go and talk to my grandmother first. Pete and Cole drove me to town and talked to my grandmother. They arranged it so that I would ride the mail truck every morning, and someone would meet me at the highway. Most days, they drove me out to the highway about 4:30 in the afternoon to meet the truck for a return to town. I spent the whole summer out there. They even paid me a small wage. That was pretty big stuff for a fourteen-year-old Indian kid."

Ben sat quietly for a while. Finally, Kasey asked, "So what happened when school started?"

"I only got out to the ranch on Saturdays. I went out for football in the fall and basketball in the winter, so there wasn't much time after practice for anything except supper and homework. Pete told me if I wanted a job the next summer, I had to study and do well in school. He wasn't going to hire a dropout. That was probably the best incentive for doing my homework," Ben grinned. "I wasn't much interested in school, but I wasn't a dummy. I was just unmotivated."

"Then, when we had our games, I noticed Pete and Anne in the crowd. Cole, too, if he was home. He was rodeoing heavy then, so he was gone a lot. But Pete and Anne came to every home game and made a point of congratulating me if they could," Ben smiled at the memories. "They even picked up my grandmother sometimes and brought her to watch me. They didn't have to do that, but they did."

Ben got up and went to his cooler for another beer. When he returned, he took up his story. "Basketball season was half over when my grandmother got sick again. She had heart problems and other problems and was sick a lot. She must have talked to Pete and Anne, though, because when the ambulance came for her, Grandmother told me Pete would come for me. And he did. He told me to pack my stuff and took me home. Grandmother went to a nursing home after she was released from the hospital. I lived with Pete and Anne for the rest of my high school career and the year after high school. They mounted me for high school rodeos, hauled me to rodeos, and still paid me a wage. You see, Cole is the way he is because that's the way his folks are. They take care of people. I was pretty lucky. I was a nowhere kid in that village. I had nowhere to go, no goals, no ambition. But out on the ranch, I found my way."

"Where were your folks?" Kasey inquired.

"Who knows?" Ben laughed bitterly. "I have no idea who my father was, and my mom was an alcoholic. Drank herself to death after I was out of high school but was always gone before that. She'd drop in sometimes, on and off, but she was a mess."

"I'm sorry," Kasey murmured. "I had such great parents. I sometimes forget that others aren't so lucky."

"Don't feel bad," Ben smiled at her. "My grandmother was pretty special; only she was old and sick a lot. Pretty much, Pete and Anne were my parents. Still are. I just found them later than most kids."

"So, do you still live with them?"

"No, a year out of high school, an Indian lease came up that bordered Pete's land. I put in for it and got it. I got a scatter site and live there now."

"Scatter site?"

Ben grinned, "There are some things that are great about the tribe. I put in for a five-acre tract of land and got a house put on it. The five acres and the house are mine if I pay them off, and I will. I make yearly payments. The leased land will support about 50 head of livestock. For now, while I am going down the road, Pete runs on my land and pays me for the pasture lease. When I quit rodeoing, I will run my own cattle. Fifty head won't support a family, but it is a start, and there are always more Indian leases coming up that I can try to get. But this was perfect because it was next to Pete's."

"What about Josie? Does she like the place?"

"Josie's family ranches north of town. She's used to living in the country, so she's pretty happy we have a place already. She wants to come back to the reservation when she graduates and teach there. Our Native kids don't always have good role models. Josie wants to come back and make a difference."

"Good for her," Kasey said. "That is a pretty good aim in life."

"So," Ben finished. "You can just stop worrying about Cole taking care of you. He comes by it naturally. These horses are his, and the rig is his. But I am buying the horses from him, and I have an older pickup at home. I'm building up. But Pete is pretty adamant I don't go deep in debt. They have taught me a lot over the years. In high school, they kept a pretty tight thumb down on me. But it was good. I had no background in any kind of finances. If they didn't teach me how to save, I'd blow my money on fast food."

"Did you ever compete in the rough stock events or just steer wrestling?" Kasey was curious.

"I wanted so damn bad to follow in Cole's footsteps and ride bulls and broncs," Ben replied. "In high school, I tried all the events. I was pretty good with the rough stock until about my junior year. I really bulked up then. You don't see a lot of bronc riders that are big men. My football seasons took off, but it didn't help me in my riding. With my size, I started having more success in doggin', so when high school was over, I focused on that. I like to rope, but I'm not good enough. I realized I was donating my money to the good ropers. I will go to some jackpots and rope, but not in the pro ranks. So, if I want to win, I stick to steer wrestling."

They sat in silence for a while, watching the fire die down. After a time, Kasey stretched and got up. "I'm catching my horses and putting them up. Then I am crashing for the night." Kasey turned and started off. She hadn't gotten far when she turned back, "Thanks, Ben. I understand Cole better now. I just don't want to be a bother to anyone."

***

The next day dawned. June was hot and windy. Kasey and Ben just lazed around, letting the horses have their freedom to graze. Kasey had a good book she curled up with for much of the day. It was mid-afternoon when Kasey heard a vehicle pull in and soon voices. Looking out her window, she saw a car pulled up by Ben's outfit. Josie and two young guys were climbing out. Kasey went back to reading. These were Ben's friends. But it wasn't long before there was a knock at the door. Kasey opened it and found Josie outside.

"Hey," Josie said, "you want to join us for supper tonight? I brought a bunch of brats and buns. Our friends are going to tent it tonight and leave in the morning."

"I'd love to if I won't crash your party," Kasey said. "I can bring a salad and chips."

"Sounds perfect," Josie replied. Then after hesitating, she asked, "And if you wouldn't mind, Ben was telling us you sing. Would you bring your guitar?"

"I'd love to," Kasey smiled. "I'll mix up a salad and be out in a bit."

***

It was a fun evening. The two extra guys were from Josie's university, a small college in the Black Hills of South Dakota. They knew Ben and were on their way home for the rest of the summer. So, they traded insults, stories, and jokes all night. Long after dark, Josie pulled out marshmallows, graham crackers, and chocolate, and they found sticks to melt the marshmallows over the fire to make s'mores. Kasey brought out her guitar, and they sang old country and campfire songs they all knew.

It had been a long time since Kasey hung out with kids her age, laughing and enjoying each other. It felt good. It was well after midnight when they packed it in. As Kasey climbed into her camper, she realized that on this night, she had been happy again. For a short time, she wasn't thinking about her family. For a short time, she felt whole.

Wednesday dawned not as hot. Josie's two friends headed out by noon. Ben and Josie headed to Sterling for the afternoon. Kasey told Ben she'd watch the horses as she had no desire to go anywhere. She was satisfied just staying put. About four in the afternoon, some pickups and stock trailers pulled in. One unloaded steers and the rest had horses. The roping club that owned the arena was having a practice. One cowboy came over and talked to Kasey, inviting her to watch them rope if she wanted. They had no concerns about her and Ben camping there. This was the West. If they could help other horsemen and women who were passing through, then that was what they would do.

And so Wednesday evening also went by fast. Ben and Josie were back before dark and watched the roping. It was a pleasant last night in their impromptu camping spot, but they would pull out the next day for Greeley. The downtime was over. Cowboy Christmas would soon be underway.

CHAPTER 4

COWBOY CHRISTMAS

The number of rodeos throughout the country over the fourth of July weekend was incredible. Cowboys called it Christmas because there were so many chances to enter and win. Most contestants picked regions of the country where they could enter rodeos within travel distance and trade out. Trading out was the practice of entering a rodeo and requesting certain days or performances to compete at so that they could enter as many rodeos as possible. Sometimes it didn't work for the rodeo to trade a contestant out, but the rodeo secretaries tried their best. It was harder for the cowboys and cowgirls that hauled horses to do this as they couldn't fly, but they could still hit several rodeos, especially if there were no more than one go-round at a rodeo. The rough stock riders who only had to haul their riggin' bags could jump in vehicles with other cowboys and hit a multitude of rodeos, crisscrossing a wide region of the country.

Kasey was entered at Greeley, Colorado where there were two go-rounds for the barrels. Greeley started before the bulk of the other July 4th rodeos, so she was entered there first. Kasey was up the first night at Greeley, on Thursday, June 29th. Then she intended to lay over one day and was in the slack on Saturday morning July 1st. After she ran that day, she would push off for Belle

Fouche, South Dakota for the evening performance on Sunday, July 2nd. Both Belle and Mobridge, SD rodeos ran the 2nd, 3rd, and 4th, every year. Belle had one go-round, but Mobridge had two goes. Kasey was up on the 3rd and 4th at Mobridge. It was a doable schedule.

Ben told her that he and Cole were both up in Greeley, but Ben was up Friday and Saturday while Cole was up both Thursday and Friday nights. Then, Cole was entered in a multitude of rodeos. Ben wasn't sure how Cole would make them all, but there were always vehicles heading in different directions with which Cole could catch a ride. Cole was off to Dickinson, North Dakota, right after Greeley and then would hit Belle, Crawford, Nebraska, and Killdeer, North Dakota, in some order before meeting Ben in Mobridge sometime on the night of July 3rd. Cole would finish up his Cowboy Christmas at Mobridge on July 4th. It would be a whirlwind week.

Greeley started out relaxed since no other rodeos were going on for the first couple of days. Kasey, Ben, and Josie headed over on Thursday and found good spots to park next to each other. Kasey liked Josie, and having another girl to talk to was fun. Josie was a ranch girl and would ride out with Ben and Kasey when they exercised their horses. A couple of years older than Kasey, Josie was a pretty Native girl in her last year of college. Kasey felt comfortable with Josie as if they had known each other for years. For Kasey, it was also nice not to be alone. She was making friends and friends were a comfort.

The first performance was well attended, and the crowd was loud. Kasey rode Roan to start this week of competitions, and he ran well. When the first performance was over, she was sitting second by hundredths of a second. She hoped it would hold but ultimately was pleased with the run. She didn't see Cole's rides that night as the arena was quite a distance from where she was parked. She was getting Roan ready for the barrel race when Cole rode his bronc and putting the horse up after her run when the bulls were on. But Josie stopped by after the rodeo and said that Cole's saddle bronc didn't have a good night, so his score was mediocre. He had a good bull, though, rode it well, and was sitting first at the end of the performance. Cole had two goes in the saddle bronc so he would be up again the next night.

Since Kasey wasn't competing during the second performance, she could watch Ben and Cole's events. Ben had a great run in the doggin' and was sitting second. It was an excellent time, so they all hoped the time would hold in the first go-round. For his second go in the bronc riding, Cole had a big paint mare that had been to the National Finals the year before. This was a match-up that the announcer made a big deal of as Cole got ready. The runner-up horse of the year with an eight-time qualifier to the National Finals would be a pair to watch. The crowd was excited, anticipating a great ride. They weren't disappointed. The big paint was strong and known for her big rear as she came out of the chute. Cole had a perfect mark-out, keeping his spurs in the horse's shoulder until the front feet hit the ground. From there, the horse came unglued, with big lunges and high kicks, but Cole got the rhythm, spurring every jump. To the bystander, it looked like the ride was effortless. To the experienced eye, it was spectacular. The judges rewarded it with the top score by several points. That ride would be hard to top as both horse and rider were awarded high scores.

Kasey watched from the fence near the chutes with Josie and Ben, where most of the rodeo people congregated to watch. It was fun to be able to watch and not worry about competing the same night. The girls smiled at each other, and Josie remarked that it had been a fantastic night. Ben just grinned at her.

"Hey, Kasey," Ben said, "we are going to head out as soon as Cole gets his riggin' bag packed and catch a bite to eat. You want to join us?"

Kasey looked from Ben to Josie. "No, you two go and enjoy; you don't need a tag-along."

"No, really," Ben went on, "Cole is coming too, so you might as well come. Cole is heading out as soon as the rodeo is over with some bull riders. He wants a good meal before he leaves."

Josie nodded, "Come with us. I hate being the only girl. It will give me someone to talk to while the guys talk broncs and steers."

So, Kasey went with them. They all crowded into Cole's pickup and found a hamburger joint near the fairgrounds. They all had burgers, and despite Kasey's efforts, she wasn't allowed to pay for her meal. It was fun to be part of a group of friends. Kasey enjoyed listening to the three people who had known each other for years. Ben and Josie were so much in love, and Cole was like an older brother to Ben. They didn't tarry, though, and the time went by quickly. They pulled into the rodeo grounds just as the bull riding was finishing up. Cole had a ride right after the rodeo with a carload of cowboys headed to North Dakota, so he needed to get back. Cowboy Christmas was definitely on.

The next few days were busy ones. By the time Kasey unloaded on July 3rd at the rodeo grounds in Mobridge, she was ready to be at the last rodeo of the long weekend. Her second run at Greeley was also good. She placed third in the first go and second in the second go to take home average money too. She rode JC in Belle. The little mare was off, and she didn't place. It wasn't a bad run, but just not fast enough. Now she was in Mobridge, where she had two goes to run. She was up in the evening performance on the third and the afternoon performance on the Fourth. She planned to ride Roan during the evening performance and JC on the Fourth in the afternoon. JC had the least experience and seemed somewhat intimidated by the lights. Kasey needed the wins, so she would try to get JC seasoned in the day performances as much as possible.

The Mobridge rodeo grounds were on the edge of town, backed up to the small airport. A carnival was up and running in the large open area between the grandstand and the highway. Kasey drove off the highway, and following a sign for the contestants' entrance, she drove alongside the carnival to the contestant's gate and pulled around to the back of the arena. It had been an easy drive from Belle Fourche to Mobridge, so Kasey had several hours to relax before the evening performance started. Maybe she'd walk over through the carnival just for fun. It had been years since she had been to a carnival.

The grounds were crowded when Kasey pulled in. Besides the usual pickups and horse trailers, there were gaily decorated floats from the parade that the town had in the morning. Mobridge went all out for the Fourth of July and had two parades, one on the third, and one on the Fourth. She didn't see many familiar faces, so she pulled toward the rear of the grounds and found a place to fall in line. She located the water hydrants, watered her horses, and then set out hay for them to munch on.

They were seasoned travelers by now and ate and drank when it was offered.

The carnival was popping when Kasey got there. Families with little children wandered from ride to ride, and teenagers in groups or pairs wove their way through the crowds, joshing and laughing, enjoying rides or trying their hand at the games of chance and skill. Kasey had more fun watching the people than the games.

As she shuffled through the crowds, a figure fell in step with her. She looked up and recognized a cowboy she had seen at North Platte. She didn't know his name, but he had been at the bar the night she sang.

"You're the singing barrel racer," the young man grinned at her.

"Is that what I'm called now?"

"Well, since I never caught your name," he stuck his hand out to her, "that's the best I can do. I'm Kolt Hanson."

Kasey smiled. "Kasey Jacobs," she said. "You're a rough stock rider, but I don't know which event."

"Barebacks and saddle broncs," Kolt replied.

Kasey studied him. He was taller than she was, but that wasn't saying much. Lean and wiry, he looked the part of a bronc rider. He was cocky; at least that was how her sister would describe him. Kasey could see he was sure of himself as he walked beside her.

"So, you must be entered here tonight," Kolt said. "I saw you were up at Belle yesterday."

"Yeah, that was wasted money," Kasey replied, "but I have done better this past month than I thought I would, so I am not complaining."

"So, was it true that you were flat broke when you sang in that bar?"

"Geesh, how did that get around?" Kasey was surprised.

"News travels fast on these circuits," Kolt laughed. "No secrets here."

They walked and visited until they reached the end of the midway and then circled back toward the rodeo grounds. By the time they walked back through the contestant gates, Kasey had a date to go dancing downtown after the performance.

***

It didn't take Kasey long to clean up after settling her horses that evening after the performance. Kasey was flying high. Roan had a flawless run, and when the dust settled, she won the first go. Going dancing was her celebratory activity tonight.

Kolt was waiting for her when she emerged from her camper, and they headed downtown in Kolt's massive boat-of-a-car. He drove a powder blue 1962 Chrysler New Yorker with a matching blue interior. Kolt saw Kasey taking in the interior as he slid in the driver's seat.

"It was my folks' car," he grinned. "Uses some gas, but I can get six guys in to help pay the fuel costs, and everyone has room. This baby flat flies out on the open road. It is a cowboy's dream."

"I would imagine," Kasey replied. "It is big enough."

Kasey could hear the music when they were still blocks away. The dance was popping by the time they reached the big tent on a side street in the center of town. There were several bars surrounding the area, and the beer was flowing. They hit the first bar, where

Kolt got a beer and was surprised that Kasey didn't want one.

"You do drink, don't you?" he inquired.

"I never have acquired the taste," Kasey told him. "Just don't like the stuff. I don't have anything against it. Just not for me."

Kolt snorted, "Don't know when I took a girl out and she didn't drink with me. Not sure what to do with you."

Kasey just smiled and said, "I like to dance."

They danced and visited with groups of cowboys that Kolt knew and meandered from one bar to another. The band in the tent was good, and Kasey was enjoying herself. She met numerous people and knew she would not remember all of their names, but it was fun being part of this noisy, boisterous rodeo crowd. She sometimes danced with other cowboys while Kolt stood with groups visiting.

It was nearly midnight when Kasey noticed that Kolt was getting pretty snookered. He began to dance with her more suggestively, holding her quite close during the slow music, and she found herself dodging his roving hands in the two steps. By the time the music stopped at 1 a.m., Kasey was ready to call it a night. It had been fun, but enough was enough.

It still took over a half hour to make it to the car. The groups didn't disperse right away, and Kolt and Kasey bounced from one set of people to another, visiting on their way to the car.

"Are you good to drive?" Kasey asked when they reached the powder blue monster.

"Hell, yes," Kolt replied belligerently. "Takes more beer than I've had to stop me."

Kasey dropped it. Luckily, they didn't have far to drive. But when they reached the rodeo grounds, Kolt sailed past her outfit, heading out to the far end of the line of campers that had come in late in the day.

"Um," Kasey began, "you just went by my pickup."

"I'm just going out to the end to turn around," Kolt replied smoothly. But when he reached the open area and turned, he slowed the car, shutting down the lights and turning it off.

"Hey baby," he said quietly, "why don't we just sit here for a while." He slid across the seat toward Kasey.

Kasey had been to a semester of college, and it wasn't much different than high school. She knew what Kolt had in mind, and she just wasn't interested.

"Kolt, I'm tired. I have to run in tomorrow's performance," she said. "I had a great time, but I'm going to head toward my camper."

Kasey opened the door and began to climb out. But Kolt was too quick for her. He reached for her and pulled her back, leaning down to kiss her. Kasey's mind told her, okay, one kiss and make a break for it. When they came up for air, Kasey pushed the door open and swung out. Kolt followed right behind her.

"We'd be more comfortable in the back seat," he said, grasping Kasey's arm and pulling her toward him.

"No, Kolt," Kasey said firmly. "I'm done. Thank you for the nice night, but I'm done here."

Kolt was well beyond taking no for an answer. He pulled Kasey back to him, pushing her up against the car. He kissed her hard while pulling her shirt tail from her jeans.

"No!" Kasey repeated, trying to pull back and struggling. "Let me go." She tried to stay calm, but she was somewhere between getting a little concerned and a lot angry. Time seemed to stand still as she fought his hands and advances, trying to free herself.

"Kolt," she finally warned, her voice rising, "let me go, or I'm going to scream and wake up the whole rodeo grounds."

"Now, don't be like that," Kolt murmured, but he reached up and put his hand across Kasey's mouth to stifle any screams.

Kasey got mad then and tried to take a swing at him. She realized almost immediately that her blows were ineffective. He was too close and holding her too tightly for her to be able to strike him at all. She pulled back once and was able to get out a loud "no," but Kolt was quick and strong. He pushed her toward the backseat of the big car. Suddenly, Kolt was pulled away from Kasey and sent staggering backward.

"Let the lady go, cowboy," she heard a familiar voice.

"Aw, shit," Kolt mumbled, "we were just having fun."

"No, you were having fun," Cole replied icily, "the lady was saying no."

"Well, fuck," Kolt said, "I took her out tonight."

"Watch your mouth," Cole told him sharply. "There's two kinds of cowboys going down the road, the real ones and the rodeo bums. Right now, you are acting like a bum. Makes me ashamed you're wearing a hat."

Giving Kolt a stern look, Cole turned to Kasey, who stood panting a few feet from them. "Let's get you home," he said, reaching for her arm. Together, they left Kolt and headed toward the camp.

"Where did you come from?" Kasey asked.

"I'm crashed in my pickup," Cole answered. "It's right beyond that trailer. I heard the car come in, and after a while, I heard you. I didn't know it was you, but I knew it wasn't right."

They approached an overhead light, and Kasey saw Cole smile. "I don't sleep bad in that pickup topper, but

I don't sleep really sound. You hear everything on these hot nights when all the windows and tailgate are open. I wasn't sure what night I'd get here so I didn't get a motel reserved, and this town is packed. Ben and Josie are at some friends of Josie's, so I have the camper bed to myself, but it still isn't great. And I am parked far enough out to hear what went on."

"Well, I thank you. I don't think he's really a bad guy, but he is a drunk guy," Kasey said wryly. "I haven't been out with a drunk before. I wasn't prepared for that."

"You get to some of these rodeo dances, and you find a lot of drunks," Cole cautioned. "Next time, leave before it gets to that point. Never hurts to be cautious."

They had reached Kasey's camper. "You came to my rescue one more time," she said. "You are going to think of me as nothing but trouble."

"Kasey Trouble Jacobs," Cole chucked her on the chin. "I'll remember that name. Maybe I'll see you around tomorrow, KT. Stay out of trouble." And he turned then and left her, heading back to his pickup.

CHAPTER 5

JULY HIGHWAYS

Kasey was sorry to leave Mobridge. The people there were very accommodating and friendly. She had many community people stop and talk to her the day after the rodeo as crews of volunteers cleaned the grounds and took down flags and signs. She even had a date that night to an outdoor movie. It had been ages since she had seen a movie, so that was fun. The young local cowboy who took her out was a nice guy and took her not-so-subtle hints that she was interested in watching the movie to heart, so she didn't have to fight him off. It was fun, but she did not linger with him in his pickup when he dropped her off.

She reflected on her Cowboy Christmas rodeos. She had placed well in Greeley, and that paid well. She had also placed in Mobridge in both runs and the average for another big check. She had run JC on the afternoon of the Fourth and the little mare had made her proud. They placed third in the go-round and with Roan's first place, they got a check for second in the average. She would have to call her sister during the week to see how her checking account was doing. She should be sitting pretty well.

Kasey saw Cole, Ben, and Josie only briefly on the Fourth and other than having a quick visit with Josie, Kasey had not had a chance to see her much. Ben and

Cole were entered in the afternoon performance and they headed out right after the bull riding was over. Josie needed to be dropped off at her college and then Ben and Cole headed home to Montana. The horses and Ben were taking the week off. They would drop the horses off at Cole's ranch. Cole was entered in Calgary. That was a big rodeo and did not take permits, but Ben wanted to experience it, so he would drive to Canada with Cole. She hadn't asked if Cole was entered anywhere else. She knew Calgary was a big rodeo, going on all week, and was far away.

Kasey spent the day after the Fourth in Mobridge at the rodeo grounds and then on Thursday, she traveled partway to Manawa, Wisconsin. When she found a nice fairground along the way that wasn't locked up, she pulled over and spent the night. She was up in Manawa on Friday night and then had two goes at Spooner over the weekend. She used Roan in Manawa and was leading it, but just barely.

Kasey pulled into Spooner, Wisconsin on Saturday afternoon. Kasey's runs at Spooner, one on Saturday night and the second on Sunday afternoon, were next. Neither Manawa nor Spooner were considered big rodeos, but they still had decent added money, so the payout, while not huge like North Platte, would be good. Kasey had been told that the arena in Spooner was a bit smaller, so that was her deciding point for running the mare in both goes. It might suit the little mare better than Roan.

Kasey didn't expect to see many people she knew at these Wisconsin rodeos. She saw a few familiar faces, and recognized a few names, but there wasn't a significant carryover of contestants from the rodeos of the plains to these. Plus, most of the big guns were in Calgary. Kasey had some friends of her folks who lived in southern Wisconsin, so she planned on stopping over to see them on Monday night before heading to some Kansas rodeos later in the week. Seeing old family friends was the draw that got her this far east.

By the end of the Saturday night performance, Kasey and JC had won the first go-round. All the really tough girls were entered at Calgary. There were some good girls here, but one hit a barrel, a second ran a new horse, and the third squeaked in behind Kasey to take second in the go-round. The second go would be determined after the Sunday afternoon performance was over.

It was almost ten Saturday night when Kasey decided to walk one more time to the public restrooms before going to bed. On the way back to her camper, she heard the murmur of low voices and tried to decipher their origin. As she rounded a pickup, she saw a young couple reclining against the front bumper of a pickup with a small camper on it. Kasey didn't want to interrupt them, so she skirted the area a little. She thought she recognized the pickup as the outfit of one of the pick-up men. She had seen him go to his pickup to switch horses between the barebacks and saddle broncs. But the pick-up man was an older man, and this was definitely a young couple. It was too dark to see them clearly, but it wasn't an older man. She thought the cowboy looked a little familiar, what she could see of him, but she couldn't place where she had seen him. Kasey just faded into the darkness and smiled to herself. She wondered if the older man knew the couple was out there, making out in front of his truck.

Sunday morning was lazy, but the grounds came alive about noon as the stock contractor began sorting stock while timed event cattle were being unloaded.

People began thinking about the early afternoon performance. The stock contractor was Bob Barnes Rodeo out of Cherokee, Iowa, and the trucks rolled in with livestock by late morning, coming in from a sale barn nearby. Kasey watched the activity as she tacked up JC and took her into the arena to warm up. She recognized the older pick-up man, and then with a start, she saw the young cowboy who she was pretty sure was out with the girl last night. He was the other pick-up man and was helping sort. That would make sense, she thought, that he would know the older man and feel comfortable sitting in front of his rig with a girl.

After the grand entry, Kasey put the mare up and returned to the arena to watch the first couple of events. She would have to get her horse ready during the saddle broncs, but she had some downtime before that. She could watch the bareback riding, the dogging, and get ready just after the saddle bronc riding started.

The saddle bronc event was getting ready to start, waiting for a clown act to get finished. The clown had a small vehicle decked out to look like a miniature ambulance. The small ambulance meandered, bucking and smoking, to the middle of the arena. The clown climbed out, and then, with assistants in white doctor's jackets, they climbed into the grandstand and selected a cute gal wearing a bright red cowboy hat. They carried the girl screaming and fighting to the arena fence and threw her over. Inside the makeshift ambulance was a coffin-like box they carried out and placed the girl in with her head out one side and her feet out the other. Then, the clown proceeded to cut the coffin in half. It was a cute act, with the false bottom of the coffin cleverly hidden by skirts. The girl screamed at all the appropriate times, the coffin was carried out, and

88

the clown jumped in his car, which bucked and smoked its way out of the arena.

The horses were loaded in the chutes, and one pick-up man rode in. Kasey looked around to see where the second man was when she heard a familiar voice next to her. Looking over her shoulder, she saw Ben coming to stand by her.

"Ben!" Kasey exclaimed. "I didn't think I would see you here. Are you entered?"

Ben Two Horse grinned at her, "Cole's entered here this afternoon, and then we are hot-footing it back to Calgary. I'm not entered here."

Kasey turned her attention back to the arena. "Ben, where's the other pick-up man?"

Ben looked out and studied the area. "He's in the chutes. He will be on the first saddle bronc out and then climb on his pick-up horse. He's Barnes' main pick-up man here. The other man just picks up at some of Bob's rodeos up here in the Wisconsin area."

The announcer started talking about the horse and the first rider.

"Here is your first bronc rider, a young South Dakota cowboy and one of your pick-up men. He's up on Barnes' good saddle bronc, Hellfire," the announcer hesitated a beat and then said, "This young man just fell in love this weekend, so let him hear you."

The chute gate opened almost immediately, and the cowboy came out on a big sorrel gelding. The horse reared high out of the gate, then settled into a steady bone-jarring buck. It was a good ride, but Kasey had no idea if it would place. She hadn't paid attention to the scores that were posted in the crow's nest.

"What was that about?" Kasey asked Ben.

Ben grinned, "Guess his girl came to the rodeo this weekend, and they have sort of been an item. Sometimes it doesn't pay to be well known to the announcer or stock contractor as they sometimes say things just to get a rise out of you."

"So, is it true," she asked, "about them being in love?"

"That I am not sure of," Ben replied, "but I hear they have been spending quite a bit of time together. He's a good guy, and the girl came with the other pick-up man and his wife. I think she's a pretty nice girl. She runs barrels some but not here."

"So, she's not a buckle bunny?" Kasey asked, referring to girls who chase after cowboys hoping to wear one of their trophy buckles or to have a night out with a real cowboy.

"Nah, I don't think so," Ben answered. "Talk is she never comes alone. She always comes with the older couple."

Cole was up next, and his horse came out of the chute with a high rear coming out over the corner of the gate, rattling chutes. The mark-out rule would have been waived, but it wasn't necessary as Cole kept his spurs in the horse's shoulder, marking him out perfectly. The rest of the ride was just as wild. The horse was strong and kicked high with each jump, but Cole rode him spurring with each jarring buck. When the whistle blew, the pick-up men veered in, plucked Cole off, and lowered him to the ground. It was an excellent ride, and Cole was sitting in the lead.

By then, Kasey had to get her horse ready, so she bid Ben good-bye and left him at the fence. It was good to have someone to visit with sometimes and catch up with the rodeo gossip. She knew now who she had almost stumbled on the night before on her way back from the restrooms. Apparently, she wasn't the only one to notice the young couple together.

Kasey's afternoon run on JC did not place. She was up later in the draw and the ground was not great. The mare seemed off this day, taking the first barrel too wide. Kasey wasn't too disappointed. She knew she couldn't place in every run, but she had hoped to collect an average check as well as the first for the first go. Still, with her first go win on JC, and if she placed in Manawa on Roan, the trip to Wisconsin wouldn't be wasted.

She didn't see either Ben or Cole anymore that day. She knew from Ben that one other guy was riding with them, and they were all heading directly back to Calgary. Cole was winning the first go-round in Calgary in the bulls and sitting in the top three in the saddle broncs. So, it was possible he could make some serious money there if the second go-around was just as good for him. Even better, Cole was in the top five nationally in both events. Barring injury or really poor luck, he was National Finals bound in December. Kasey knew Cole wanted to make the Finals once more. Not many men were nine-time qualifiers. Cole wanted to be in that elite group.

***

The rest of July flew by for Kasey. She continued to rack up wins or placings. After Spooner, Kasey had a couple of down days and could stop in southern Wisconsin and stay with friends of her parents, people she had known from her childhood. Seeing old friends and talking about her family with these kind people was good. They lived in the country, and while they did not have animals of their own, they had enough land for Kasey to camp and let her horses graze on hobbles during the day. It was fun being at a house and getting a good shower. But after two days there, she was ready to be off again. The rodeo road was calling to her.

The end of the third week of July took Kasey to Pretty Prairie and Burden, Kansas. There was one go-round at Burden and two at Pretty Prairie. She split the runs between both of her horses, and they ran well, placing in each. Because she was helped by that kind rancher when she had a tire blowout in Nebraska, Kasey felt she needed to enter McCook. It was such a pleasant fairground that she looked forward to returning. She was up Saturday afternoon and planned to stay that night and head out the next morning for the next rodeo.

Kasey rode JC at McCook. It was a one go-round, and she was sitting first after the Saturday performance. There was a big-name country music star performing that night at the grandstand so Kasey had been warned that if she left the infield where the rodeo contestants camped, she would have to pay to reenter the grounds because of the concert. Kasey was perusing her cupboards for a possible supper when there was a knock at the camper door. Kasey looked out the screen, and recognized a barrel racer she had seen at other rodeos.

"There's going to be a feed out here in a bit," the girl said. "Everyone is invited."

"Really? For everyone?" Kasey replied. "I don't really know anyone here."

"Erv Korkow, the stock contractor, went to town for hot dogs and burgers. He can get back in with his contractor card. Some guys went into the field next door and picked some corn. Bring chips if you can, or whatever, and join the fun." The girl smiled and was gone, spreading the word.

It was an unusual barbeque. A couple cowboys dug a shallow hole in the ground, and a fire was built in it. Then a portable panel was laid over the top and a five-gallon metal bucket, filled with water and fresh ear corn, was set on top over the fire. A couple of contestants had charcoal grills to use for the hot dogs and burgers. Whatever any of the other campers could scrounge up was laid out to be shared by all. Kasey had two cans of black olives and a jar of green so that was her contribution. Paper plates and plastic silverware appeared, and little groups of people sat telling stories and jokes. Kasey joined a group of girls who were also barrel racers. The concert started at the grandstand just before dark, and by the third song, everyone at the barbeque wandered over, finding empty seats and enjoying a night of music. Kasey enjoyed the barbeque, the camaraderie, and the music. She was glad she had decided to return to McCook for this rodeo weekend. She had been able to visit again with the rancher who had helped her with her tire in June and see a concert as well. If her time in the barrels held up, she would get money from this rodeo too.

Kasey decided to stay in Nebraska and Kansas for the rest of the month. There were rodeos at Hays, Ft. Scott, and Colby, Kansas. She also hit Burwell, Nebraska. She didn't place in each rodeo, but placed or won in most of them, so she was beginning to fly high. Her checkbook was looking pretty good too. She even had enough padding to feel comfortable to find a phone booth, and with a pocketful of change, she called her sister for a long, overdue chat. Life was much nicer when she didn't have to worry about money.

Cheyenne Frontier Days was going on at the same time as most rodeos where Kasey was competing, and Cheyenne was a big rodeo that didn't take permit holders. She knew that Cole would be at Cheyenne. Ben, on the other hand, would enter in Salt Lake City because that rodeo allowed permit holders in steer wrestling. Kasey saw neither of them for the rest of the month. She was getting to know more people but not well enough to seek anyone out for company. She did have several dates to rodeo dances in the small towns she was at, and she enjoyed herself, but she was careful to end the evening if her date drank too much alcohol or began to make too many advances. She didn't want any more complications in her life right then. The wound of losing most of her family was too painful. She did not want any strings attached to anyone at the moment. So, she kept her distance, even on a date.

CHAPTER 6

DEADWOOD

The two-lane road from Sturgis to Deadwood wound up and through pine-covered hills. Kasey remembered coming to the Black Hills of South Dakota once as a youngster with her family on a vacation. She couldn't remember exactly where they went but knew they camped in a cabin at Custer State Park for a week. Those were good times, and she remembered her whole family enjoyed being in the Black Hills.

Now Kasey was returning, heading for the Days of '76 rodeo in Deadwood. She had never been to the rodeo there, but everyone on the circuit considered it one of the best. Comments ranged from the pleasant mountain climate, the great parades, and the well-run rodeo, to the unique old mining town. Kasey had been warned to arrive early if she came on the day of one of the rodeo performances. The roads coming into Deadwood could get plugged up quickly with all the people arriving, and several people told her horror stories of waiting in long lines of cars so far out that the town wasn't even in sight. So, Kasey decided she would hit town the day before the first performance and try to get a good camping spot. There were two go-rounds in the barrel race, so Kasey decided to stay in Deadwood for the whole three-day weekend. She was tired of rushing from one fairground to another. She was looking forward to staying put and enjoying Deadwood.

The first thing she noticed as she pulled into the Days of '76 parking area behind the big arena was the Korkow Rodeo tack van parked behind the chutes. Erv Korkow was the stock contractor at the Mobridge and McCook rodeos which were well-run rodeos, so Kasey expected the same precision at Deadwood. Kasey was glad she was starting to recognize some of the names she encountered at these rodeos. She wasn't feeling quite like such a newcomer now. As she drove around the tack van, she saw a group of people lounging outside the van. She knew the stock contractor and his crew were probably busy getting stock lined up for the performances, visiting with rodeo officials, and getting tack and flags unpacked. She drove on to the beginning of a line of pickups and trailers in the parking area and pulled in next to another camper pulling a trailer.

Kasey had the horses unloaded and a bucket in hand, trying to locate the closest water source when she heard her name called.

"Kasey, you looking for water?" Cole called. He was walking from the direction of the Korkow trailer.

"Seems I am always asking you for directions," Kasey laughed, "and yes, I might as well get water before I think about resting."

"It's this way," Cole said, reaching for her bucket. "I'll walk with you. Haven't seen you for a while. You've been doing well, I hear."

"I have. No missed meals lately," Kasey smiled. "That might come again, but not for a while. My horses are running well. How about you? How was Cheyenne? I hear you did very well at Calgary."

"July has treated me well," Cole replied grinning. "I can't complain at all. I'm sitting near the top of the standings, so barring injury, I am Finals bound again in December."

"Good for you. Maybe this year you will bring home a title," Kasey smiled up at him.

They walked in silence for a few minutes and reached the water hydrant. Filling the bucket, Kasey waited while her horses drank. They were close to the arena, and Kasey looked around the grounds. Across the arena sat the stately log grandstand with its massive support logs. Nestled between two steep mountainsides, the arena and grandstand seemed to echo the majesty of the surrounding countryside.

"This is really a cool rodeo grounds," she said. "I heard it was quite the place, but this is more than I imagined. That grandstand is magnificent."

"Deadwood is one of my favorite places to compete," Cole answered. "There is just something about this place. The town is an old-time mining town, and the people here go all out. The parades are full of horse-drawn vehicles from the museum in town, and the rodeo is well done. It's just a fun place. It's not a rodeo I ever get tired of."

They were halfway back to Kasey's outfit when she turned to Cole. "Hey, you don't have to walk me all the way back with an empty bucket. I think I can handle the horses and bucket. I am sure you were on your way somewhere."

"Well, actually," Cole replied, "I saw you drive in. I was over at Korkow's. A bunch of us are invited to a cabin a few miles out of town tonight. The night before the rodeo starts, there is always a big feed at this anesthetist's place. He's a big game hunter and a friend of

Korkow's. He and his friends have all this wild meat in a pit, cooking all day. It's quite the party, not wild, but just fun people. Why don't you come along with me? Ben and Josie are off to friends of Josie. Her college is just north of here. So, I'm heading out with an empty vehicle."

Kasey thought about that for a moment, then smiled and said, "I'd like that if I won't be imposing. I've never had wild meat or anything cooked in a pit."

"You need more experiences, youngster," Cole smiled. "Be ready at six."

***

Cole was outside promptly at six. They drove about five miles out of town to a gravel drive that wound up through the pines and came out on a small clearing packed with cars and pickups. Nestled in the trees was a log cabin and in front was a crowd of people sitting on chairs, logs, or on the ground. A pit with steam and smoke rising from it was off to the side with the most marvelous smells of cooking meat. Kasey saw the size of the crowd and was immediately hesitant. She didn't see anyone she recognized. She wished that Josie and Ben were here.

Cole noticed Kasey's hesitation and laughed at her. "You can stand up in front of a group of strangers in a bar, but you are spooked at a crowd sitting around a yard?"

"Yeah, that's about right," she smiled tentatively. "Remember I told you I become the music on a stage. Here, I have to rely on my bubbly self. I seem to have lost that part of me."

Cole grinned and took her elbow steering her toward the crowd. "You will do fine. Let's get a drink first."

Inside, the cabin was packed with all sorts of people milling around. Cole guided Kasey toward the makeshift bar, dodging around small groups. Cole got a Coors, and Kasey asked for a Coke.

"You don't drink either?" Cole asked.

"Tasted stuff at college," Kasey answered. "Just never found anything that tasted good. I never felt like I needed anything to have fun, and if it doesn't taste good, why do it?"

"Smart girl," Cole replied. "Stay that way."

They moved slowly to the door, Cole stopping here and there to introduce her to several people he knew. There were other contestants there, but the majority of the people were either cowboys working for Korkow's or rodeo committee members from the area. Kasey found she didn't have to worry about fitting in. The people were friendly and most knew Cole. She was finding that some knew her too. One lady said she had recognized Kasey's name from seeing it in the rookie standings for the Women's Professional Rodeo Association. That was news to Kasey. She had no idea she had won enough to be in the rookie standings. But it was good to hear. She'd have to see if she could run down the WPRA's magazine and see for herself.

The evening was fun. The tables loaded with all kinds of food were impressive. There was antelope, deer, moose, bear, and elk meat. There were salads, chips, and vegetable trays. When Kasey came to the assortment of meats, she wasn't sure which was which, so she took a small serving of each. Last along the long tables were all kinds of desserts. Her plate was loaded when she let Cole led her to a picnic table where they found two empty seats.

Kasey was content just listening to the conversations around her and watching the people. It was then that she spied what she thought was a familiar face. When Cole was quiet, intent on his food, she had to ask him. "Isn't that the pick-up man who was at Barnes' rodeo last month? If it isn't him, he sure is a look-a-like."

Cole looked up. "Yup, that's him. I visited with him at the tack trailer this afternoon. He came out to work for Korkow's. Good move to get him out here. He's a good pick-up man. He bought a semi and is going to truck for Erv when they aren't rodeoing. He's getting married after Christmas and wants a steady job."

"So, is that girl with him the one he is marrying? Is she the same girl he was sparking in Wisconsin?" Kasey asked. "How'd she get way out here? I thought she was from Wisconsin or Illinois or something."

"The way I heard it, she was from the Midwest, but her folks moved. In the summer, they are somewhere in the mountains of Colorado." Cole chewed a piece of meat before going on. "I think her folks are over there eating with them." Cole indicated an older couple sitting with the young couple. "The way I heard it, the girl was in South Dakota meeting his folks. Her parents brought her horse to Deadwood and she's running barrels here."

Kasey thought about that while she ate. She envied the girl having her folks here. What Kasey would give for her folks to be here right now. She shook her head. She had to let that go. But Kasey wondered if that girl knew how lucky she was.

After eating, Cole and Kasey moved into the yard. A fire pit burned and as the evening shadows fell, the air began to cool. Many people stopped to visit with both of them. While Kasey carried on a conversation with a daughter of a local rancher, she heard a man greet Cole and stop to visit.

"Where's Callie this weekend, Cole?" the man inquired. "I thought she'd come with you?"

"She was at Calgary for the whole week," Cole answered. "That was pretty much enough for both of us. There is a limit to good times." The two men laughed before Cole continued, "She's back in Omaha working on an ad campaign. She's not much of a country girl anymore."

People started leaving around eleven. By then, Kasey was feeling pretty comfortable and found herself visiting with many different people. In between, she enjoyed just watching the crowd. Who would have thought she would be part of a sure enough rodeo crowd two years ago? Because so many of the people were committee members, area ranchers, and older people, the party was, as Cole described earlier, a great time but not a wild time. Cole collected Kasey at about eleven, and they made their way back to town.

"Enjoy yourself?" Cole asked as they got underway.

"I did," Kasey smiled. "Nice people. I was sitting there thinking I sure never thought I'd be part of a rodeo crowd two years ago. It's fun. I like these people."

"There are bad eggs in every crowd, but I always think that the rodeo world overall is a pretty good bunch," Cole thought about that. "Most of us were raised on God and country and hard work. It is a pretty good combination. We don't have the big salaries of other athletes, and we get no guarantees, but maybe we are too independent for that anyway. Basically, these are my kind of people."

"Well, I like your kind of people," Kasey replied. "What about the wild meat," she continued, changing the subject. "Did you try it all?"

"I stayed away from the bear meat. Someone mentioned it was pretty strong. How about you?" Cole asked.

"I could have used that tip," Kasey laughed. "I think I got a little chunk of that and I couldn't even keep it in my mouth. It was awful. The rest was marvelous though. I am stuffed!"

The day had taken its toll on Kasey and by the time they returned to the rodeo grounds, she was starting to yawn. Cole dropped her off at her camper and said good night. He had a motel room somewhere. Kasey checked on her horses and headed to bed. It had been a long day with her drive to Deadwood and then the party this evening. But it was a good day. She was having more and more good days as the summer went on.

***

Deadwood was definitely a tourist town, and the grandstand was packed with a noisy crowd, both those familiar with rodeo and those not. Colorful flags decorated the outside of the arena, the grand entry was fast, and the rodeo moved quickly and smoothly. Kasey could see why Deadwood was such a well-loved rodeo. All the performances were in the afternoons, and she could see the lines of cars coming in off the highway right up until rodeo time. It was a wonder that they could get that many vehicles in this town, tucked as it was between the surrounding peaks. Kasey was thankful she didn't arrive today.

Kasey was up in the first performance, so she had to get ready and ride in the grand entry. The rodeo moved quickly after that. Kasey was parked far enough from the entry gate that it was quite a trek to get to where her contestant's pass would get her in to watch the rodeo. So she stayed out at her outfit, listening to the announcer. She would have time on Sunday to relax and watch the rodeo since her second run was on Saturday.

With the big arena and the sizeable crowd, Kasey opted to ride Roan in this first go. She was the seventh girl to go, so the ground was not dug in too deep. Kasey saw that girl who was with the pickup man the night before. She ran third and had a typy little bay quarter horse mare. Fine boned, but all business, they made a correct run but not blistering fast. The girl's time was just a second too slow. She wouldn't place.

The run to the first barrel was long, but Roan was a seasoned barrel horse now. He checked and turned at just the right moment. With his long ground-eating stride, he ate up the space between the three barrels. When she crossed the timeline, Kasey knew he had run well but was overjoyed to have that confirmed by the announcer.

"And that run puts this Colorado girl in first place, folks," he stated. Kasey could only hope it would hold.

As Kasey walked Roan to cool him off, she listened to the times of the next eight girls. She was still in first place when they had all run. That didn't mean her time would win, though. There was slack in the morning that would finish out the first go-round. But it was a good beginning for Kasey at Deadwood.

***

Kasey waited until the vehicles leaving the contestants' parking area cleared out. All the vehicles jockeying to get out of the area made walking to the water hydrant difficult. She needed water, but not for the horses. She had already walked them over for water and even brought a bucket back for later. Now Kasey needed water for a shower. The Deadwood dust settled over everything as vehicles moved through the gravel lots, and Kasey felt gritty.

Kasey's camper was never intended as a full-time living space. Despite its high-end finishes, it was meant as a weekend outfit. It had a stovetop on one side, along with a counter. There was no sink or water storage. Kasey had a plastic camping sink that stored almost two gallons of water within its plastic walls. A little hand pump on it ejected water for washing hands or filling the little sink with water. To get hot water, Kasey had to heat it on the stove and add it to the cold water in the plastic sink. There was no shower and no stool. She did have a porta-potty in the tack room in the trailer, but most places had restrooms she could use. Many fairgrounds had showers available, and when that was the case, Kasey made good use of them. But here in Deadwood, if Kasey wanted a shower, she had to set up her portable shower.

Kasey's portable shower consisted of a battery-operated little pump that pumped water up to a tiny shower head she hung from a hook on the ceiling in the camper. She hung a shower curtain from ceiling hooks, and the curtain hung down into a round tin bucket that just fit on the floor of the camper. Finally, she needed three or four gallons of water. She would heat a half gallon on the stove to boiling and add it to the cold water in a five-gallon pail. Usually, the water temperature was just right for a shower if one hurried. It wasn't particularly easy to set up, especially getting the water, but it worked when there weren't showers available.

Kasey had blue two-gallon water containers that she usually kept filled for washing up or for her sink, but on this day, they were both empty. It was time to walk for water for her needs, not the horses. Kasey gathered her water containers and headed off to the water hydrant. Rounding a small bumper camper, she came almost face to face with a card game. Surprised, she altered course to skirt the cowboys seated around a table when she heard her name called.

"Kasey, are you after more water? I thought I just saw you coming back with your horses a bit ago," it was Cole. Three men were with Cole, playing cards around the table, and one was preparing to deal.

"This time, it's for me," Kasey stopped to say. "I need a shower and find myself somewhat short of water."

"You have a shower in that camper? Where do you have that hidden?" Cole smiled.

"Actually, I set up a portable one. It's a hassle, but it works when no shower houses are around," Kasey explained.

"Well, hell, don't bother with that," Cole dug in his pocket, and pulling out a motel key held it out to Kasey. "Run up that hill to the motel up there," he gestured toward the road, "room 23. There's a real good shower there, and the water comes right out of the faucet." The other cowboys laughed at this.

"I can't do that," Kasey protested. "That's your room."

"Well, I am here and intend to stay for quite some time. Go and use it. They don't charge by the number of showers, just by the night."

"But . . ." Kasey began but Cole interrupted her.

"Ben is off with Josie. He isn't staying with me this weekend. Now go, get a good shower," Cole thrust the key at Kasey. It was too tempting; a real shower with ample running water. She took the key.

"Thanks, Cole," she smiled. "I will enjoy it." Turning on her heels, Kasey headed back to her pickup to unhook it from the trailer. Not only could she get a good shower, but she could take her water containers with her and bring them back full. That was a bonus.

***

The man dealing the cards stopped what he was doing to watch Kasey's retreating figure. Then, looking up at Cole, he said, "You are going up there too, aren't you?"

"What?" Cole looked surprised. "Why would I do that?"

"Hell man, that girl is hot, and she's gonna be using your shower. If it were me, I'd be following her up there in a few minutes."

"Well first," Cole said patiently, "I am a nicer guy than you, and second, that gal is over ten years younger than me. She's not much more than a kid."

"Humff, she's a looker. You must be getting old, Cole," the dealer commented mildly.

"Old? Yes," Cole agreed. "And I feel old more and more. But I'm not too old to notice, just too old to be a shit. Deal the damn cards."

***

Saturday morning dawned clear and cool with the crisp air of the mountains. As Kasey was watering her horses, she saw a yellow pickup with a topper pull up, and the girl she had seen with the pick-up man untied a little bay mare from a trailer and walked over with a bucket to get water.

"You had a nice run yesterday," Kasey smiled at the girl.

"Thank you," the girl replied, recognizing Kasey. "I'm just a weekend barrel racer, but it was fun. I don't think my mare is in the same class as yours, but she's honest."

"I'm pretty lucky my horses turned out as good as they are," Kasey commented. "It has been a learning experience for me."

"Well, I have a lot to learn," the girl replied, "like learning how to back up a pickup using mirrors when there is a topper on the bed. We are staying at the Franklin Hotel downtown, and I borrowed my fiancée's pick up to come out here this morning. I backed up and hit a parking meter at the edge of the hotel parking lot. If you get up Main Street, look down the line of the meters next to the Franklin Hotel parking lot, and you will see one bent over! I'm just hoping no one saw me do that."

Kasey laughed at that. "Do you really think anyone else will be out at this hour in the morning to see you? It is only us who are taking care of our precious horses that would get up this early!"

"I hope you are right," the girl answered smiling. "Hey, have a good run today. I saw you were in the rookie standings. Good for you!" Nodding good-bye, the girl led her horse back toward her trailer.

***

Kasey was tidying up the camper after a quick breakfast on Saturday when a knock came at the door. She opened it to find Josie outside.

"We are going up to watch the parade," Josie said. "We've got room in my car, so you better come with us. It is a pretty cool parade."

Kasey made quick work of pulling on boots and heading out. Ben was driving Josie's little hatchback car with Cole in the passenger seat. Kasey climbed into the backseat with Josie. Deadwood was an old mining town situated in a gulch with mountainsides rising from both sides and a creek running the length of it. Main Street was narrow with old buildings crowded along each side. The town was packed, but Ben knew his way around and found parking in a back alley not far from the parade route. The parade was spectacular in a very historical way. The town museum had a multitude of horse-drawn vehicles, and people with driving horses and teams came from all over to pull these relics in the two parades that weekend. In addition, men dressed as old prospectors and their mules and donkeys walked along the route as did horseback riders, antique cars and trucks. Even the Korkow stock contractor riders carried the American flag and the Korkow flag in the parade. Kasey recognized the pick-up man and his fiancée among the riders. She waved, happy to recognize someone. The parade was everything she had heard about and more. Kasey was glad Josie had stopped for her.

The Saturday afternoon performance was well run, the weather perfect, and so was Kasey's run. The slack that morning had two girls who beat Kasey's time in the first go-round, so Kasey placed third. Kasey wanted an equally good run in the second go, get another check, and maybe to sneak in for an average check too. When the last girl ran during the Saturday night performance, Kasey again was sitting first. She would have the whole performance on Sunday to wait and see if her time held.

But she was hopeful. Her time was even better than the winner in the first go-round. She thought she would at least place.

After getting Roan and JC comfortable, Kasey walked to the arena to watch the rest of the performance. She had missed Cole's saddle bronc ride but heard the announcer say he was sitting in first place. She hoped that would hold. Ben had his doggin' run the day before and had a perfect run too. He was sitting second and hoped his time wouldn't be beat so he would place. Kasey got to the arena just as the bull riding was starting. She knew that Cole wasn't up in the bulls that day, but she wanted to watch the rides anyway. As she approached the fence, she saw Cole standing nearby and went to stand by him.

"I thought I heard the announcer say you were sitting first in the bronc riding," she commented. "Did I hear that right?"

"At the moment, I am," Cole replied. "It's a one go-round, so I will have to wait until tomorrow to see if it holds up. You are in the same position in the barrels, aren't you?"

"Well, it's not a one go-round, but I will have to wait until after the runs tomorrow to see if my time places in the second go."

"It will. I saw your run." Cole was thoughtful. "Your run was flawless. There are maybe only one or two girls up tomorrow who have the ability and horsepower to beat that time, so you will place."

"I hope so," Kasey smiled. "I might get an average check that way too. It should pay pretty well."

***

The rodeo grounds became relatively quiet as the crowd dispersed, and the few contestants who camped in the parking area quieted down for the evening. Kasey was just about ready to curl up for a few hours with a book when a knock came at the door.

"We are going uptown to walk the streets and the carnival," Josie said. "It's a kick. Come with us."

With Cole navigating, Ben again found parking near Main Street. They spent a leisurely couple of hours wandering the streets, popping in and out of stores that interested Josie and Kasey. The men mainly stood on the street watching the tourists meandering along or visiting with other rodeo people they knew. Cole treated them all to ice cream cones at a little corner store. It was well past dark by the time they got to the carnival. They passed several groups of people that either Ben or Cole knew, stopping to visit before moving on. They were nearing the end of the carnival strip when Cole stopped, and grinning, pointed at the booth ahead of them.

"This is going to be good," he said. "Let's watch."

What Cole was pointing at was the young pick-up man of Korkow's. He was weaving his way to the booth. It was one of those basketball booths where one paid for three basketballs. If all three balls went through the hoop, the winner could pick a prize.

"It looks like he's pretty plastered," Ben grinned, his arm over Josie's shoulder.

Kasey could see the man's fiancée waiting with the older couple whom Kasey recognized as the girl's parents from the cookout at the cabin on Thursday night. They were all laughing at something the pick-up man said.

The young man put down his money, and the carney set three basketballs on the counter. The cowboy felt the ball in his hand, eyed the basket, and threw. The ball came close but bounced off. He took the second ball. Again, he palmed the ball, took aim, and shot. Again, the ball sailed through the air, and rattled around the hoop before bouncing off. Taking the last ball, the cowboy shot again. This time, he staggered back as if losing his balance. But the ball went true and fell through the hoop. The few onlookers grinned.

The cowboy took out another bill and put it on the counter.

"He's going to go broke," Kasey laughed. "He can hardly stand straight."

"Just wait," Cole grinned down at her. "It ain't over yet."

And it wasn't. The young man sank three baskets, nearly losing his balance on two. Grinning, the cowboy picked out an orange stuffed snake and handed it to his girlfriend before putting down another bill and picking up the first of the next three balls. Set after set continued with wins, until the girl began giving away stuffed animals to other people in the crowd. Kasey and Josie each got a stuffed bear. The cowboy couldn't miss. A crowd gathered to watch the show. Occasionally, the cowboy took a rest, leaning on his girl, grinning, and letting someone else take a turn, but eventually, he was back at it. He could hardly stand up straight, but he sank almost every shot.

"How did you know this was going to be so good?" Kasey looked up at Cole.

"I heard he was a hell of a basketball player in high school," Cole replied. "He just needed to get the weight of the ball in his hands to figure out what had to be done. They make those balls a bit different from regulation balls, and the hoops are smaller. Your aim has to be exact to sink a basket."

"But he's drunk!" Kasey laughed. "He can barely keep his balance."

"He's feeling no pain," Cole agreed, "but I don't think he's as drunk as he acts."

The walls of the carney's booth were half empty when, finally, the carney threw in the towel.

"Closing up!" he called, dropping curtains. The crowd laughed and began to disperse. The show was over.

***

Kasey was enjoying the Sunday performance. With her two runs over, she could sit and watch the entire afternoon performance. For most of the summer, if she wasn't up in a performance, she was usually on her way to another rodeo. So, she enjoyed this day of rest.

Cole had drawn a big, red brindle bull that had a reputation of being not only good at bucking, but also dangerous in the chutes. From a distance, Kasey could see Cole gingerly lower himself into the chute. He made short work of getting set before he nodded for the gate. She breathed a sigh of relief that the bull didn't erupt before the chute gate opened.

But the bull did erupt when they pulled the gate. With a big rear, the bull leaped one stride before going into a spin to the right, into Cole's hand. But the bull didn't just spin. He came high off the ground on each jump, then kicked out high behind. Cole stuck to the bull, only slightly getting off to one side when the bull suddenly switched directions. But Cole adjusted his position, getting square again on the big beast's back. To Kasey, it seemed an eternity before the whistle blew, signaling the end of the eight-second ride. The crowd went wild. It had been a superb ride. The judges rewarded it with the highest score of the rodeo. Deadwood, it appeared, was a good rodeo for them all this year.

The contestants and their families and friends had seats in the smaller grandstand across the arena from the massive log grandstand that sold reserved seats. Kasey waited for people to clear the seats before heading down. She was in no hurry and could wait. As she stepped off the last row of seats, she saw Cole making his way from behind the chutes, riggin' bag in hand.

"Congratulations," she called to him. "Great ride."

Cole changed directions and came to meet her. "It was a good bull. Last time I had him he threw me at six seconds when he changed directions. I wasn't going to let that happen again," Cole grinned, and they fell in step together. "So, are you heading out this afternoon?"

"Yes and no, actually," Kasey answered. "I'm going to wait for the checks to be cut, and then I saw a committee member from the St. Onge rodeo grounds. I asked him if anyone would mind if I stayed out there a day or two. I figured no one would mind, but it is nice to ask. Anyway, I will head over there when the traffic clears out and camp tonight. The horses can graze and be untied. They will like that."

"How'd you end up in the barrels?"

"I won the second go, and with the third in the first go, I should get either first or second in the average," Kasey smiled. "I'm kind of excited to see what that pays."

"So where are you heading next?"

They had reached Kasey's outfit and stopped. "I'm going to hit three Colorado rodeos next," Kasey answered. "I'll hit Yuma and Colorado Springs first. I was lucky to get into Colorado Springs because they only take so many permits. There is a lot of money up there. But then I am going over to Loveland. I can stay with my sister for a couple of days at Ft. Collins, so I didn't specify a performance. I'll stick around for all three perfs, anyway. But after that, I don't know. I got a copy of the *Sports News* and will study it tonight when I get settled. I was going to let the horses rest after the Colorado run, but now that I'm in the rookie standings, I'm wondering if I shouldn't maybe go for it. See how far I can get." Kasey looked up at Cole. "I mean, I was just trying to pay my way with this rodeo thing when I started out this spring, but to get in the standings, any standings, well, I don't know. I didn't expect that."

"You need to go for it," Cole got serious. "If you don't, you will regret it. Your horses are fit and running well. You are on a roll. You have all winter to take off. Now is the time to hit the rodeos hard." Cole looked toward the parking lot, watching the line of vehicles trying to get out. It would take a good hour or more to clear the lot and get these people out of this gulch. "Tell you what. I'll get my checks when the secretary has them ready and the horses from Ben. I'll head over to St. Onge with you. Ben wants to stay tonight with Josie. She can bring him over in the morning. She's got some mini course she's taking for a couple of weeks, so she's staying in Spearfish. We can all look through the *Sports News*, see what rodeos pay best and figure out a plan. How's that sound?"

***

The night was pleasant, cooling from the summer heat but not cold. Cole and Kasey sat in easy companionship on two folding chairs that Kasey produced from the tack room in her trailer. The two pairs of horses grazed around the rodeo grounds, grateful for the grass and the freedom. After being near each other at rodeos, often tied to their respective trailers, the horses were not strangers. They kept in pairs, not bothering each other. "How long have you been rodeoing, Cole," Kasey asked. "I know you have been to the finals many times, but I'm not sure how many."

Cole thought about the question before answering. "I hit my first professional rodeo right after graduating high school. I had a rodeo scholarship offered to me, but I just wanted to rodeo. I knew I was going back to take over the ranch eventually, so I wasn't much interested in college. Then the Army got me, so I spent two years with Uncle Sam. So, figuring two years in the service, I have been on the rodeo road for twelve years. I have been to the finals eight times. If I make it this year, it will be my ninth."

"Do you get tired of it?"

"Oh, yeah," Cole chuckled. "But after a week or so of rest, it's like the rodeos are calling to me, pulling me back. I used to be so stir-crazy over the Christmas holidays that I couldn't wait to get back on the road. I find it easier to stay away now, but not much easier. You thinking of quitting soon?" Cole turned the question back to Kasey.

"Oh, no," she said, startled at his take on her question. "I'm surprised about that, though. This was supposed to be just a couple of summer months of traveling that my mom and I had planned before school would start again in the fall. Then my folks got killed, my sister married, and I decided to try my luck alone. But now that I am actually going down the road, I like it. I don't think I am ready to stop moving," Kasey looked over at Cole. "The excitement of it helps me forget my other life, at least for a time."

Cole nodded thoughtfully. "It gets in your blood, doesn't it?"

"It does," Kasey agreed. "I think part of it is the adrenalin of the competition. Some of it is going the grueling miles between rodeos, but a huge role is being part of something bigger than myself. I feel a part of the rodeo scene and that I belong here, like I did when I had a family. I look forward to seeing familiar faces. More people seem to know me. I guess I never expected that."

"I suspect we all think just about the competition going into this sport," Cole commented, "and then we get into it, make friendships, have our wins and losses, and suddenly it is more than just entering. For me, sometimes it is that bull or bronc that I didn't get covered, and I'll go for years hoping to draw that animal again to give me another chance. Like that bull I had at Deadwood. I knew I could ride him if I just had a chance again. I was happy I got him in Deadwood."

"Well, the second time worked," Kasey smiled. "I bet it paid well too."

They sat quietly, watching the horses grazing in the fading light before Kasey continued the conversation. "So, how long will you keep this up? How will you know when you are ready to go back to the ranch?"

"I've thought about that some, especially lately," Cole said casually. "I think a lot of factors come into play. One might be my dad, and when he needs me to come and take a lot of the responsibility off his shoulders. He's not ready to step back yet, but that time is coming one of these days. Another is whether I stay healthy or not. That is a big deal at my age. I'm not going to bounce back so quickly if I get hurt now. Otherwise, it might depend on when it quits being fun. I'm older than a good portion of these guys now. But I still enjoy it all. I'll admit I don't do the carousing I did ten years ago. I steer clear of the young hotheads, and the wild parties. Rodeo is my job, and to do it well, I need to focus on taking care of myself. I'm no Freckles Brown. He's fifty-three and just retiring. I respect the hell out of him, but I won't keep on that long," Cole chuckled. "What about you? How many years do you have in you?"

Kasey thought about that. "Well, I don't have a ranch or a family to go home to. I mean, I have my sister, and she and I are close, but she's already become a city girl, and I'm not going there. I don't want to live the town life. I guess I'll be done when I get tired of it. Might depend on my horses or maybe new horses if it comes to that. Right now, rodeo has become a lifeline to me. Getting in the rookie standings was a wake-up call that I can go places in this sport. I already feel the energy coming from that knowledge. I'm enjoying kicking back here at the St. Onge rodeo grounds for a day or two, but then I will be chomping on the bit to get on the road."

"I believe you have got the rodeo bug," Cole replied. "Happens to the best of us."

They sat watching the sun setting behind the Black Hills. The breeze was light, and there were few insects to bother them. For a while, they didn't need words to fill the silence. It was fully dark before Kasey had another question.

"So, when you finally quit rodeoing, will your girl settle down at the ranch with you?"

Cole looked at Kasey quizzically, "My girl?"

"Well, I wasn't eavesdropping or anything, but at the barbeque, a man asked you where Callie was. Is Callie your girlfriend?"

"Ah, I see," Cole replied casually, "You heard Callie was in Calgary with me, so you figured she is a girlfriend."

"Well, apparently, others do too, if they know about her," Kasey added. Kasey could see the flash of Cole's teeth as he smiled in the murky darkness.

"Callie and I were a couple in high school," Cole began. "That was a long time ago. I suppose for a while there, we both thought we would stick, but then high school ended. She went off to college, and I went to rodeos and Vietnam. She's running one of her dad's ad agencies in Omaha. She's a confirmed city executive and only comes out to play cowgirl at the largest rodeos, the ones that are the most fun. So, I see her every now and then, but we aren't a couple anymore, just pretty good friends."

"Does that bother you?"

"Not at all. Our lifestyles would never mesh anymore, and we both know it. We go our own directions, but we can still have fun when we meet up," Cole didn't elaborate more. "How about you? Any serious boyfriends?"

"Ha," Kasey smiled, "I had all the usual high school crushes and one brief boyfriend the first month of college, but we realized almost right away we were better as friends. He got married this spring, and I am happy for him." Kasey got quiet, thinking. "I am afraid right now that I might meet someone and fall head over heels thinking I am in love, and really, what I am looking for is the security of the family I lost. So, I'll date, but that is it. I need to learn to live by myself before I learn to live with or for someone else."

"Smart girl," Cole agreed. "You have plenty of time. And speaking of time, I think I'll put out a couple of buckets of water for the horses and turn in. It's been a good weekend, but I feel my bed calling."

***

Josie brought Ben out early the following morning. Ben brought doughnuts, and they all sat on the tailgate of Cole's pickup, eating the sweets and drinking coffee Kasey brewed up. It would be a month before Ben saw Josie again. So, they enjoyed the lazy morning watching the sun bathe the hills. But finally, Josie had to head back to Spearfish. Her class would begin that morning, and she didn't want to be late.

The rest of the day, Ben, Cole, and Kasey studied the *Rodeo Sports News* for the rodeos that were the most lucrative to them. They studied maps, checked mileage, and finally decided on the routes they would be taking. Kasey was already entered in Ponca City, Oklahoma, but Cole pointed out that Great Bend, Kansas, was only 200 miles from Ponca City. If Kasey could get traded, she could make both rodeos easily. From there, she would head back to Colorado for Stirling and Keensburg. Pueblo, Colorado, followed right after the first two Colorado rodeos, and Cole told Kasey that while Pueblo was a big rodeo, they did take some permit holders. With her rise into the rookie standings and being classified as a Colorado resident, she had a good chance to get accepted there. The prize money at Pueblo was big, so Cole felt she should try to get in. With the rest of August mapped out, phone numbers, entry open dates, and times listed, they went in search of the nearest phone booth to get their entries called in. Each rodeo had entry offices that opened a few days before the rodeo started. Contestants needed to call in their entries during that window of time. Sometimes, a contestant had to stop at multiple phone booths or gas stations to make a call, only to get a busy signal. It was a frustrating process at times.

Ben, who was also hauling horses and driving to the rodeos, entered many of the same ones as Kasey. It would depend on which performances he drew whether he would be there at the same time. On the other hand, Cole would enter these and also fly to Washington to enter Bremerton and Kennewick there. The rodeo year went until the end of October, so with a little over two months left, it was important to hit as many as possible. For Kasey, she found she was chasing a goal she had never dreamt of achieving in her first year. Being in the rookie standings revived her for the travel and the competition. Suddenly, she was galvanized to get down the road to the next rodeo.

CHAPTER 7

CHASING A DREAM

A
s it turned out, Kasey only saw Ben briefly at Pueblo. They didn't get traded the same for the Colorado rodeos, so they only met one other time, on the highway between Stirling and Keensburg, both going the other way and waving like crazy. As for Cole, Kasey only heard of his rides. He had placed several times in the Colorado rodeos in both bulls and broncs, but then he had flown off to the West Coast, and she hadn't heard how he did out there. With the rookie standings to chase, Kasey was busy and focused on her own goals. This paid off with big wins at Keensburg and Pueblo and a third-place run in Stirling. Kasey had money in her pocket and the bank. She wouldn't go hungry for quite some time now.

On the first day of Pueblo, a veteran barrel racer stopped by Kasey's trailer on the way to exercise her horse in the arena. Kasey had never talked to Mara Olson, but she was well aware of the lady. Mara had qualified for the National Finals rodeo several times, and Kasey had competed against her a few times that summer, only placing above her once.

"You're Kasey Jacobs, right?" Mara asked.

Kasey nodded, "Yes, ma'am."

"Have you seen the latest rookie standings that just came out?"

"No," Kasey shook her head, "I haven't called home to see if the magazine got there yet."

"Well, kid," Mara smiled at Kasey, "welcome to the big time. You just rose to first in the rookie standings. Congratulations." Mara urged her horse on, leaving a stunned Kasey staring after her. Later that day, she put in a call to her sister to look at the *Women's Professional Rodeo* magazine to make sure she heard that right. It turned out she had.

***

It was old home week for Kasey at the Littleton rodeo. At first, Kasey intended to stay with Kelly instead of at the rodeo grounds, but since the rodeo was two go-rounds, Kasey decided it would be just as easy to simply stay put at the rodeo grounds. Her sister was busy, so they planned to meet between the activities of each.

As it turned out, Cole and Ben pulled in the first day and parked next to Kasey. Because they didn't have motel rooms, they were both bunking for the night in Cole's topper. After the rodeo performance finished, Ben and Cole saw Kasey's big pickup pulling out of the rodeo grounds as they walked back to their outfit. They prepared to get in their own vehicle to go for food when Ted Langley pulled up beside them.

"Hey, we are heading for a drink and some food," Ted said. "I have room for two more if you two want to ride with."

"Sounds good to me," Cole said, climbing in the rear seat beside another cowboy. "I don't have to unhook then."

They pulled out of the rodeo grounds and headed toward town. As they approached a busy area, Ted saw Kasey's pickup pulling into a parking lot.

"Isn't Kasey from around here?" he asked. "She's pulling in on the right. Maybe this is a good honkytonk and steak house. I'll follow her."

By the time Ted found a parking space, Kasey had disappeared inside the establishment. One of the cowboys with them eyed the bar quizzically. "The Pink Pony doesn't especially sound like a cowboy bar," he commented dryly.

"Well, if anyone makes advances towards you," Ted said, "we will protect you. Come on, it says steaks too, and I am hungry."

The men could almost immediately see it wasn't a cowboy bar. There wasn't a cowboy hat in the place. There was a band at the far end playing some folk song, a bar down the right side, and tables spread out from the door to the stage. Kasey was at the far end of the bar, chatting with the barman. As they watched, she leaned over the bar to give the burly man a hug. The group hesitated.

A waitress approached. "You cowboys lost?"

"You sell beer and steaks?" Cole asked dryly.

"Best steaks around," the waitress answered.

"Then we aren't lost," Cole cast around, and seeing an empty table, the men headed to it.

"This looks like a hippie joint," Ted remarked softly, looking around. "What's Kasey doing in a hippy joint?"

"It appears she knows people here," Ben mentioned. They watched as Kasey made her way down the side of the room, sometimes stopping for a hug from one person or another. She raised her finger to her lips at the crowd to keep them quiet as she made her way to the side of the stage. It was obvious from the reaction of those sitting near the edge that Kasey was known by many.

The band consisted of a drummer, two guitar players, a young long-haired man singing, and a young woman at the piano. Kasey made her way to the back of the stage, still with her finger to her mouth to keep the crowd from giving her approach away. She moved among the band members behind the main singer, smiling and whispering. When the song came to an end, the band immediately broke into the Peter, Paul, and Mary song "Leaving on a Jet Plane." When the surprised lead singer turned to his band, Kasey began the song, softly singing into a microphone she had taken from one of the guitarists.

"I'm leaving on a jet plane, don't know when I'll be back again. . ."

Like when Kasey sang her heart out in North Platte, she mesmerized the crowd. Kasey sang to the lead singer, advancing toward him. It was apparent they had performed together. The man joined her in appropriate places, sometimes singing a verse. When the song ended, he embraced Kasey, leaned her back, and gave her a kiss on stage. The crowd went wild. After that, Kasey went to all the band members for hugs, and then they swung into another folk tune. The crowd shouted for their favorite songs, and Kasey and the band complied.

"I think they know Kasey here," Ted remarked as their steaks came. "Apparently, she didn't start out singing in a honkytonk bar."

***

Cole heard Kasey's diesel pickup roll in after the sun was barely over the horizon. She had never returned that night. Ted and his friends sat around with Cole and Ben until nearly midnight before pushing off to their beds. A couple of the younger men with them were grumbling that Kasey was so prim and proper with them but not afraid to stay out all night with some long-haired musician. Cole refrained from commenting. He was a little concerned that Kasey hadn't returned to the rodeo grounds, but this was her stomping grounds. She knew a lot of people here.

"Morning," Kasey called as she got out of her truck. "I hope I didn't wake you pulling in so early."

"I was up," Cole said, sitting on the tailgate of his pickup. "You get lost last night? I was worried some hippie got you in the backseat of a car with no one to rescue you." The last sentence was a bit clipped.

"Oh, for goodness sakes," Kasey said, "I was with my sister and brother-in-law. Met them at a hippie dive and crashed on their couch."

"A carload of us saw you going in the Pink Pony," Cole retorted. "Thought it was a cowboy bar. We all had a steak there. Saw you on the stage. Apparently, country music isn't your only genre of music."

"Really?" Kasey said, surprised. "I didn't see you. But yes, I like country music, folk, and even some rock and roll. I used to sing with that band. That was my sister, Kelly, on the piano, and my brother-in-law, who sings. That is where I have a standing job offer if I want."

"Your brother-in-law was the singer? Looked like you knew him well. Couple of young guys with us were a bit put off at how well you knew him."

Kasey eyed Cole. "Hmm, that is interesting," she said, slightly annoyed. "You have to remember that on stage, we are the music. And Blake and I were an item for about a month in the first semester of college. But we knew we were better friends. There was no spark between us. Then my sister and Blake became close right after that, and I am so happy for them. Blake is in my life as my brother-in-law now. That works best for all of us."

Cole nodded, feeling surprised at his relief. "Well, guess I'll spread the word you aren't taken. You don't want to break all the young men's hearts," he said wryly.

***

It wasn't until Kasey hit Salt Lake City in mid-September that she met up with Cole and Ben again. Salt Lake was a big rodeo, and again, she got in because she was listed in the rookie standings. At the same time, she was also entered in Ely, Nevada, and Eads, Colorado, and was lucky to get traded so she could make all three rodeos.

When Kasey saw Cole and Ben walking toward her as she unloaded her horses, she called to them. "Did you hear? I moved up to first in the rookie standings!"

The two men grinned as they stopped and waited for her to tie her horses to the trailer.

"I heard that. Congratulations." Cole answered. "But have you seen the latest *Sports* News?"

"No, why?" Kasey called over her shoulder as she secured Roan. "Hey, did you move up? Are you in first place?"

"Well, yeah, in the broncs I'm sitting first, but that's not what I want you to look at." Cole walked over and handed a *Sports News* to Kasey, already folded to a page. "Check out the barrel racing standings."

While the *Rodeo Sports News* was the official newspaper of the Rodeo Cowboys Association, it always had the top twenty barrel racers listed. The top fifteen would make it to the Finals in December, but they listed the top twenty in each edition.

Kasey looked quizzically at Cole but took the paper. "Well, Mara has moved to first place, but I sort of expected that."

"Keep looking," Cole commanded.

Kasey's eyes drifted down the list, and suddenly, her breath caught. "Holy. . ." she whispered. "That's my name in the twentieth spot. Is that a misprint?" She raised wide eyes to Cole.

Cole just laughed. "I think, kiddo, you have got to stop thinking of the rookie standings. You have about six weeks to move up five places. You need to start thinking of the National Finals."

Kasey suddenly had a new focus, and it took her breath away to think about it. The first performance at Salt Lake found her nervous, thinking of her new goal of making the Finals. But when her name was called, she shook off her anxiety, trusted her horse, and flew. When the first go-round was over, she was second behind Mara. In the second go, Kasey again placed second but behind another tough competitor. Mara had tipped a barrel. That left Kasey in the winning hole for the average. Her confidence surged. Maybe there was a chance.

The end of September was a flurry of rodeos. Kasey's horses continued to run well, and they continued to place or win at several. She got in the habit of finding a phone booth when she thought her mail at her sister's home would contain the *Sports News*. Her sister complained that Kasey called more now to ask her to look at the standings instead of just saying hi. But in truth, Kelly was just as excited for Kasey as Kasey was herself.

It was the second week of October when all the miles paid off. Kasey had risen to fifteenth in the standings. If she could just keep that place, she was Oklahoma-bound in December.

***

The month of October ground by. There were fewer rodeos now, and only on the weekends. So, there was a lot of down time during the week. Kasey hunted down fairgrounds where she and the horses could rest between rodeos. She was entered in Fort Leonard Wood, Missouri, on the third weekend of October and St. Louis, Missouri, the last weekend. With the limited travel, the horses and Kasey felt refreshed and ready for both rodeos. She placed high in Fort Lenard Wood and won it all at St. Louis. By the end of the season, Kasey had not only held her place in the standings but had inched up to thirteenth.

There was no question about it Kasey was Oklahoma-bound in December. Suddenly, she was scared. She was a rookie, after all. Not just a rookie, but a very new competitor to the professional ranks. What business did she have going to the National Finals Rodeo her first year? But Cole just laughed at her when she voiced that fear after the final performance at St. Louis.

"What do you mean you don't belong there?" Cole chucked her on the arm lightly. "You won enough money to get you there. You belong. You earned it."

"But I haven't even competed against most of the girls who are heading to the Finals," Kasey argued. "I haven't even run up against them."

"Well, of course not," Cole answered patiently, "there are rodeos all over this great country of ours. Most of the gals out in the West Coast area – California, Washington, and Oregon – seldom cross the mountains to hit the rodeos to the east. The girls along the East Coast or the southern states hit rodeos in their geographical area. You have mainly rodeoed between the Rocky Mountains and the Missouri River. There is no reason for you to compete against most of those other girls in a regular season. That is the purpose of the Finals. It brings all the greats together in one place."

"Greats! I'm not a great. I'm just a rookie!"

"Kasey," Cole said sternly. "You have great horses. You have won the money. You belong. Get it out of your head that you aren't as good as the other girls. Trust your horses. That's really all you need to do."

Kasey might not have been entirely convinced, but Cole's words helped. She did trust her horses. She believed in them. It was her ability that scared her. Being at the Finals, competing against all the well-known names of barrel racers she had only heard about was what scared her. Take a breath, she told herself. Wait until December to panic.

***

At first, Kasey thought of taking off the whole month of November. But on Cole's advice, she decided to hit two rodeos in November. These would be the first rodeos of the new season. She wanted to give her horses a well-needed rest before the Finals. But Cole told her she should hit a couple of the bigger rodeos to get an edge on the new season. So, she had chosen a South Dakota rodeo called The Flying Buckskins Rodeo in Sioux Falls and a St. Paul rodeo over the Thanksgiving weekend. These both had pretty good payouts and were both indoor rodeos. So far, all of Kasey's runs had been in outdoor rodeos, so hitting some indoor ones would be good practice before going to the Finals. All ten rounds of the Finals were held indoors. Her horses needed some experience with that.

The Flying Buckskins rodeo was the first November rodeo. It was getting cold, and Kasey wanted to keep her horses from growing their winter coats, so she started blanketing them. She also headed to Sioux Falls a couple of days before the rodeo. She found a phone booth and called three veterinarians in the area before she got a good recommendation for a stable near the city where she could board her horses and camp until the rodeo started. She found a nice private place with the added bonus of a heated stable and an indoor practice arena. The owners were former rodeo people who had heard of her and were happy for Kasey to stay with them.

It turned out that there were three performances for this rodeo, and in the barrel race, there were two go-arounds. Kasey drew the slack on Saturday morning with her second run during the Sunday afternoon performance. That suited Kasey just fine. The Saturday morning slack would be less chaotic, and with almost no crowd, it would be quieter. That would be a perfect way to get her horses used to an indoor arena. She had been running Roan hard toward the end of the season, so she decided that JC would run in the slack. Depending on how the little mare handled that, Kasey would determine if she wanted to change horses for Sunday or keep riding JC.

Kasey went to the Friday night performance and watched the rodeo. She also familiarized herself with the layout of the coliseum and where the timed event people kept their horses while waiting for their event. The coliseum had a big back room where horses were tied all along portable panels as they waited to be used and a small area where the competitors could warm up their horses. Kasey's horses were so well-mannered and seasoned, that they were not barn or buddy sour, so she had no fear of bringing one or both over to the coliseum when she competed. However, because neither horse had any indoor arena experience, she decided to come early on Saturday and bring both. Maybe she could get them both in the arena and give them a feeling for being indoors. The sights and sounds in a coliseum were quite different from those the horses were used to when competing outdoors.

The arena opened at seven a.m. and Kasey was there with both horses saddled and ready. There was an hour for contestants to ride in the arena before the calf roping slack started at eight a.m. Kasey made good use of that hour. She began by riding Roan. He was nervous going into the arena, head high and swinging it back and forth as he took in the surroundings. JC trotted along beside him, curious but not nervous. JC was content to let Roan be nervous for both of them. After three rounds of the arena, Kasey pushed Roan into an easy lope, JC breaking into a lope beside him. Slowly, Roan's head relaxed and came down to a more normal level. He had decided that no monster was going to jump out at him. Kasey rode Roan for another ten minutes, then pulled over into a corner and switched horses. Because the horses had such different conformation, she had a different saddle for each horse. The bonus of having two saddles was both horses could be saddled and ready at the same time. She could easily switch horses.

After the third time around the arena, Kasey took Roan out to the waiting area and tied him to a panel. When she returned to the arena with JC, she could see it was filling up with contestants. She recognized Ben exercising his horses. She wondered if Cole was here with Ben. But there was no time to think about that. It wasn't long before the announcer gave the command to clear the arena. Slack was about to start.

It took almost two hours before it was time for the barrel slack to start. Kasey was up seventh out of fifteen girls. When it was Kasey's turn, she had JC positioned at the end of a long alley that led into the arena. It had a tunnel feeling, but JC did not let the surroundings upset her, so Kasey felt reasonably confident. When the gate man motioned to her, she bent over the little mare and asked her to run, and by the time they entered the arena, JC was at full flight. What surprised Kasey was how fast they came to the first barrel. It surprised JC, too and for the first time since spring, JC turned too tight on the first barrel, grazing it with her shoulder as she turned, and it tipped over. Kasey knew immediately that she would not place in that round and had no chance at the average. The rest of the run was a training run for Kasey and JC. Kasey pushed JC forward, guiding her a little wide around the second and third barrels. She wanted JC to leave the rest standing. They carried only one five second penalty when they exited the arena, but that was enough. There would be no paycheck for the first go-round.

While Kasey walked the little mare to cool her off before leaving the staging area, she heard a familiar voice calling to her, and she turned to see Cole hurrying to catch up.

"A bit of tough luck there," Cole commented. "Is this the first time your mare has been in an indoor arena?"

Kasey nodded. "She seemed to take it all in stride, so I wasn't expecting her to tip a barrel. She hasn't tipped all season except one time in May. I'm not sure what came over her."

"It's the walls coming at her," Cole responded. "Outdoors, you have panels that can be seen through. In an indoor arena like this, they see the barrel but also this expanse of a solid wall. The patterns are smaller to accommodate the size of the coliseum so that throws most horses off too. She will figure it out, but you have to push her into the barrel, almost as if you are pushing her past it. It might be a ragged run for a time or two, but that little mare should be perfect for indoor arenas. She just needs a little more experience."

"There's not a lot of time before Oklahoma," Kasey commented.

"No, there isn't, but there are ten runs at the Finals, and you get arena time to practice. That will help you quite a lot," Cole told her. "Are you riding the roan horse for tomorrow's performance?"

"Well, I thought I would ride JC again here and Roan in St. Paul. Do you think that is a bad idea?"

"No, I would suggest the same," Cole looked thoughtful. "Give the little mare a second chance here while you can, and then focus on the roan at the next rodeo. Those two will get the hang of these indoor arenas. It just takes some time and experience."

Cole was right about JC. She seemed to understand the walls wouldn't close in on her when she ran again. Kasey was also careful, pushing the mare toward the barrel and ensuring she left plenty of room. Her time in the second go-round didn't win it, but she ended up with a third-place check, and that was enough to give her some added confidence going into the new season.

Kasey let the horses rest tied to a panel with the rest of the competitors' horses until after the rodeo was over. She was in no hurry, and it was cold outside. She would wait for the parking lot to clear some before she took her horses out to unsaddle and load. She planned on staying at the same stable until the middle of the week before heading to Minneapolis.

She watched the bull riding and saw the Korkow pick-up man make a super ride, knocking Cole out of first place and taking the lead. Cole had been up Saturday night in both of his events, and Ben was up on Sunday, so they were both here on this last day.

As she left the arena to collect her horses, she heard Cole call to her. "Hey, Kasey, they are awarding the All-Around Saddle. Want to walk out and watch with me?"

Kasey changed directions and went to join Cole. "I didn't know they had an All-Around Award here," she said. "Are you in the running?"

"Nope," Cole answered easily. "My horse bucked just a hair harder than I rode," he grinned. "I think I was sleeping. Anyway, it's better to get bucked off here than at the Finals. I think you will recognize who won it though."

A small crowd gathered around a new saddle sitting on a stand in the center of the arena. Inscribed on the saddle, Kasey saw the words, Flying Buckskins Rodeo All Around. And moving up to get the award was the Korkow pick-up man.

"I'll be darned," Kasey smiled. "What other event did he place in? Saddle bronc?"

"He didn't actually place in the broncs," Cole responded, "but he got a score, and with the win in the bull riding, he won the most money. He's a good guy. I'm happy for him."

Kasey nodded, watching the young man wait while pictures were taken. Along the edge of onlookers, she saw the cowboy's fiancée smiling proudly as she waited, and the stock contractor Erv Korkow shake the young man's hand. It was a good day for Korkow Rodeos. A successful rodeo was in the books, and one of their own won the All-Around Saddle.

***

It turned out Ben was heading back to the Black Hills to spend a few days with Josie. He hitched a ride with some cowboys he knew and would meet Cole in St. Paul. Cole decided to leave his horses at the same stable as Kasey. Kasey would take care of them while Cole went to Nebraska. He had some business there with a rancher who usually purchased calves from Cole and his dad. The tradeoff was that when Cole returned, he would load up Ben's doggin' horses and head to St. Paul. Kasey could follow him into the cities. That was a relief to Kasey as she had no idea where to go in St. Paul. She didn't know where to stable the horses and could envision herself getting completely lost. Cole had competed in the Twin Cities several times and had stabling already set up.

Just knowing she wasn't alone going into the city was a big thing for Kasey. So, the days she spent alone in Sioux Falls with the horses were relaxing ones for her. She exercised the horses lightly, hers and Ben's, and could even give them turn-out for a few hours each day in a wintery grass lot. She was ready to move on when she heard from Cole Wednesday evening. He would be hooked up and ready to load at dawn on Thanksgiving morning to head to St. Paul.

"We can miss a lot of traffic if we go in on the holiday," Cole explained. "Get there and get the horses settled and rested before the Friday performance. And as a bonus," Cole smiled at her, "I know where there is a Thanksgiving dinner we can hit."

***

The traffic was light on Thanksgiving, but Kasey was glad to follow Cole as they arrived in the city; even light traffic in a city as large as St. Paul had many vehicles on the road. Cole had arranged to keep the horses at the same livestock barn where the stock contractor kept the bucking stock. That was as close as they would find to the coliseum. The sale barn had large, clean inside pens where Cole and Kasey put their horses. With the Thanksgiving holiday, there were no cattle sales that week, so the place was quiet. A bonus was an electrical outlet by the barns that Kasey could use while she camped there for the weekend.

They no sooner got the horses settled, and Cole had his pickup unhooked than Cole told Kasey to jump in with him. It was only one o'clock, and he knew where they could get a Thanksgiving dinner. Kasey wondered if there was a chain restaurant that was open for Thanksgiving, but she was content to see where he was taking her. So, she was surprised to see him head deeper into the city and pull into the massive parking lot of the coliseum. A few trucks, a couple of cars, and one of Korkow's big semis were parked near the big building.

"This is the coliseum, isn't it?" Kasey asked, looking around. "Is this where the rodeo is being held this weekend?"

Cole nodded. "The rodeo office is in one of the rooms here. Might as well pay our fees."

They went in a back door near the semi. The Korkow truck was pulling a set of portable chutes behind it.

"You never think of all the extra things needed for a rodeo, do you? Korkow's have to haul all these panels as well as the stock to put this on." Kasey said as they walked in. "When do they set up the chutes and arena fence?"

"I suppose the ground crew will come in either tonight or first thing in the morning and haul in dirt," Cole answered. "The dirt has to be in before the chutes can be set up. Tomorrow will be a busy day."

They walked down a hallway, and it wasn't long before Kasey smelled the turkey roasting. "The Thanksgiving dinner is here?" she asked, surprised.

Cole grinned down at her. "Erv and Lafola and the rodeo secretary have a Thanksgiving meal here for their crew and for whoever gets here early," he replied. "Jim told me about it. He said I should come if I get to town today. I figured it beat a café somewhere along the road. Plus, I like coming into the city before traffic is heavy."

"So, remind me who's who?" Kasey whispered as they began to hear voices coming from a nearby room. "Erv and Lafola?"

"Erv is the stock contractor, Lafola is his wife, and Jim is their son who works in the business. Jim used to clown, but now he is one of the pick-up men at Korkow rodeos. Jim is married to Carol. Another son, Kenny, and his wife, Liz, are here too. There will be some other guys

that work for Korkows. You might recognize some faces," Cole whispered back. "It's sort of a family dinner,
but the family just got extra-large with Korkow em-
ployees and friends. Come on, you'll be welcome."

They walked into a large room, a big table spread
before them with turkey and all the fixings. Kasey expected to feel out of place, but it didn't take long for her
to get comfortable. There were familiar faces, people
she didn't know but recognized from the Korkow rodeos where she had competed. She recognized Jim then,
having seen him at Korkow rodeos. She also recognized
the other pick-up man and his fiancée who she spoke
to at Deadwood. She saw a couple of men who looked
familiar and recognized the stock contractor, Erv, and
the rodeo secretary, Marian Urbanek. She might not
know any of these people personally, but she was beginning to recognize who they were.

More importantly, Kasey was welcomed to this
Thanksgiving meal as if she were expected to be there.
Marian Urbanek was responsible for putting on this
sumptuous meal for everyone. Erv and Lafola were
gracious hosts. With their infectious smiles, the two
Korkow men, Jim and Kenny, welcomed Cole and Kasey
into the large rodeo office room, introducing Kasey to
people she didn't know. Carol and Liz introduced themselves and made Kasey feel at home. As the turkey was
dressed and the food laid out on long tables, the rodeo
stories and jokes kept everyone laughing.

Kasey might not tell anyone this, but she had been
dreading the holidays. This was the first Thanksgiving
since she lost most of her family. But this was such an
unexpected Thanksgiving dinner, with such a fun rodeo crowd, that Kasey had no time to reflect on what
she missed. By the time Cole got her back to her camper

that night, she realized she had gotten through this first Thanksgiving without the heavy sadness that holidays without family could bring. These people may not have been her family, but as she lay in her camper that night and thought about it, today, they had been her family and friends. And for that, she was very, very grateful.

***

The St. Paul coliseum was used for various events, one of which was hockey. For the rodeo, tons of dirt had to be brought in to cover the arena floor. The problem that year was the dirt that was hauled in had been wet and then frozen. When it was laid in the arena on Thursday night, the heaters under the flooring were turned on to thaw the dirt. Unfortunately, when the dirt was thawed, it turned to mud. Kasey had not been in many indoor arenas, but this was the first one that she had seen where the footing was mud. It was a thick sticky mess.

As it turned out, the St. Paul rodeo was a family affair for the Korkow family. At other rodeos such as Deadwood, Erv was the stock contractor, Lafola and Carol helped with secretarial duties, and Jim was a pick-up man. But at St. Paul, Kasey also noticed Erv's younger son, Kenny and his wife Liz. Kenny was the rodeo announcer at St. Paul, and Liz was helping behind the scenes wherever she was needed. Kasey watched the family work together. This rodeo family worked well together and put on excellent rodeos. It was fun to see how each had their place in the business.

About halfway through the performance between events, a stagecoach was brought into the arena carrying dignitaries. As Kasey watched, the stagecoach, pulled by a single team of horses, bogged down in the mud at the far end of the arena. The team could not pull it out. Kasey watched as Jim Korkow, waiting for the bull riding to start, rode in on his bull horse, a stout sorrel gelding he called Snoopy. He used Snoopy in the bull riding in case a bull decided to overstay his time in the arena. If Jim had to rope a bull, Snoopy was stout enough to drag the bull out. Seeing the trouble the stagecoach was in, Jim was ready. Looping his lariat around the front of the stagecoach, he got in position to pull.

"What do you think you are doing?" called the astounded stagecoach driver.

Jim didn't answer. He just asked Snoopy to pull and that stout gelding pulled that stagecoach right onto the team's rear ends before the surprised coach driver got in gear to urge his horses on. The crowd loved it as the pick-up horse pulled the stagecoach out of the arena.

"Never underestimate the ability or brawn of a horse that can pull bulls out of an arena," Ben said to Kasey as they watched the show.

Again, there were two go-rounds in the barrels. Kasey had drawn Friday night and Saturday afternoon. She had studied the ground, and knew she would run in that sticky mud, but then everyone else would too. She was glad she was riding Roan because he was a big stout gelding with big feet. He would handle the mud better than JC with her dainty little hooves. Kasey was able to get Roan into the arena late Friday afternoon after the coliseum had been transformed from a hockey arena to a rodeo arena. Nervous at first, Roan settled down to the strange sounds only an indoor coliseum can have. When the two made their first run that night, Kasey thought she was ready, but the run was still ragged. Roan tried to shut down as he ran toward the first barrel, but Kasey was ready to urge him on. It took a full second off her run, and she was well off the time. Still, she hadn't tipped a barrel, so she had another run to see if she could improve.

On Saturday, Roan ran much better as he became more confident running in the small arena. When they left the arena on Saturday, Kasey was sitting first in the second go. But, she was knocked to fourth by the end of the Sunday performance. She was out of the average too. Still, the trip had been worth it. Roan got experience, and Kasey, with her fourth place, had a few more dollars added to her winnings for the new year.

Kasey was able to watch the bull riding on Saturday night and see Cole ride. He had a huge Korkow bull called High Tower. High Tower came out strong and bucked hard. It was a stupendous ride, and when the buzzer sounded, Cole baled off and walked away. High Tower was not a man-eating bull and once his job was done, he walked away, looking for the turnout gate. Cole was sitting in first place at the end of the ride, but the go-round wasn't over until after Sunday's performance.

Right after Cole's ride, the last bull of the night was turned out. This was a little black bull called Hellcat. Hellcat had the reputation of eating cowboys, in other words, he was mean. When the cowboy bucked off, or bailed out after the whistle, it was time for the clown to come to the rescue. The clown at St. Paul was Bunky Boger and he was one of the best. When Hellcat's rider was ejected, Bunky enticed the beast away from the cowboy. When the cowboy was safe, and Hellcat had taken some runs at Bunky, the clown suddenly lay down on the arena floor. The surprised bull didn't know how to act with that. He shook his head, snorted, and pawed the ground, but the clown just lay there. Finally, the black bull was so frustrated that he couldn't get Bunky up to chase, that the animal turned and left the arena. The crowd had a lot to love with that performance. It was a fitting end to a good night of rodeo.

Now Kasey had three weeks to rest her horses. She planned to drive towards Oklahoma and find a place where she and her horses could take a well-needed rest. She'd find a rodeo arena or a fairground to camp at and hopefully find room for her horses to graze and relax. The next rodeo she would compete at was the National Finals Rodeo in Oklahoma City. Just thinking about that gave Kasey chills.

CHAPTER 8

BEYOND HER WILDEST DREAMS

Kasey gripped the wheel in a death grip, and then, realizing this, she forced herself to relax. It wasn't as if the traffic was terrible. Yes, she was entering Oklahoma City in the afternoon, but she had driven in cities before. The traffic wasn't even very congested. It was her nerves that were causing her anxiety. It was more than nerves. It was simple raw fear, and she couldn't rid her mind of it. She was going to the National Finals Rodeo in Oklahoma City, and she was just plain scared stiff.

Kasey had spent part of the week after Minneapolis at Sioux Falls, South Dakota, where her sister flew in and spent three days with her. During those days, Kasey relaxed and enjoyed being with Kelly. They had shopped and laughed and even ridden together. Kelly had never been the rider that Kasey was, but she did enjoy riding for pleasure. That was just what Kasey's horses needed—some nice, long, relaxing rides in the country, and the two sisters took them out each day. But like all good times, there was an end. Three days were all the sisters had together. On the evening of the third day, Kelly's husband had driven in from Colorado, and the next morning, he and Kelly headed east. They had gotten a good music gig and were on their way. It would be quite some time before Kasey would see her sister again.

After Kelly left, Kasey loaded up and headed south. It was cold in South Dakota, and with only a little over a week until the Finals started, Kasey headed toward Oklahoma, keeping an eye out for a nice rodeo arena to camp at for a few days. She found the perfect spot outside of Guthrie, Oklahoma. It was a private arena set apart from the distant ranch buildings. Kasey could see lights and a water hydrant at the arena, so she drove up to the ranch buildings and inquired about the possibility of staying at the arena for a few days. The owners were gracious, not wanting anything for electric usage, but Kasey insisted. The arena was completely fenced, and roping cattle grazed in the enclosed pasture area. The owners gave Kasey permission to let her horses graze also, so it turned out to be a perfect place to hold up for a few days.

The only downside was that other than a couple of evenings when there was team roping practice at the arena, Kasey was mainly alone. And with each day closer to the Finals, Kasey's fear and imagination ramped up. One day, she drove into Oklahoma City and found the coliseum where the Finals would be held, hoping that finding the site would ease her anxiety. It didn't. So, other than that one drive into the city, Kasey stayed put and worried. It wasn't a mentally healthy week for her.

So here she was, driving into Oklahoma City for the Finals. The first performance would be the following night. But Kasey could arrive today, find the stabling assigned to her horses, a camping spot for her outfit, and be ready to take advantage of arena time in the morning to work her horses. And with every passing mile, her fear increased. *I made it to 13th place,* Kasey would tell herself, *I deserve to be here.* Then her alter ego would pipe in that *she was a rookie* and *got some lucky breaks. She would fall apart in the pressure of the Finals. I have great horses,* she would argue back. *They will fall apart under pressure,* her mind retorted. Over and over in her head, Kasey would argue back and forth. By the time she reached the coliseum gates, it took all her willpower to turn the outfit into the contestants' entrance and come to a stop by the entrance attendant.

"Name," the middle-aged man with a clipboard asked.

"Kasey Jacobs."

The man consulted his clipboard. "You have two horses?"

"Yes."

"They have stalls twelve and thirteen in barn two," he told her. "And you can find any space in the parking lot around the barns for your outfit. There are some electrical hookups; just look for them."

Kasey looked around, confused. The coliseum loomed large and foreboding before her, and a vast parking lot was in front of her and on both sides of the coliseum, but she saw no barns or parked vehicles.

"Um," she began hesitantly, "which way are the barns?"

The man studied her. "First time here?"

Kasey could only nod.

"Take a right here and go around the coliseum," the man smiled kindly. "You will see the barns once you get around there. They are just tents, really, but they work. Behind the barns are the electrical hookups. You might have to share with a neighbor."

Kasey took a breath and nodded again.

"Scared?" the man asked.

"Petrified," Kasey managed a smile.

"I've heard of you," the man said. "My daughter says she's going to be just like you when she grows up. She wants to make the Finals her rookie year."

"If how I feel right now is any indication, I'd advise her to start rodeoing at an earlier age and work into it slowly," Kasey croaked.

The man chuckled at that. "I'm sure it is overwhelming," he said reassuringly, "but honey, you earned this trip. You'll do fine. Just give it a day or two to get the nerves settled."

Kasey looked at his kind face and nodded. "I am trying to do that. So far, the nerves are winning."

The barns did come into sight as Kasey rounded the coliseum building. There was a row of tents with two doorways in the front of each, leading to large alleyways. Kasey stopped before tent two and went in to find her stalls. They were the second to the last stalls in the first alleyway. Returning to her trailer, she unloaded the horses and took them into the barn. The stalls were roomy, and there was ample room in front of the stalls to haul in the bales of hay she had in her trailer. A hydrant served both barns one and two, but a long hose reached to the end of the alleyway. Kasey filled water buckets and left them in the stalls.

After getting the horses settled, Kasey took a walk and checked out the parking area. Behind the barns, there were electrical outlets on posts. Several campers were already lined up and hooked up to electricity, but there was room for many more. Kasey drove around behind the barns and found an empty electrical hookup almost directly behind barn two. She wouldn't have to walk far to reach the horses. Little activity was going on, and Kasey didn't recognize any other pickups and trailers. She wished she could see Ben and Cole's outfit parked close to hers, but since Ben hadn't qualified for the Finals, she knew his horses, and thus, Cole's outfit, wouldn't be here. Cole might not come to Oklahoma until the next day. Without having horses to get settled and use the arena time in the morning for practice, there was no need to come early.

Kasey spent a restless afternoon. She tried to read. She went for a walk around the grounds. She checked on the horses. She could not shake the overwhelming anxiety she was feeling. It wasn't until Kasey went out to feed her horses that evening that she saw the first familiar face. Coming out of the back of barn three, she saw Mara Olson. Mara had slipped a little in the standings coming into the Finals in second place, but she was so close to first place that it would be interesting to see if Mara could retake that place. Mara looked up, saw Kasey, and smiled at her.

"So, you made it, kid," Mara remarked as she got close.

"I did," Kasey agreed, "and it scares me to death."

"I remember that first year," Mara chuckled, but then she got serious. "Just remember you made it here by skill, not luck. Don't let the nerves ruin it for you."

"I'm trying," Kasey said, "but I'm not winning that battle yet."

"Get your practice time in tomorrow morning and just try to think of this as just another rodeo," Mara advised. Then she stopped and smiled at Kasey. "I don't know why I am giving you advice. You will probably get out there and kick my ass." And with that, she walked off, leaving Kasey feeling better, but not by much.

***

147

If Kasey thought her nerves would improve by the time the rodeo started, she was wrong. She had forgotten to switch her reins from straight reins to roping reins before the Grand Entry. She couldn't find the skid boots she wanted on Roan and hunted all over the trailer for them before finding them right where they should be. She had to return to the trailer for her back number, or she would get fined for not wearing it. She had to have her back number on whenever she was in the coliseum. She started clicking off in her mind all the things she needed and double-checking that she had them. By the time she joined the rest of the barrel racers working in the warm-up arena, she had checked and rechecked her equipment. It didn't make her feel any better.

At the National Finals, it was required that every contestant ride in the Grand Entry. Only the bareback riders were exempted because that was the first event. Whatever horse Kasey was not riding in the performance each day would be the horse that Kasey rode in the Grand Entry. While it demanded that Kasey switch horses, she thought it was best. It afforded each horse a turn around the arena each day, but the horse she chose to compete on, would not have the excitement of the Grand Entry on the same day they competed. Kasey would ride JC in the first Grand Entry and the little mare seemed to take it all in without concern. Kasey, though, felt her own fear ratchet up as they raced with the other contestants into the arena with the deafening noise of the crowd in their ears. To Kasey, it seemed the whole world was inside that coliseum. The first Grand Entry did nothing to ease Kasey's anxiety.

Kasey was thirteenth in the barrel racing draw out of fifteen. The line-up of the girls running never changed, but each night, they rotated one place. She ran thirteenth the first night, fourteenth the next, then fifteenth. Then Kasey started at the beginning of the runs as first, then second, and so on. By the last performance, she would be running seventh. The earlier the run, the better the ground. Kasey watched as Mara entered the arena. Mara was starting in the fifth spot tonight. She would be in sixth tomorrow and then seventh. Eventually, Mara would end up in the fourteenth spot. It was as fair as possible when the ground was not raked during the performance to level the dirt after several runs. Every girl rotated into ten of the fifteen spots.

Kasey was riding Roan. He was the most seasoned of her two horses, and she hoped he would handle her nerves better than JC. She had to shake this feeling, but no matter what she tried, she could tell she was close to falling apart with nerves. She just hoped she could focus on her run when she entered the arena.

There was a long alleyway the girls and their horses rode down to get to the arena. It came into the main alleyway at an angle. About thirty feet from the mouth of the arena, the alley fed into the run-in, run-out main alley. Once the girl competing in the arena exited in a full run, the gate was opened, and the next girl would move her horse into the main alley and start toward the arena. Horses were in full flight by the time they entered the arena and full flight when they exited. Kasey felt like she was in a fog as she watched the girls in front of her, one by one, head into the arena to the roar of the crowd. Finally, it was her turn.

When the gate opened, Roan stalled. He had never done that before, and it threw Kasey for an instant as she urged him forward. At first, he refused again. Roan's head was up, and he was nervous. Kasey, already in almost panic mode, kicked him hard. Roan reacted by jumping jerkily forward. Kasey couldn't quite get with him as he whirled once, not wanting to turn toward the arena gate. Finally, she got him lined out toward the arena and urged him forward, breaking into a run. They came out onto the arena hunting the first barrel.

In Kasey's mind, it was an awful run. It was a full second and a half off the time. Kasey miscued Roan, and he shut down too early before the first barrel. Seeing her mistake, she had urged him forward, and Roan overshot it. But they did get the next two barrels turned, although they were not pretty. The only saving grace was they had not tipped a barrel. And that hadn't been because they hadn't tried. The second barrel was only saved from falling by Kasey's quick reach down to stop its descent. But that save had cost them time too. The turn at the third barrel looked good, but by then, it was too late. The run had been a disaster. Kasey left the arena despondent and embarrassed. She felt like an amateur. By the time all fifteen runs were in, Kasey had the slowest time except for the three girls who tipped barrels and had penalties added. Again, Kasey had the overwhelming feeling that she didn't deserve to be here.

She knew she should have gone back and watched the bulls to see how Cole did, but Kasey didn't want to face anyone. She cooled Roan off, brushed him down, fed her horses, and then curled up in Roan's stall on a pile of straw, watching him eat. Occasionally, she would talk to him, telling him how sorry she was and how that run was her fault, not his. She dozed some, too, finally feeling exhaustion from her nerves and the previous sleepless night overtake her.

"So, are you hiding here or just found a new place to sleep?"

The question woke Kasey, and she blinked, getting her bearings. She looked up and saw Cole leaning over the half door into Roan's stall. He wasn't smiling. "I think I am doing both," she replied. "Well, hiding and sleeping, that is."

"I think it is time you come out of there and quit feeling sorry for yourself then," Cole's voice was brusque.

"Oh, Cole," Kasey wailed, "I shouldn't be here. I don't belong. Did you see my run tonight?" Her words came out in a rush. "Roan refused! Then he whirled when coming down the alley. I miscued him on the first barrel and probably the second too. It was awful. Can I just get a vet's release and go home?"

Cole unlatched the stall door and came in, offering his hand to Kasey. "Get up and come out of there," he ordered. "It's bad enough you are feeling sorry for yourself, but you don't have to subject your poor horse to your mood."

Reluctantly, Kasey gave him her hand, and he pulled her up and guided her out of the stall. They walked in silence out of the barn, heading toward Kasey's pickup and camper. As they drew close, Kasey saw that Cole's pickup was pulled up nose-to-nose with her outfit. He guided Kasey to the back of his pickup, dropped the tailgate, and picking her up lightly, he placed her on it before climbing up to sit beside her.

"You know why Roan acted the way he did going into the arena?" Cole asked gently.

"Well, he was nervous, I suppose," Kasey answered.

"He was more than nervous," Cole responded. "He was looking for the monster that your anxiety told him must be out there. You were scaring that poor horse out of his wits with your own fear. He was only trying to avoid what was scaring you."

Kasey hung her head but didn't respond. She knew Cole spoke the truth.

"Kasey, look at me," Cole was firm. She raised her eyes to him. His voice softened then. "I get that you are scared. This is a big step for anyone, but you are taking your fear a bit too far. You are freaking yourself out, and it is carrying over to your horse. You say you believe in your horses. Well, you earned the right to be here with them. You already have beaten some of these girls. Time to put on your big girl pants and fight for yourself and your horses."

Kasey watched Cole for a minute before replying, "You think I can really do that?"

"Good God, Kasey, of course I do," Cole said, exasperation in his tone. "I have watched you blossom this year with those two horses. I think you have the ability to beat every one of these girls," he hesitated. "But honey, you have to believe it too. And hiding in the stall isn't going to do it."

Kasey took a deep breath. "I know, but I just. . ." she hesitated. "I just want to hide." She looked up at Cole and smiled weakly.

"Okay, that is over. It's time for action," Cole said, slipping off the tailgate. "Come on, time you got rid of some of the nerves." He reached for her hand and pulled her toward the passenger door of his pickup.

"What? Where are we going?" she asked.

"We are going dancing," Cole grinned at her. "By the time we get back, you should be tired enough to sleep."

Cole knew all of the venues for rodeo parties after the rodeo. As he drove through the streets, Kasey thought to ask about his rides.

"Did you place in either event?" she asked.

"Second in both," Cole answered. "So, I don't have to attend the buckle presentation tonight." Cole was referring to the buckles presented each night to the contestants who won go-arounds. Each night, there was a buckle presentation for the winners of each event. Cole looked over at Kasey and grinned. "I don't expect to make this a habit. I plan to get more buckles while I am here. You should too."

They stopped at a large hotel and made their way to a big convention room. Here, there were tables and a bar set up, and a band playing. It was crowded, smokey, and noisy, overflowing with rodeo people.

"What is this place?" Kasey asked.

"Well, this is the hotel where I'm staying, but it is also where the buckle presentations are every night," Cole answered. "So, it is always crowded. The presentations were going on while I was looking for you. So, now it is just the after-party."

And a party it was. It wasn't long before Kasey saw Ben and Josie. They were saving seats for Cole and Kasey at a small table. Kasey began to see a few other familiar faces among the crowd. No one said anything to Kasey about her run, and after a bit, she started to relax and enjoy herself. Cole had her out dancing often, and when they were at the table with Ben and Josie, along with other people who knew Cole, the stories and jokes were fun to hear. Kasey was surprised to admit it, but the night wasn't quite as much a disaster as it started out to be.

***

Kasey was up in the morning and had Roan saddled, ready to ride in the arena as soon as she was allowed in for her practice time. She hadn't gotten much sleep since Cole had her out dancing for at least two hours, but when her head hit the pillow, she was out like a light. She could take a nap in the afternoon. Sleep she wasn't worried about. Instead, she felt renewed. Yes, she was still nervous, still afraid. But in her heart, she knew Cole was right. She was the cause of Roan's nervousness, and she was the cause of the poor run. She had to get over it. Using this time and focusing only on Roan might help. She would ride him again this second night. Roan needed to know everything was good and he would only do that if Kasey rode that way. She knew her horse trusted her. She had to trust the horse.

After the arena time, Kasey collected JC from her stall, and for over an hour, she rode JC and ponied Roan around the parking area. Kasey practiced breathing deeply and relaxing in the saddle. She couldn't do much more than walk in the cement parking lot, but she knew the horses enjoyed getting out of the stalls. And while she rode, Kasey repeatedly told herself this was just another rodeo. Now, if she could only believe it.

***

The day passed more quickly than Kasey expected. She had just gotten the horses back in their stalls and headed back to her camper to rest when Josie stopped by. Ben and Cole were off somewhere, and she was wondering if she could hang out with Kasey. Kasey welcomed the company. It kept her from thinking about the upcoming performance. At noon, Cole and Ben returned, picked up the two girls, and they went out for lunch at a cowboy café that Cole knew about. It was well after two in the afternoon before Kasey was dropped off at her camper. She was tired and ready for a nap. With the performance at night and the late night afterward, Kasey had her days and nights mixed up. She got almost two hours of sleep before she had to start getting ready for the evening performance.

To say her nerves were settled on this second day would be incorrect. But there was a difference. She hadn't been alone all day, stressing. It felt more like just another rodeo, albeit a big one, because she had interacted with friends. By the time Kasey rode Roan to the coliseum for the barrels, she could feel the difference in herself. Now if she could only hold it together while she waited.

So, Kasey was surprised when she rode into the coliseum alleyway to see Ben and Josie waiting for her. They stood together, leaning against the alleyway panels.

"Hey," she smiled at the pair. "Are you lost?"

"Nope," Josie replied. "We are your escorts. We are supposed to keep you from going crazy scared."

"Yeah," Ben piped in, "Cole said not to leave you alone until you fly into that arena. He said to tell you to believe in your horse, and the rest will fall in place."

"Well, I have to admit that it is good to see you," Kasey grinned. "I am better now than I was this time yesterday, but I was starting to worry. I hope this works!"

And it did. Ben and Josie did not break Kasey's concentration for the upcoming run, but they also did not let her slide into the deep anxiety that plagued Kasey the night before. When the gate opened, and Kasey urged Roan through it, he went willingly. When they reached the arena floor, they were flying. From there, it was almost like they were on autopilot. When they exited the arena, they were sitting second. By the time the event ended, Kasey had been pushed to third. She'd be getting a check for that, but more importantly, she knew she was over the hump. Kasey belonged at the Finals, and now she knew it.

Kasey rushed to settle Roan in his stall and hustled back to the arena to watch Cole in the bulls. Through visiting with Ben and Josie before the barrels, she knew Cole had won the saddle bronc riding go-round, so Kasey knew he would be headed to the buckle presentation after the performance. She hoped he'd get two buckles that night, but that thought was dashed when Cole couldn't make the final half-second on his bull. He would have won it if he could have just held on. The bull was one of the few great animals that had never before been ridden. So, for the bull, it was a good night.

On the third night, Kasey was riding Roan once more. She felt both his and her confidence got a big boost with the third-place win on day two. She would give him another night and hope they improved more. And improve they did. Roan went down the alley like the seasoned horse he was. He was hunting the first barrel as he came out of the alley and into the arena. Once again, they were a team, taking each barrel in stride. When her time was announced as she left the arena, she was sitting in first place. The horses that followed didn't catch her.

Again, Kasey rushed to catch Cole's bull ride, but after Cole's ride, Kasey headed back to her camper. Quickly, she cleaned up, putting on clean jeans and a pretty blouse. Because Kasey placed first, she had to attend the buckle presentation that night. She was outside unhooking her pickup from the trailer when Cole pulled up.

"What are you doing?" he called as he sat in his idling pickup.

"I won!" Kasey called, hardly believing it herself. "I actually won the go-round! I'm unhooking. I have to go to the buckle presentation if I can find it!"

"Silly girl, come climb in with me," Cole laughed. "You don't want to drive that big camper around town."

And so, she did. Cole had already won a couple of go-round buckles by then, one in broncs and one in bulls. He was an old hand at this. Cole could see how excited Kasey was, and it tickled him. He teased her as she got in the pickup and then grew serious.

"I told you that you could do this," he said quietly. "I hope you see that now."

"I think," Kasey began slowly, "I can do almost anything with these two horses. But it is so hard to believe. It's like a fairy tale. I just wish my folks were here to see this."

"They are here, Kasey," Cole said softly. "Trust me, they are here."

***

Kasey thought about the week as she saddled JC. It was the ninth round of the Finals, so there were just two more runs to make. Roan had done his job, and JC would finish up. Kasey had ridden Roan three more times after her third-place win in the second round. On the fourth night, Kasey was up last. It was the worst of the ground, so she was just hoping for a clean run. Roan ran his heart out and came in second by a hundredth of a second. She couldn't have been more pleased. Then, on the fifth night, running on the top of the ground, Roan had flown, cinching her next buckle for a go-round win. She switched to JC after that and won the next two performances. JC slipped going around the third barrel in the eighth round and they ended up in fourth place. Cole teased her that she had so many buckles that she would need another truck to haul them home. The thrill never got old to Kasey.

So here Kasey was, saddling JC for the ninth round. Kasey hadn't won enough money coming into the Finals to move up to first or even close to that in the world standings. It just wasn't possible to win enough to advance that far in ten performances. But she had moved up from the thirteenth spot to seventh. Currently, though, Kasey was neck and neck with Mara for the average. There were two winners at the National Finals Rodeo. There was the overall winner, the contestant in each event who won the most money during the year, including what was won in the Finals. Kasey had no chance of being number one in that. But the Finals average was hers if she could just nail good runs in these last two performances. It was beyond her wildest dreams that she would even make it to the Finals, and then to be in the race for the average was beyond imagining.

***

Kasey and JC won the ninth go-round. That made five go-round wins for Kasey. She had to keep looking at the buckles to believe this was really happening. Kasey had four buckles sitting on her countertop, but the fifth she was wearing. She'd glance down occasionally to make sure she wasn't dreaming.

Kasey sat outside her camper on a lawn chair, watching any activity in the contestants parking area. Some young ropers were roping a bale of hay three outfits down from her. A card game was played on a folding table just beyond that. This was the last day. One more performance and then this parking lot would become a ghost town. Because the last performance was held on Sunday afternoon, everyone would be busy once the performance started. But for this last morning, the community of the contestants parked around the barns was a place of relaxed activity. Most afternoons found contestants and their families gathering outside if the weather allowed. It was a long time between the performances and most people just wanted to relax in the afternoons. Even contestants who stayed in motels gravitated to the contestants' parking area on many afternoons. But this was the last morning, and the weather was mild, so people came out of their campers or drove in from motels. Kasey had enjoyed the week visiting with people who passed by her camper. Many afternoons, Josie came and sat with her, and on several days, Ben and Cole sat in lawn chairs with her. The Oklahoma sun was warm, and Kasey only needed a light jacket.

This was the last day, and she wanted to absorb every minute of this amazing week. Besides the actual rodeo performances and the buckle presentations, there were a multitude of activities going on in and around the city. Kasey had several times gone with Cole, Ben, and Josie to visit stores during the day or go dancing after a performance. They had visited the National Cowboy and Western Heritage Museum in Oklahoma City and spent a good portion of the day there. Kasey had been surprised when, as the week progressed, she was called upon by different news outlets for interviews. Her blistering record at the National Finals was attracting attention.

Kasey saw Cole's pickup as it rounded the coliseum and came to park nose-to-nose with hers. She smiled in greeting as Cole reached for the spare chair folded up against her trailer. He waved to someone in the card game and sat down next to Kasey.

"So, last day," he commented. "Has it been all you thought it was going to be?"

"Oh, my gosh," Kasey breathed, "this has been so much more. I never even dreamt of this."

Cole grinned. "It's been fun seeing it again through your eyes. Making the Finals will always be exciting, but I'd forgotten how if felt that first time."

They sat for a while, watching the activity around them. Some rough stock riders wandered by and stopped to visit with Cole for a while. Kasey relaxed, listening to them. They talked about the horses they'd drawn for the night, discussing the animals' strengths and weaknesses. After a while, the men wandered off leaving Cole and Kasey alone.

"So, are you excited to go home and spend Christmas with your sister?" Cole asked suddenly.

"Well, um, no. I mean, no, I am not going home," Kasey replied slowly. "My sister and her husband are off on a tour. They are renting out the house while they are gone."

"You said they had a gig, but won't that be over by Christmas?"

Kasey smiled and looked away before answering. "They were hired to be the opening act for a big-name rock band. They have an eighteen-month contract. They are in Europe. All their concerts are in Europe. I won't see Kelly until after Christmas next year."

"Oh," Cole said, surprised. "I would have thought you two would want to spend this Christmas together." Kasey knew what he meant. He meant this "first Christmas" after the accident.

"It was a big decision," Kasey said slowly, "but I told them they had to take this opportunity while they could. Just like I had to make the Finals." Kasey sat quietly for a while. "I think we both knew we couldn't go back to what we had before, so maybe this is best. Christmas will be so different for us, and it has to be. This might be better than sitting and moping together."

Cole digested this before he asked, "So where are you spending Christmas then?"

Kasey didn't answer at once. She watched the ropers. Finally, she spoke. "Well, when I leave here tomorrow, I thought I'd go back to that ranch I stayed at the week before the Finals. I'm sure those people will let me stay there again. The horses liked the place and could get out and graze." She hesitated before continuing, "Then the weather is supposed to turn cold next week, so I was thinking of heading into Texas and finding a place to hold up somewhere. Maybe a state park or a rodeo grounds, or even a ranch somewhere. I'm not sure I want to stay in the camper if the temperature gets below freezing."

Cole sat quietly, letting her words sink in. Finally, he turned toward her.

"So, what you are saying," Cole said, irritation in his tone, "is you are just going to bum around for the next three or four weeks? Over Christmas and New Year's? Alone?"

"Well, yeah, I guess. What's wrong with that?" Kasey was defensive.

"Girl," Cole said, turning on her, "you spent a week alone before the Finals and got here a blubbering mess. Now you think you are going to spend a month alone over the holidays? That sure as shit isn't healthy."

Kasey was taken aback by his response. "I'll be all right," she said weakly.

"No, you will not be all right," Cole said, exasperated. "You will be alone, and the depression will hit you, and you will sink lower than you thought you could go," Cole stopped, thinking before continuing. "So, what you will do is come home with me and spend a decent holiday with people who will help you through this first Christmas."

"I can't do that!" Kasey responded. "I can't impose on your family over the holidays."

"You won't be imposing. You'd be welcome."

"I can't do that. You said a while back that your sister and her family come for Christmas every year. I can't just barge in! I mean, you haven't even talked this over with your folks."

Cole regarded her for a minute, then stood up and put his hand out to her. "Get up," he said. "Come with me."

"Where? Where are we going?" Kasey asked, but Cole just grasped her hand and headed toward the coliseum, dragging her behind him.

Cole pulled Kasey, who had to almost trot to keep up, into the coliseum through the contestants' entrance. Just inside the door there was a wall of pay phones. Going to one, Cole deposited a coin, dialed a number, waited, and then deposited more coins. Finally, a call went through.

"Hey, Dad," Cole said cheerily into the receiver. "What's the weather like?"

For a minute, Cole chatted with his father, then asked to speak to his mother.

"Hey, Mom," Cole asked after visiting briefly, "you have any problem with me bringing a friend home for the holiday break?" Cole listened, then said, "I didn't think so, but my friend wanted me to make sure. We should be rolling in by Tuesday night at the latest." Cole visited a moment longer before signing off. Turning to Kasey he smiled.

"See," he said, "it's settled. You are coming home with me."

"Cole," Kasey started, exasperated, "you didn't even tell them I'm a girl!"

"And that makes a difference?" he asked as they walked out of the building.

"Well, of course, it does," Kasey said. "I mean, they probably think you are bringing another guy who could, you know, stay with you."

Cole started to laugh. Looking down at Kasey, he smiled. "Kasey, my folks' place has plenty of room. Quit worrying."

***

The tenth performance was over. The awards for that performance were presented immediately after the rodeo in the arena. Kasey and JC had placed second in the last round, so she had no new go-round buckle. She wasn't too disappointed after winning five of them. But with that tenth-round second-place win, Kasey had cinched the Finals barrel racing average. Besides the extra money the average carried with it, she also won a trophy saddle. Mara stood in the line of presentations beside Kasey. Mara had won the World Title, and the accompanying saddle that year, but Kasey had edged Mara out of the average win.

"I knew I should never have given you advice," Mara smiled at Kasey. "Congratulations, kid."

Kasey smiled back. "It was good advice," she said. "Thank you."

Cole had won the Saddle Bronc World title. This was his ninth Finals, and he finally won a World Title. He was edged out of the Bull Riding title by a nose this year, placing second for the second year in a row. He also placed second in the All-Around average, edged out of the average saddle by a cowboy who was a calf roper and a team roper. Cole stood behind the trophy saddle for the bronc riding title and smiled across at Kasey. It had been a good Finals for both of them.

CHAPTER 9

SANDERS' RANCH

B en and Josie dropped Cole off just before eight the following morning. Ben would take Cole's pickup home, stopping by Spearfish on the way to get Josie's things from her apartment. Josie had one semester of college remaining and was student teaching close to her family's home. She wouldn't return to the campus except for a few short weeks of Methods classes. For those, she would stay with a friend and let her apartment lease go. When Kasey protested that Cole didn't have to drive with her, he had just grinned and said he was glad to have an excuse not to help with Josie's move.

Cole and Kasey headed toward Denver on Monday morning. Cole knew rodeo people who lived between Colorado Springs and Denver, where they could stay that night. They could make Cole's ranch by Tuesday evening.

The trip was far more enjoyable to Kasey than all her travels that summer. Cole drove almost the entire way, and Kasey had no objection. Cole's friends had a small ranchette not far off the interstate where Kasey's horses had a large indoor pen, big enough for both of them and room to move around. Cole's friends welcomed her and insisted she stay in a spare bedroom. Kasey didn't object to that either. It was December in Colorado, and her camper would be drafty, despite a furnace.

They got a late start Tuesday morning after having breakfast with Cole's friends, so it was dark when they pulled into Cole's ranch. While Kasey couldn't see the mountains well in the darkness, she knew the terrain was mountainous as they wound their way along the last miles of gravel. They had stopped in Sheridan, Wyoming, and had a quick supper, and as they pulled into the ranch yard, Kasey knew she was ready to stop. The last two weeks had taken its toll, the adrenaline from the Finals was wearing off, and she was weary.

The Sanders' home was a large two-story frame house with a porch that stretched the length of it towards the drive. It was lit up like a Christmas tree with lights strung along the porch and railing. Kasey could see a decorated tree in the picture window facing the road, and colored lights also twinkled from the yard fence. As Cole drove slowly up to the large barn, lights came on outside the barn.

"I knew Dad would be watching," he grinned at Kasey. "Good thing I called them at noon and told them we'd be late, or they would have sat by the window watching for us since before dark." He put the pickup in park. "Come on. Let's get your horses settled. Dad said he would have stalls ready for them."

It didn't take them long to get the horses out of the trailer. The barn had stalls and an indoor arena. Kasey was able to turn her horses into the arena to roll before putting their blankets back on and getting them comfortable in their stalls. She was going to haul in the hay bales she had with her, but Cole told her to leave them for January when she headed out. They had plenty of hay in the barn. Kasey was too tired to argue. She would try to pay later for the hay and the stalls.

Kasey thought she might be nervous meeting Cole's parents, but she remembered visiting with Ben when they camped during the summer outside Sterling, Colorado, and how Ben said Cole's folks were such good people. Kasey had to believe that because Cole himself was so good to her. Kasey found she was looking forward to meeting them.

Pete and Anne Sanders were waiting at the door for Cole and Kasey. In their mid-sixties, they greeted Kasey warmly. If they were surprised that Cole's friend was a girl, they didn't show it. Kasey assumed Cole might have mentioned that fact when he called his folks when they stopped for lunch. *Or maybe*, Kasey thought, *Cole had brought other women home in the past.* In any case, the couple welcomed Kasey.

Pete Sanders was an older version of Cole. Medium height with a tanned face from hours in the sun, he looked every bit the cowboy. For a man in his mid-sixties, he carried no extra weight and looked as fit as a younger man of fifty. Anne Sanders was shorter than Pete and slim in a middle-aged way. Her smile was welcoming, and her eyes twinkled. Anne was a handsome woman with medium-length brown hair that fell just short of her shoulders. Kasey had no problem seeing where Cole's good looks came from. Anne must have been a stunner in her younger days.

"This is Kasey Jacobs," Cole introduced her to his parents.

"I know that name," Anne responded with a smile. "You are the rookie barrel racer who took the Finals by storm. We watched an interview with you on our local news channel last week."

"You have certainly had a good first trip to the Finals," Pete added.

Kasey was surprised. She had given some interviews during the Finals but thought they just went out to local Oklahoma City news shows. She didn't realize they were sent out to other television stations.

"I don't know about taking the Finals by storm," she answered, "but I tried to shape up my act after my first disastrous run."

"Apparently, you did just fine," Pete said. "Everyone knows who you are now."

The four of them retired to the living room, a large comfortable great room with overstuffed leather chairs, a sofa, and a cheery fire crackling in the fireplace. Despite the large room, it was cozy and warm. The conversation turned to the Finals and how the week went for them both. But as Cole and his folks carried most of the conversation, Kasey felt herself getting drowsy. The crackling fire, the end of the long journey, and the security of being with other people were lulling Kasey to sleep. She tried to fight off the feeling, but her yawns gave her away.

"You look like you need a bed," Cole said to Kasey. "I'll show you to your room if you want."

Kasey smiled gratefully. "I don't know why I am so tired all of a sudden, but I think you are right. I am about to crash right here on the couch."

Cole took her bag and led her up the stairs to the second floor. At the top of the stairs, they were in a U-shaped hallway that wound around the stairs.

"My folks built a bedroom years ago on the main floor, but that room on the right used to be the master bedroom," Cole pointed to a doorway. "My sister and her husband stay in there when they come. They have a private bathroom in there. Straight ahead is the up-stairs bathroom. You will only share with my niece and nephew when they get here closer to Christmas." Cole turned to the left and went to the first door. "This is where you can stay. My niece will share this with you when she gets here if that is okay with you."

"No problem," Kasey said, peering into the room through the door Cole opened. It was a big room with two twin beds, a double closet, and a dresser in be-tween the beds. "This is nice."

"I'll leave you then," Cole turned to go, then hesitated. "The bathroom has towels. Help yourself. The shower works but give the hot water a minute to make it up here. My nephew will stay in the next room past this, and that last door at the end leads to my room. Holler if you need anything." And with that, Cole was gone.

***

Pete and Anne were sitting in the same easy chairs when Cole returned. He sat down in front of the fire facing them.

"So, how did you become acquainted with the rookie barrel racer everyone is talking about?" Anne asked. "Have you known her long, or just meet her at the Finals?"

Cole smiled. He knew his mom, who longed for him to find the perfect wife, would ask something along those lines. He hated to disappoint her with the truth.

"Remember when I stopped for a few days after St. Onge last summer and told you about a young girl who lost her dog?"

"Didn't you say that gal also lost most of her family in a car accident?" Pete asked.

"She did, between Christmas and New Year's last year," Cole answered, his tone solemn. "That girl is Kasey. I seemed to run into her several times over the summer. Ben and I got to parking near her outfit if we could, and Kasey would watch over our horses if we stayed in a motel. I think she was lonely, or at least very alone. Maybe I felt like I had to watch over her, too. I had to pull a drunk cowboy off her one night," Cole chuckled at that. "She wasn't too experienced dating cowboys."

"Then Ben had Josie along with him some of the summer. Josie and Kasey really hit it off, so we'd take Kasey with us out to eat. Stuff like that. Anyway, over the summer, we all got to be good friends. It sometimes made me feel like the "big brother" with those three young ones, but it made me feel good to help her out."

"So, she has no other family?" Anne asked.

"She has a twin sister," Cole answered. "Her twin got married early last spring. I thought Kasey would spend Christmas with Kelly, but when I asked her at the end of the Finals what she was doing for the holiday, she told me she was going to be alone; just bumming around. Her sister and brother-in-law had the opportunity to open for a big-name band in Europe. They have a band and have an eighteen-month contract and left at the end of November."

Cole kicked off his boots and made himself more comfortable. "Kasey spent over a week alone before the Finals and got to Oklahoma City a nervous wreck. Her mind had imagined all the awful things that could happen. She about had herself convinced that she shouldn't be there. It showed in her first run. I chewed her butt that night. And she came out of it." Cole leaned back, relaxing. "When she told me she planned to be alone for the holidays, I knew that was a recipe for disaster. She'd spend all that time thinking of the family she lost. That just isn't healthy."

"I am glad you brought her here," Anne said. "You are right. No one should be alone over the holidays."

***

Kasey woke to the delicious smell of frying bacon and the tantalizing smell of baking bread. It was still dark outside, but her watch said it was almost seven. She had slept so hard that she was still groggy, but she got up and dressed. Downstairs, she found Anne frying bacon and trays of warm buns were cooling.

"Oh, my," Kasey said, entering the large kitchen, "I overslept. I better head out and feed my horses."

"Cole said he would throw your horses some hay and check their water," Anne answered. "Pete and Cole went to feed the work horses and will be right in for breakfast. Cole said you can turn your horses out for the day after breakfast when the sun is up."

"Well, that sounds good," Kasey smiled. "I'm sure you know it, but you raised a very nice man."

Anne smiled back, "I do know that, but a mother always likes to hear someone else say it."

"How can I help?" Kasey asked, coming to the stove.

"Watch the bacon. I have more buns ready to come out of the oven."

"They smell heavenly," Kasey commented. "I don't know anything about making bread, but you must have been up at midnight making them."

"No, this is an old family recipe. I started the dough yesterday at about noon. Let it rise a couple of times, and I mixed them out into buns before you came last night. They rise one more time overnight and bake first thing in the morning," Anne explained as she took out a tray, and with a spatula, moved the buns to a cooling tray. She reached for a semi-cooled bun and handed it to Kasey. "Try one right out of the oven. I cannot resist eating them before they cool." Anne pointed to the counter. "Slather some butter on them, and they are really good."

Kasey lost no time in following directions and taking a bite. "Oh my gosh, these are good," she breathed. "They are almost like a sweet roll."

"They have sugar in them," Anne agreed. "They are great for sandwiches and hamburgers. We are kind of spoiled. Regular bread just doesn't do the trick most of the time."

It was then that the men came stomping in, leaving overshoes and coats in the mud room.

"I knew you'd have fresh buns this morning," Cole said, going to the counter and plucking a still-hot bun from the tray. He looked over at Kasey, "Mom always has fresh buns when I get home."

"Ha," Anne retorted, "I always have fresh buns baking. You just think they are for you."

Breakfast was hearty with talk of the weather and how the animals were doing thrown out between bites. Pete and Cole discussed the cattle market, how the fall calves sold, and how many were held back to sell after the New Year. While Kasey's dad had bought the Colorado ranch where she had lived for the last several years, he had left the management of it up to a foreman. Kasey had little working knowledge of the nuts and bolts of ranching and found the conversation interesting.

As they finished eating, Cole looked over at Kasey. "You want to come with us to feed cows? See how an old-time cowboy does it?" he asked.

"I'd love to, but I should help your mom clean up," Kasey answered.

"You go," Anne told her. "I have nothing on my calendar and don't want to step out into the cold. I have plenty of time to clean up. Lunch is sandwiches on fresh buns, so it is easy."

Kasey had to run out to her camper and find her coveralls and warm winter boots, but it didn't take her long to join Cole and Pete in the barn where her horses waited. After giving the horses their morning grain, Kasey turned them out. The stalls opened to a small outside pen the horses could share. They still had hay and water in their stalls so they would be content for the day.

In the daylight, Kasey could see the size of this barn. It was fairly new and had eight stalls on one side, which opened up to a large indoor arena. "This is nice," Kasey told Cole.

"This is what several good years on the circuit buys," Cole said. "I was tired of seeing Dad freeze all winter riding his young stock. It isn't heated, but it keeps the elements out, and we have a heated tack room to go into and warm up on the coldest days."

"Does your dad ride colts?"

"He used to ride them from the first saddle on, but now he does the groundwork, and I put a few rides on them whenever I am home," Cole answered. "Then Dad goes on with them. We usually sell six or eight horses a year. It's called ranch diversification. When I retire, I will do more of the riding, but Dad is one hell of a horseman. I don't think he will give up his horses."

They walked out of the arena, and Kasey saw a big, red, wooden barn behind it. It was one of those big old barns with a center aisle and a large hay mow above. The center aisle door was slid shut, and they entered through a walk-in door at the side. Inside, Kasey saw that the hay mow was on either side of the aisle. The mow was stacked with square bales of hay. Along the sides of the aisle were big, roomy horse stalls. Her first thought was that these were stud stalls or foaling stalls because they were so large, but as she peered inside the first one, she saw she was wrong. These stalls were for draft horses. The barn was warmed by the big animals and smelled of hay and horses.

Almost blocking the aisle was a large hay wagon, already loaded with hay. Pete and another man were harnessing two large draft horses to the wagon.

"This hombre is Stan," Cole introduced Kasey. "He's the man who keeps Dad in line while I am gone."

Stan and Pete both grinned at that, neither denying it.

Kasey shook hands with Stan. He was about fifty, a slight man with a firm handshake and a gentle smile. As Kasey watched, she saw that the two men seemed to know exactly what to do, as if they had done this job for years, which, on reflection, she was sure they had.

"Stan and his wife used to have an old cabin where the arena is, but when we built the arena, we put in an apartment in the barn, and they live there now," Cole told Kasey. "Stan has been here since I was just a kid. It's always been like having two dads."

Cole helped Kasey climb onto the wagon, clambering up to the top. The hay was loose, not baled.

"I thought maybe you would use the square bales from the loft," Kasey commented.

"That is our winter insurance hay," Cole told her. "If we get a bad storm, we can load the wagon inside and not fight the weather. But otherwise, we load from the loose haystacks. Cheaper to put up loose stacks. We use a tractor to load the hay onto the wagon, though.

We don't have anything against tractors or mechanical things, but Dad has always fed with a team. We keep several draft horses, always breaking in one or two a year. Then, when we get a seasoned young team, we sell them. The old horses that we use year after year will die here. They are the old trusted ones we use to break in the young ones. After a horse gives us a lifetime of use, it deserves to be retired here and live out its life in peace."

"Nice practice," Kasey replied. "I wish everyone thought that way. There wouldn't be so many old broken-down horses going to sale barns and from there, worse."

The wagon lurched and started gliding out of the barn on runners. Riding high up on the hay, Kasey could see the layout of the whole barnyard. She could see back toward the house as they pulled beyond the arena. It sat white against the pine-covered hills behind it. White snow glistened all around.

"It's like a picture postcard of some idyllic place," Kasey whispered. "This is so beautiful."

***

That first week at the Sanders' ranch was one of discovery for Kasey. Riding with the men and helping with the feeding in the morning was so different from anything she had ever done before. In the afternoons, Kasey either rode her horses or stayed in the house and helped Anne. With the indoor arena, Kasey could ride any day, but there were some warm winter days when she and Cole rode out into the surrounding fields and even up into the low mountains. These mountains were like the Black Hills of South Dakota. The Wolf Mountains had gentle slopes and tree-covered hillsides. Cole told Kasey there was some rough country on the ranch, but a good many of the slopes were not rocky or steep. It was a beautiful setting for the Sanders' ranch with the tree-covered mountainsides surrounding meadows.

One day, Josie drove over and she and Kasey headed to Sheridan for Christmas shopping. Kasey wanted to give everyone a gift, so she welcomed any help Josie could give her. Since Ben had been part of the family for many years and Josie had been going with him since high school, she knew all the Sanders well. With Josie's help, Kasey was able to find a gift for Pete and Anne. Josie was also familiar with the Sander family's Christmas Eve tradition where in lieu of gifts between all the family, everyone brought a single gift for a family gift exchange. But for Kasey, it was Cole she had the most trouble deciding what gift to get. When Kasey went by the window of a jewelry store and saw a small gold hat pin, she knew she had found the right present. The Black Hills Gold hat pin in the figure of a bucking horse and rider would be perfect for Cole, especially since this was the year, he won the title in the bronc riding.

Twice before Christmas, Ben and Josie came for supper, and several times, Ben showed up for an afternoon to help with chores or to go off with Cole and Pete to a livestock auction. It wasn't long before it was time for Cole's sister and her family to arrive and for the holiday activities to begin. In reflection, Kasey was glad she had been busy so that she didn't have much time to think about her family's past holidays.

Two days before the rest of the family was due to arrive, Anne headed to town to stock up on groceries for the holiday gathering. Cole, Pete, and Ben headed to a neighboring ranch to help work some cattle, and Kasey opted to stay home. It was a cold blustery day, so after being out for a short while, she was glad to get back inside the house. She had seen the piano in the great room, so she wandered in and sat on the piano bench. She fingered the keys. The piano was not her instrument of choice, but she could peck out some melodies. There was a hymnal that she thumbed through and found the Christmas carols. She sat and began to play, losing herself in the music and her memories.

***

Cole and Pete drove into the yard right behind Anne, which was good because Anne had a trunk load of groceries to carry in. As Anne opened the trunk and began handing out paper bags of food to the men, she straightened and stood still.

"What am I hearing?" she asked.

Cole looked toward the house, hearing what Anne heard. "It's Kasey," he said. "She's singing Christmas carols."

Anne looked at Cole. "She has a beautiful voice. But it's . . ." Anne stopped, thinking. "It sounds so sad the way she is singing them."

Cole nodded. "She's only been alone here an afternoon, and the sadness crept in," he said. "I was afraid of that."

"Sometimes, you just have to work through the sadness," Anne responded gently.

"I agree, but only for a while," Cole said. "Then you have to go on with life. So, let's go help her move on."

***

177

Cole wasn't sure at first what woke him. He lay in bed, alert and listening. Then he heard it again, a faint moaning or a cry. He got up and pulled on his jeans. Going to the bedroom door, he pulled it open and waited. It was a cry, and it was coming from Kasey's room. Turning on a light, Cole walked down the hall and stood silent outside her room. Again, he heard her cry, almost a moan this time. Softly, he tapped on her door.

"Kasey," he called softly, "are you okay?" When there was no answer, he tried again. Again, there was no answer, but when he heard her cry out again, he tried the knob and it opened. Bathed in the hall light, Cole could see Kasey lying on her bed, and it was evident she was in the throes of a nightmare. He crossed the room and went to her side. Reaching down, he shook her gently.

"Kasey, wake up," he said.

Cole shook her again, repeating the words. It took a few seconds to wake her, and then Cole could see she was struggling to climb out of the nightmare. She looked around wildly and then sank back to the pillows, seeing Cole.

"I'm sorry," her voice caught. "I . . ." She looked confused.

"You were having a nightmare," Cole told her. He sat down on the edge of the bed. "Do you remember it?"

Kasey took a ragged breath. "It was the accident. I was back at the accident."

"Have you had the nightmare before?"

"Yes, but it always sort of surprises me."

"How often do you have these dreams?" Cole questioned.

"It varies," Kasey answered, closing her eyes. "I haven't had one since before the Finals. I always hope they quit, and then one comes again."

"Have you ever talked to anyone about the accident?"

"You mean like a shrink?" Kasey opened her eyes and looked at Cole.

"No, not like a shrink, but like anyone?" Cole answered. "Have you ever just talked to anyone about what you went through then?"

"No, I just wanted to forget that night."

"So, you hold it in, and it comes out to haunt you at night," Cole prodded her gently. "Tell me about that night."

"You think it will help?"

"It has been a year, and you are still getting nightmares," Cole said. "I have no idea if it will help, but can it hurt? Isn't it worth a try?"

Kasey lay quiet, thinking. Cole moved to settle himself at the head of the bed, sitting upright. "Here, come up here and talk to me," he said, patting the pillow beside him.

Kasey pushed herself into a sitting position next to him and he drew her toward him. Cole could feel her warm curves as she let herself be held. She was wearing an oversized T-shirt with the sheets pulled to her waist. She felt rigid to him, probably uncomfortable with his touch as well as the nightmare. Still, he held her as he waited for her to begin.

"We were driving to Denver, to the airport," Kasey whispered. "We were all trying to be cheerful, but it was forced. My brother was going back to Vietnam, and we knew he would be in danger there. We knew it was going to be hard to say good-bye, but I think we all wanted to make those last hours happy for him. It was dark and snowing. We didn't know that we were coming to an area in the mountains that had gotten sleet. Dad wasn't driving fast, but as we rounded a curve, the car hit black ice and started to slide. Then around the bend came a big truck. It was veering too wide. Our car grazed the truck, and that sent us into a spin, and the car went through the guard rail and down the mountain."

Kasey stopped abruptly. Cole didn't prod her. He had felt her body stiffen when she said the car went over the side. He wanted to give her some time. Finally, she began to speak again.

"It was so dark. The car rolled, and we were all bounced around. It was like being in a movie when they spin the picture. When the car stopped, I was on top of Kelly, and we were both on Mom. I heard Kelly moaning, and I was able to crawl off her. The car came to a stop on the passenger side. I saw Dad in the front seat, but he was against the passenger door, not behind the steering wheel. I couldn't see my brother at all. Windows were blown out, and my brother was gone." Kasey took a big breath, and Cole could feel her fighting for control. "I hurt all over, but I could move. I was able to pull Kelly out. She was in a lot of pain; she had a broken leg and ribs and a concussion, but she was able to help me pull her out. I went back for Mom and was able to pull her out, but I was pretty sure she was gone. I couldn't get her to respond, and I couldn't find a pulse. I couldn't get my dad out, and I could smell fuel. The trucker we hit on the highway had gotten his rig stopped quite a way down the road. He had a two-way radio and he had called for help. He climbed down the mountain to the car and helped me pull Dad out. I knew my dad was dead then. The trucker had a flashlight and he left us and found my brother. Bob had been thrown from the car, and he was dead too." Kasey gave a short, bitter laugh. "We were so worried about him going back to Vietnam, and here he gets killed in a car accident. I just can't wrap my mind around that."

Cole could feel Kasey begin to sag in his arms, the tension draining out and weariness taking over. "How long did you have to wait for more help to arrive?" Cole asked gently.

"It seemed like forever, but I think it was more like a half hour. The trucker found some blankets we had in the car before it started to burn. Between the blankets and the flames, Kelly and I didn't freeze. Kelly was in the hospital for over a week, but they only kept me overnight. I came out of the whole thing without anything broken, but I had a concussion and an assortment of cuts and bruises. I'd give anything if the rest of the family could have been so lucky."

Cole knew there wasn't anything he could say to help with her hurt. And to relive the accident over and over again in her sleep was a burden she shouldn't have to endure. However, the mind is not something a person can always control. He just sat quietly and held her. She didn't cry, but he felt her pain. As the minutes passed, he felt her relax.

"Maybe you can rest now," Cole said. "Lie down and let me rub your back. I still remember my mom doing that to me when I was a kid and something was wrong. I'm not a mom, but I don't suppose rubbing a back is skilled labor."

Kasey looked up at Cole for a moment, then she nodded. She moved away from him and lay down with her back to him. Gently, Cole rubbed her back with a slow circular motion. He saw her eyes close, and it wasn't long before her breathing slowed. Cole knew she had dropped off to sleep. He sat still beside her, watching her breathe. But what he was remembering was the feeling of her in his arms. She's just a kid, he told himself. A kid with a lot of sadness and vulnerability. He had to remember that. He stood up, and closing the door quietly, he went back to his own bed.

CHAPTER 10

HOLIDAYS

Three days before Christmas, Cole's sister Carla and her family arrived. Carla was a younger version of Anne, slim and cute with a warm smile. She gave Kasey a friendly hug and introduced Kasey to the rest of the family. Carla's husband, Mitch, was a tall, lean man who seemed as comfortable as an old shoe. Anne had told Kasey that the couple had bought a small-town newspaper a hundred miles away seven years earlier, but they both looked more like ranchers than journalists. Kasey remembered Cole telling her that Mitch and Carla lived at the Sanders' ranch for years while starting their family. This had been their home as Mitch finished his master's program, Carla taught at a nearby school, and their two children were born. The two children, Libby and Matt, were seventeen and sixteen, respectively. Kasey knew right away she would like the whole family.

The house seemed filled that first night when Ben and Josie also joined them for supper and cards. Cole, Ben, and Carla joked and teased each other like siblings do, and Kasey longed for those days she had with her own brother and sister. Kasey could see that Ben was indeed a part of this family, and Josie had been his girlfriend long enough to fit right in with the rest of them.

After the party was winding down and the cards were being put away, Ben stood, pulling Josie with him.

"We have an announcement," Ben said, his grin wide. "I asked Josie to marry me."

"And I said yes," Josie chimed in, laughing. "I didn't want to give him a chance to back out."

There were congratulations all around. They were considering a wedding date right after the St. Onge rodeo in June. The St. Onge rodeo was close to home, and Ben and Cole could take a week off from their rodeo schedule for a wedding. Josie would be finished with student teaching, and she could travel with Ben most of the summer after the wedding. Kasey could see the excitement of the young couple, and she was happy for them. As Josie and Ben bundled up to leave, Josie pulled Kasey aside.

"I want you to be there," Josie said. "Will you sing at the wedding?"

Kasey was honored and told her, of course. No matter how she was doing in the standings then, she would come and sing at the wedding.

***

The next two days flew by. Ben and Josie came to pick up Libby, Matt, and Kasey for a day of skiing at a small nearby ski slope. Cole had business in Sheridan for the day, so he bowed out.

"I didn't know you skied," Kasey commented when his niece and nephew hounded him to accompany them.

"I ski, but haven't lately," Cole said. "At this point in my life, when I know I only have a few years of rodeo left in me, the last thing I want to do is break a leg on a ski slope. And I do have business in town. You go and have a good time."

So, Kasey went and did have fun. She hadn't skied for over a year, but it was a sport she enjoyed and might have excelled at if she had stuck to it. It was late afternoon when they returned, laughing and boisterous as they came into the ranch house.

Cole was home from Sheridan by then and smiled as the young people entered. Kasey was younger than Ben and Josie and just a few years older than Libby and Matt. As Cole watched the young folks come in, he suddenly felt old. He watched Kasey as she teased and kidded with the others and was aware that he was well over ten years her senior.

***

Christmas Eve dawned cold but clear. The men were out early doing chores. Kasey knew only that the family gathered food and their gifts for a Christmas game and took them to a mountain cabin somewhere. Going to this cabin was a tradition the family did every year. Ben and Josie arrived before chores were finished and went out to help. The women were all in the kitchen putting together the food for the day.

Anne and Carla had made homemade buns the day before, and Kasey had helped Libby make Christmas cookies. An apple crisp appeared from the freezer to cook at the cabin, and a big roast, complete with potatoes and carrots, was cooking in an electric roaster. A cooler with ice cream was set out in the snow to load when they were ready to leave.

Kasey helped cart things to the covered porch as they were packed and finally, the men came to carry everything outside. That was when Kasey looked outside and saw one of the big teams of draft horses hitched to the smaller of the two hay wagons the Sanders ranch used. The wagon was mounted on runners, and the back of the wagon had hay bales stacked around the edge for the family to sit on.

"We are going somewhere on that?" Kasey asked Cole, who came up to grab a box to load.

"Did I forget to tell you that?" he grinned. The family had kept where they were going a secret from Kasey, wanting to surprise her. "We are going up the mountain to my grandfather's original old log cabin. We spend every Christmas Eve there during the day."

It took about an hour with the team to get to the cabin, although it wasn't far. The snow got deeper as the group went farther up the mountain, and once the men got out with shovels to help make a path through a drift. Kasey saw a log cabin nestled against the wooded hillside, when they came out on a small meadow. Pete drove the team up to the cabin, and everyone pitched in to carry things inside. Then Pete unhitched the team and tied them to the wagon where they could eat their fill of the hay on the wagon.

The cabin was one big room with a rough wooden floor. A big stone fireplace was at one end and a cooking stove was at the other. Cole started a fire in the fireplace, while Ben started a fire in the cookstove. No one took off their outerwear until the heat from both ends of the cabin began warming the frigid air. Around the room were scattered couches and chairs, and, at one end, was a big wooden trestle table with benches around it. The roast, with its potatoes and carrots, was popped into the cook stove oven to reheat, along with the apple crisp, and soon, marvelous smells filled the room.

While the family waited for the food to finish cooking and the room to warm, they told stories of past

Christmas gatherings and stories they had heard from their grandfather, the original settler of this land. Josie told of some of her family's traditions. Her family did all their Christmas activities on Christmas Day, so she and Ben could join the Sanders for Christmas Eve and spend Christmas Day with Josie's family. Kasey listened to the stories and remembered her own past Christmases.

"Did you have Christmas traditions?" Anne asked Kasey, breaking into her thoughts. "If it is painful, you don't have to talk about it."

"Actually, no, sometimes it is good to remember the good times," Kasey smiled at Anne, pleased to be included. "Our Christmas traditions when we lived in Illinois consisted of going to our Swedish relatives on Christmas Eve. It used to be a big gathering, but by the time I was ten, it was getting smaller and smaller as the older folks died and the young folks moved away. When we moved to Colorado, my brother was off to the service, so it was just my folks, my sister, and me. We didn't really have ties to anyone in Colorado, so sometimes we went skiing for the holidays, and sometimes we just stayed home together. It was the one time Dad wasn't off doing business, so having time just for us was fun. Then last year, with Bob home, there were the five of us, and we enjoyed that. We spent some days skiing, some days sledding, and some days eating popcorn in front of the fire. I think we were just content to be together."

"Well, we can't replace your family," Anne said gently, "but I think we are all glad you have joined our family this year."

Kasey felt unwanted tears threaten, but she blinked them away. "You can't know how nice it is to be here,"

Kasey replied. "I am so glad Cole insisted." Kasey shot a smile at Cole. "He can be sort of a bully at times, in a good way," she finished.

***

By the time they finished eating, the entire cabin was toasty, and the family piled their presents on the table. The Christmas "game" they played consisted of drawing numbers and they picked a present of their choice in the order of the number they drew. Everyone watched as the present was opened. Some presents were more on the gag gift spectrum, while others were thoughtful. As each subsequent person came up to choose a gift, they also had the choice of taking a gift from one of the already opened gifts. That sent the original possessor of that gift back to the table for another wrapped present. Kasey drew the number five. She chose a brightly wrapped rectangular box, only to find it filled with a dozen men's black socks. When Ben, with the number eight, took the socks from her, Kasey chose again between the remaining two boxes. This time, she tore off the wrapping to find a box full of crushed pop cans filled with change. Everyone laughed as she shook a can and saw an assortment of change fall out. Pete was the last to draw, and he took the cans and change from Kasey.

"I'm in the ranching business," he laughed, taking the box from Kasey, "I always need extra money. I'll keep shaking those cans and let you take the last gift."

Kasey laughed too, going for the third time to unwrap a gift. This was the last gift and was a flat box. She tore off the wrapping paper and opened the lid. Pulling back the tissue paper, she just stared. Then, her eyes filled with tears as she read the message on a wall plaque.

Friends are the family that you find along the way.

Kasey looked up at the people grouped around her. Suddenly, she knew they all knew what was in this package and that it was meant for her. She smiled through her tears.

"Thank you," she whispered, her throat tight. She started to say more, then just smiled and shook her head.

"I found it," Libby exclaimed. "I hope you have room for it in your little camper. It sort of says how we feel about you being here with us this year. I hope it doesn't make you sad."

"I love it," Kasey choked out. "I just love it."

***

The party broke up before the afternoon sun was too far down in the sky. Everyone knew their jobs, and in no time, the fires were put out, the horses hitched, the leftover food and gifts were loaded onto the hay wagon, and they were heading down the mountain, singing Christmas carols at the tops of their voices.

Back at the ranch, the family unloaded the gifts and leftover food, fed the team and the horses in the barn for the night, and prepared to attend the Christmas Eve service. Anne was the pianist, so they had to get there early so she could play.

Kasey rummaged in the trunk, which she kept in the saddle compartment of her trailer, for a dress. When she left her sister's home, Kasey took primarily jeans and shirts, but put two summer and two winter dresses, shoes, and a nice coat in her trunk. Not knowing when she would have a place to put down roots, she thought she better have at least a couple of nice outfits with her. This was the first time she had a need for anything nicer than jeans.

***

Only a few people were in the church when the Sanders' clan walked in, but the pastor was waiting at the door for Anne.

"Anne," the pastor whispered urgently, "Mary Ellen has laryngitis and can't sing the solo we planned. We will have to drop that from the program. I know you have practiced a lot on the song, but I don't know what else to do."

Anne looked thoughtfully at her family as they started to seat themselves midway down the church. "Pastor, don't throw in the towel just yet," she replied. "I think I might have a substitute staying with us."

Before going to the piano, Anne detoured past the family and conferred with Kasey. Kasey smiled and nodded. Anne pointed at a place in the program. Kasey nodded again. Smiling her thanks, Anne went to the piano and began playing as more people began to enter the church.

Cole slid into the pew next to Kasey. "I don't think I've ever seen you in a dress," he whispered. "Not a bad look." He grinned at her.

Kasey was wearing a cream-colored, bell-sleeved tunic dress with matching sparkling tights. She wore knee-high boots with three-inch heels. It had been so long since Kasey wore a dress that Cole's words helped her relax. She was glad she had packed some nice clothes because she didn't think jeans suited the Christmas Eve church affair.

When the service got to the place for the solo, Kasey squeezed past Cole and went to join Anne at the piano. Cole, Ben, and the rest of the Sanders' clan were the only ones in the congregation who knew the quality of Kasey's voice. As Kasey began singing the hymn, "What Child is This?" Cole saw people around them straighten up. Her voice rang out clear and sweet as she sang,

What Child is this
Who lay to rest
On Mary's lap is sleeping
Whom Angels greet with anthems sweet
While shepherds watch are keeping

Cole looked at Ben, and they smiled. They watched the congregation as Kasey sang. Like in that smoky bar last summer when Cole and Ben first heard Kasey sing, the crowd in the church was equally mesmerized. Even the rest of the Sanders' group, who had heard Kasey sing Christmas carols with them on the wagon that day, and Anne, who had heard her the one afternoon in the ranch house, were enthralled with her beautiful voice. She looks like an angel up there, Cole thought. He watched her as she sang, and in his heart, he was glad she was here.

It took quite some time after the service for the family to get away from the crowd of people who wanted to talk to Kasey and Cole. Many people wanted to congratulate Cole on his Saddle Bronc World Title that year. When introduced to Kasey, most people had heard of her meteoric rise in barrel racing standings at the Finals. Between that and her solo during church, just about everyone wanted to meet her. By the time the

Sanders family loaded up and got home, it was late. All the fresh air and excitement of the day had worn them out. Christmas morning would come soon enough. It didn't take long for the ranch house to quiet as everyone went off to bed.

Christmas morning on the Sanders' ranch started with feeding the animals as always, but chores were done quickly. A big breakfast awaited them and right after, the family retired to the living room and opened presents. Kasey had bought silk neckerchiefs for Ben and Pete. This was a favorite winter weather accessory in the west, and both men wore them. Kasey had found soft cardigan sweaters for Anne and Josie, a blue one for Josie and tan for Anne. Cole was surprised when he opened the little box with the tiny gold hatpin in the shape of a bucking horse and rider.

"Never had one of these before," he commented, smiling. He got up and retrieved his hat from the hat hanger at the door. "Sort of fits this year, doesn't it?" he asked, looking at Kasey, fitting it to his hat. "I love it. Thank you."

The day was filled with laughter, singing, eating, and even a sledding party in the surrounding hills. By evening, when Kasey climbed the stairs with the gifts she had received that day, she was tired. Libby was sound asleep, the bedroom light still blazing, before Kasey got out of the shower. Kasey sat on her bed and looked at her gifts. Pete and Anne had given her a new saddle blanket with her initials carved in leather and sewn into the back corner of the blanket. Josie and Ben had given Kasey a southwest-colored shawl. Kasey remembered admiring it in a store the day she and Josie went shopping.

From Cole, she had gotten a book of the National Finals Rodeo highlights from that year. Kasey hadn't realized there was a highlights book. But here it was, and in the section on the barrel race results was a picture of her riding Roan around the third barrel, and on another page, Kasey stood in the arena behind her trophy saddle along with Cole and the other event and average winners.

"I ordered that the last day of the Finals," Cole told her. "I was guaranteed it would be here by Christmas, and it made it with one day to spare." Inside the front cover, Cole had written, "*To Kasey, who took the Finals by storm.*"

Kasey sat and looked at the National Finals Rodeo book and then at the little plaque that she had gotten on Christmas Eve. "*Friends are the family that you find along the way.*" Kasey missed her own family, but she knew this little plaque was telling her she still had family. She just had to find them along the way. She had made it through this year of "firsts." It had been a tough year in many respects, but she had survived. She had made it through this first Christmas with the help of these wonderful people. Her heart was full.

***

Two days after Christmas, Carla, Mitch, and the kids had to head home. The ranch seemed so quiet after they left. At breakfast the next morning, Cole mentioned that he would try to top out several young colts for his dad and wondered if Kasey would like to help him.

"If you'd like to pony me on them, I could get more of them started today," he said casually. "I like to get a half dozen or more rides on each before I leave in January, and Dad takes over riding them. With your help, I'd get a head start."

"He doesn't think his old man can ride the rough stock anymore," Pete grinned across the table at Kasey. "I try to humor him."

Cole grinned and answered, "Good practice for me if they buck."

So, Kasey spent all day in the indoor arena with Pete and Cole, ponying colts with and without a rider on them. Anne brought sandwiches to the barn and they ate together in the heated tack room. By suppertime, Kasey was spent, but it had felt good to be out with the horses all day. As she ate, she glanced up and saw the calendar hanging on the wall. With a start, she realized what day it was.

"It was a year ago today," she said, looking at Cole. "You knew that, didn't you? You kept me busy all day so I'd forget."

"Did it work?" Cole asked seriously.

"Until right now," Kasey answered. "And I think I'm so tired now, I will be able to sleep despite the date."

"Good," Cole told her. "That was the intention."

"You were all in on this too," Kasey said, looking at Pete and Anne, who nodded. "Well, thank you. I dreaded this day and then missed it entirely."

***

Two days before New Year's, Cole broached the plans for New Year's with Kasey and his folks over supper.

"Saw Callie in town last week, and she reminded me of the Triangle X Ranch New Year's Eve party. Wanted me to mention it to you both," Cole said casually to his parents. "There's going to be the usual feed, music, and drink."

"Not me," Anne answered. "I am getting too old for the late night. We are going to have Stan and Margie over for drinks and cards on New Year's Eve. That way, we can say 'Happy New Year' at ten and go to bed."

Anne and Pete looked at each other and chuckled. "You young people go. That is a young crowd, anyway."

"So, how about you, Kasey?" Cole asked. "You want to go dancing on New Year's Eve?"

"What is this Triangle X Ranch?" Kasey asked, trying to remember where she heard the name Callie before.

"The Triangle X is a big ranch about ten miles west of here," Cole explained. "It is owned by Will Bonder, a businessman, who bought it twenty-five years ago. He wanted to raise his kids away from the city. He has a foreman who runs the place, but Will built this mansion of a house that he lives in when he is here. His wife died ten years ago, and his kids are both executives in businesses in the city, but every year, they come home for the holidays and have a big New Year's Eve bash for the area."

"Sounds like fun," Kasey said. "The food and dancing, anyway."

"So, Callie is home now?" Pete asked nonchalantly.

"I don't think Callie would miss Christmas in the mountains," Cole answered. "She might not give a rip about the country any other time, but she loves Christmas here."

Suddenly, Kasey knew where she had heard the name before. When Cole took her to the barbecue in Deadwood, someone asked Cole if Callie was in Deadwood with him. He had said that Callie had been in Calgary with him. Callie had to be his old high school flame but Cole had said last summer that Callie was not his girlfriend. Still, she wondered if going to this New Year's Eve party was the right thing to do. She broached the subject later when she followed Cole to the living room before his folks joined them.

"Cole," she said tentatively, "about this party? I don't want to cause any problems with you and Callie. You don't have to feel bad just going without me."

"Callie?" Cole grinned. "I told you before that Callie and I haven't been more than friends since high school. She won't mind your coming."

"Friends . . . with benefits? Did I get that wrong?" Kasey doubted this Callie woman stayed a whole week in Calgary with Cole without "benefits."

Cole laughed outright at that. "Okay, maybe there are some benefits, but there are no strings. We both know we will never be more than friends." Cole got serious then. "Come to the party. Half the area knows you are here for the holidays, and whoever didn't get to meet you on Christmas Eve at our church will be sorely disappointed if you don't show up at the party. It's a good time. You'll enjoy it."

***

New Year's Eve was a cold, clear night. As Cole and Kasey drove up the drive to the Triangle X, Kasey saw a line of cars parked in the plowed area in front of the massive log home. The house was lit up like Las Vegas with lights hanging from the porch, along the walk, and on the decorative fence in front. Every window twinkled with lights, and a massive pine in front of the house was decorated.

"Wow," Kasey breathed, "this is one big place. Impressive."

"Yeah, when they built it, it was the talk of the area," Cole said. "It took a while for the townsfolk to accept the Bonders, but Will is a good guy. He has done a lot for the town and the area. Both of his kids went to school here and that made them part of the community. Will might not be a full-time resident anymore, but he is well-liked regardless of his obvious wealth."

The plowed area was filled to overflowing with vehicles. Cole found a place at the edge, partly burying his four-wheel drive in a drift. Kasey had to slide to the driver's side to get out without climbing through the snow.

"There are a lot of people here," she said. "Will they be the people we met Christmas Eve at church?"

"Oh, there will be some you might have met," Cole replied, "but this is more of a rancher and cowboy's New Year's Eve party. People here will have come from miles around. And when I say miles, it may be forty or more miles. This is an annual event, and anyone who ranches, rodeos, or cowboys knows about it. Some of these people I only see a couple of times a year at brandings or rodeos. You'll like the crowd."

They were met at the door by an elegant woman dressed in a flowing tan and maroon wool covering, resembling a poncho but opening in the front. She wore this over a silk blouse and with a corduroy skirt. Fancy high-top boots completed the outfit. Kasey, who wore her new shawl over dress jeans, boots, and colorful blouse, felt outclassed by the obviously understated, but expensive outfit of her hostess.

"About time you got here," the woman said to Cole, kissing him on the cheek. "I have been fielding questions about whether you were coming for an hour already."

"Thought I'd make an entrance," Cole replied, helping Kasey out of her coat and handing hers and his over to the woman.

"Callie, this is Kasey Jacobs."

"I have been looking forward to meeting you, Kasey," Callie said warmly. "Not every day we meet someone who took the Finals by storm."

"It is very nice to be here," Kasey replied. "But I keep telling people I didn't take the Finals by storm. Basically, I got over the sheer terror of being there and let my horses carry me to some wins."

"For the rest of the rodeo world, what you accomplished was amazing," Callie said. "Now go and enjoy my party."

"See, what did I tell you?" Cole whispered in Kasey's ear as they walked down the hall toward the sounds of the party. "If there is anything I can say about Callie, she isn't concerned that you came with me. We are friends, just friends."

It turned out that Cole did make an entrance. A roar went up as he and Kasey walked into a large open room filled with people. Shouts of "about time," "congratulations," and "nine times must be the charm" came from around the room. As Cole and Kasey worked their way deeper into the room, men came forward to shake Cole's hand while many women gave him quick hugs. It was apparent to Kasey that Cole was one of the area's favorite sons, and they rejoiced with him for his Saddle Bronc World Title. As the hoopla started to die down, Cole introduced Kasey and then she became the object of the crowd's attention. Most of the rodeo people had heard of her. While the National Finals were not televised nationally, most western states covered the finals in their nightly news. Kasey found that quite a few western television stations carried her interviews. The night was fun for Kasey. The buffet table was crowded with all types of food. A three-piece band was playing in one corner, and people wandered from the food to the dance floor, and to couches or tables that were pushed back away from the dance floor. Kasey had a variety of dance partners. Cole danced with her several times, but kept getting cut in on by other men.

Ben and Josie were there, and Kasey sat and visited with them for quite some time, resting her feet from dancing. Looking at the clock, Kasey was surprised that it was almost midnight. She noticed Ben leaning over to Josie and whispering in her ear, nodding toward the door. Kasey looked that way also and saw Callie moving toward Cole, catching his hand and pulling him from the room. Josie shook her head at Ben, nodding slightly in Kasey's direction. It took Kasey only a short time to catch the meaning.

"Oh, Josie, don't worry," Kasey smiled at her friend. "I know all about Cole and Callie. Cole says they are just friends, but I think we all know that it is deeper than that. And Cole and I are just friends, so you don't have to be secretive around me."

"That's good," Ben laughed, "because I think Cole and Callie have sneaked off every New Year's Eve for the last ten just about this time. Give 'em an hour, and he'll be back."

***

Callie pulled Cole into the hall, backing up to the wall and pulling him to her. She was a tall woman, almost reaching Cole's height. With her heels, she didn't have to stretch much to reach him for a kiss.

This wasn't a surprise to Cole. They had welcomed the New Year in every year in Callie's bed for as long as he could remember. It was never anything Cole planned, but he did find it enjoyable. He pulled her close, her familiar body easy in his arms. It was then they heard the music stop in the great room, followed with the whoops of "Happy New Year" coming from the crowd. As the crowd noise lowered, he heard Kasey's voice come clearly over the mic.

"This is an old favorite for this night, but I heard it sung with a cowboy twist to it," she said. "I hope you enjoy it as much as I do."

The crowd quieted, and in the silence, Cole heard Kasey's voice rise clear and sweet, singing "Auld Lang Syne."

"For old acquaintance be forgot, and never brought to mind."

Cole stiffened, pulling back from Callie and listening. When Kasey got farther in the song, he heard new words with a cowboy twist. Kasey sang a line about drinking a shot of whiskey for old times' sake.

Cole looked back down the hall, thinking. Looking back at Callie, he smiled gently. "What are we doing here, Callie?" he asked.

"Having fun," Callie answered. "That is what we always do."

"But it's just for tonight," Cole said reflectively. "And that has always been enough for both of us. But I think I want more, and we both know neither one of us wants that for us. And suddenly, I think I know who I want that with."

Callie studied Cole for a moment before answering. "That girl is more than just a friend, isn't she?"

"Not yet," Cole answered, "but I think maybe I would like her to be."

"Cole, she's just a kid. Is she even out of her teens?"

"She's out of her teens, but not by much," Cole admitted. "I'm willing to let her grow up some, see what comes. Maybe it won't work out, but for the first time in my life, I want to give it a shot. And that has to start now." He pushed away from Callie. "Sorry, doll, I'm going to stand you up this year."

Callie smiled at him, and leaning toward him, she gave him a peck on the cheek. "You go, see what comes. If it doesn't work out, you know where to find me." As Cole turned to go, he heard Callie whisper behind him, "Be happy, Cole. That is all we ever wanted for each other."

Cole reached Kasey just as she was finishing her song. When the crowd burst into applause, Cole went to her and pulled her off the stool she was sitting on as she sang.

"Happy New Year, Kasey," he said softly. "The next dance is mine."

***

It was after one in the morning when Cole and Kasey left the party. They rode back to the ranch, laughing about different stories they had heard that night. Kasey wanted to know about many of the people that she had met that night. Cole pulled the pickup into the yard a half hour later.

"That didn't seem to take long," Kasey said, "but I am glad to be back. I think the pickup just started to warm up finally, and the cold has seeped into my bones. I wasn't ready for this much winter this fast!"

Cole laughed. "Staying south until mid-December makes coming home a bit harder when it gets as cold as it is tonight," Cole agreed. "Want to have some hot chocolate to warm you up?"

"That sounds great."

Cole reached for Kasey's hand as she headed to the front door. "This way," he said, pulling her in a different direction.

They went through the walk-in door in the garage. It was an oversized two-car garage that housed Anne's car and Pete's big pickup. Along the far side was a staircase leading up to the loft above the garage. It was here that Cole led Kasey.

"Is there a storeroom up here?" Kasey asked as they climbed the stairs.

"Well, I suppose you could say that," Cole agreed, as he opened the door at the landing at the top of the stairs and switched on a light inside. Kasey walked through the door and just stared.

"You could sort of say I am stored up here," Cole grinned.

It was an apartment. On the left was a living room, complete with a free-standing wood-burning fireplace and a picture window overlooking the backyard. On the right was a small kitchen with a table nestled against the wall. There was a door to a bathroom, and another door where Kasey could see the end of a bed.

"This is a complete apartment," she exclaimed. "Did you do this?"

Cole shook his head. "When my sister was first married, she got a teaching job in town, and Mitch still had two years of graduate school. Mom wanted a garage in the worst way, and she got Dad to build one by suggesting that they build one with a loft, and Carla and Mitch could rent it for a few years while they got on their feet. Dad was all for that. I was in Vietnam then, and Dad knew I'd be going down the road when I got home. Both Carla and Mitch were good help on the ranch when Dad needed it. They actually lived here for ten years. Both of their kids were born here. They moved a few years ago when they bought the newspaper."

Cole went to the fireplace and opening the glass door, built a fire. "I couldn't see this going to waste, so I moved in. I don't live here that much, but it is a place to store my things, and it gives me a feeling that I am not living with my folks, even though I am," he chuckled at that.

Going to the kitchen, Cole ran water in a kettle and put it on the stove. From the cupboard, he took out a plastic container and two mugs. Opening the plastic container, Cole served heaping spoonfuls of a powdery mix into each mug. "Mom makes this hot chocolate mix with powdered milk and cocoa, and I love the stuff when I'm home," he said. "I keep this container full so I can make hot chocolate on cold nights. I like coffee the rest of the time, but there is something about hot chocolate before a fire late at night that's comforting."

Pouring hot water into the mugs, Cole handed one to Kasey with a stirring spoon and took one for himself. He put his hand on Kasey's back, guiding her to the couch in front of the fire. The hot chocolate was steaming, and Kasey held hers in her cold hands, relishing the warmth.

"Warming up?" Cole asked.

"Hmmm," Kasey nodded, sipping the hot brew.

They sat in silence, watching the fire and enjoying the drink. After a bit, Kasey looked up at Cole. "Cole, I really dreaded the holidays. I can't tell you how much it has meant to me to be with your family. You were right; I shouldn't be alone. I thought being with someone else's family would be harder than being alone, but I was wrong. This was what I needed. I have had such a good time here. It doesn't seem like saying thank you is enough."

Cole looked down at Kasey fondly. "I think your being here has been the highlight of the holidays for my family too. It was meant to be."

They sat in silence again for a while before Kasey broke it. "So, this isn't your last year on the road, I'm guessing."

Cole smiled, and putting his arm over her, pulled her close, liking the feeling of her leaning into him. "I got too close this year to quit now," he said. "I got the one title, but I want the other. If I push hard this year, maybe it will happen. You know," he said reflectively, "I was not far from the all-around title. That roper was just too good this year, working the calf roping and team roping. Getting the title in the bulls would be wonderful, and the all-around title would be the icing. If I can stay healthy, I'm going to make another year. How about you? You more than a one-year wonder?"

Kasey laughed. "Not sure of the wonder part, but I've been bitten. It would be fun to see where I can get if I start the year out with these big winter rodeos. After that, I guess I'll take it day by day."

She relaxed against Cole, her head leaning on his shoulder. It felt safe, right. The fire and the hot chocolate were warming her, and she felt the excitement of the New Year's party fading away, and weariness taking over.

Cole felt her relax. He looked down at her, and his fingers reached over and pushed her hair off her cheek.

Without thinking, he moved away just enough to lean down and kiss her. If Kasey was startled, she didn't show it. Instead, Cole felt her kiss him back. He kissed her gently at first, then the kiss became more heated. Pulling Kasey toward him, he held her close, knowing he wanted more. That was when he stopped.

"You are so young," he whispered, fingering her hair.

"I'm going to be twenty-one soon," Kasey replied softly, "that's not that young."

"To me, it is," Cole answered. "I'm almost old enough to be your father."

"No, you're not." Kasey looked surprised, "You're only twelve or thirteen years older, aren't you? I mean, gosh, a guy has to be . . ." She cut off in mid-sentence.

Cole laughed outright. "I suppose guys are different, but if you can get it on, you can get it done," Cole chucked her on the chin. "I think I was about fifteen. And that is more than you need to know. I think it is time I escort you home and we hit the hay."

They walked through Cole's bedroom to the door leading to the hallway and down the hall to Kasey's bedroom door.

"I had a good time tonight," Cole whispered, kissing Kasey's forehead. "Sleep well, young 'un." Then he turned and went back to his apartment.

CHAPTER 11

ANOTHER SEASON, NEW BEGINNINGS

K asey had never been to any of the big indoor winter rodeos the year before, but after competing in the National Finals, the early season rodeos didn't scare her. Both Kasey and her horses were now seasoned. Kasey set a goal of getting to the Finals again, and since she was starting earlier in the season this year, she wanted to be higher in the standings by the end of the rodeo year.

Following Ben and Josie's outfit, Cole rode with Kasey in her rig and did most of the driving while the four of them headed to Odessa, Texas right after New Year's Eve. From there they headed back north to the Denver Stock Show. Josie left them in Denver, flying home to start her last semester of college and student teaching. The big rodeos were sometimes over a week long, and Cole traded out when he could, also hitting smaller rodeos, catching rides with whomever he could find. Ben and Kasey, though, were content to stay at the big venues, letting the horses rest between the performances. With two or three days between the big rodeos, travel wasn't as frantic trying to cover the distances between events.

After Denver, there were a slew of big rodeos from Ft. Worth to Montgomery, Alabama. Cole, Kasey, and Ben planned their routes. Because Ben hauled horses too, he and Kasey were usually at the same rodeos simultaneously. Cole, on the other hand, wandered in and out depending on where and when he drew up at smaller or more distant rodeos, like Great Falls, Montana, and Baton Rouge, Louisiana. But whenever it worked, Cole would jump in with Kasey, helping her drive when they moved from one big rodeo to the next.

The rodeos that finished with a short-go, or finals, Denver, Ft. Worth, and Houston, for instance, usually found all three of them competing. Kasey placed or won every rodeo she entered in the first three months of the year. Her streak from the National Finals wasn't over yet. Cole too, was in every short-go performance, but was also winning at the smaller rodeos he entered. And Ben had finally come into his own. By the end of March, he had climbed into the top fifteen in the steer wrestling and hoped to move up as the season progressed. Kasey and Cole dominated their events, both sitting in the number one spot in their chosen events.

After Denver, many rodeos that Kasey and Ben entered were in the South. They crisscrossed Texas and Arizona, hitting rodeos in Tucson and Phoenix, Arizona, and Lubbock and Nacogdoches, TX. Cole flew a wider path, sometimes flying and sometimes catching rides north to Rapid City, South Dakota, Valley City, North Dakota, Tacoma, Washington, and Cedar Rapids, Iowa. The three months flew by.

By May, the big winter rodeos had petered out. The rodeos ranged from Texas, such as Jasper and Mesquite, to Sioux Falls, South Dakota, with stops at Oklahoma rodeos, like Guymon, in between. The purses got smaller, and the rodeos became one-, two-, and three-day affairs, but the promise of summer would bring some big fair rodeos too. The season was well underway.

This second season was entirely different for Kasey. It wasn't just that she had confidence this second year, both in herself and her horses, but now she didn't have the anxiety she had the year before. It was even more than that. Kasey suddenly felt like she belonged. There were few people who didn't recognize her when she pulled up to a rodeo now. There were always people stopping to visit when they saw her or to wave as she rode by. It wasn't unusual for someone to come and bang on her camper door and ask her to join a group when there was downtime. Often, she was asked to bring her guitar and sing. There were always others with a guitar, and it was fun to sit and jam.

In the beginning of the year, Kasey could have had a date every night of each big rodeo. She accepted several and had a good time at most. She was much more careful about who she dated now. But the endless nights out were starting to wear on Kasey, and she often would beg off, wanting extra hours of sleep. She was seldom alone, after all. Cole and Ben would stop by her camper and take her to a café or restaurant almost every day they spent in the same town. Ben loved to sit in on card games, so when he was preoccupied, Cole would often pick up Kasey, and they'd catch a bite somewhere. Kasey sometimes felt she had two big brothers watching over her and didn't mind that in the least.

***

It was mid-June, and Kasey was heading toward St. Onge from a rodeo in Wyoming. The road sometimes seemed endless, and Kasey checked the map for the next town. She was hungry and needed to stop. She was coming up on a junction, Mule Creek Junction, the map called it. According to the map, there was no town at the junction, but if she turned east, she'd eventually come to Hot Springs, South Dakota. She estimated in her mind how long it would take to get to Hot Springs. Maybe an hour at the most. She would just have to wait, she decided.

So, it was with some surprise she saw a lonely, tumble-down café as she approached the junction. There was a wide parking area around the café, and Cole and Ben's pickup and horse trailer were resting at the edge of the parked cars. Kasey navigated to the outskirts of the gravel lot and parked next to Cole. It wasn't too hot to leave the horses in the trailer, so giving them a quick check, she headed to the café. As she approached the café door, she had to weave through a maze of a half dozen big motorcycles. They were all colors and gleamed in the summer sun.

As Kasey's eyes adjusted to the inside of the café, she spotted Cole sitting in a booth with another man. Ben was at a table at the back with some younger men. Cole saw Kasey enter and motioned for her to come and join him, which is where Kasey headed. Cole slid out of the booth, letting Kasey in, and slid back in beside her.

"You know this guy?" Cole asked Kasey, indicating the man sitting opposite of him.

Kasey had seen this man around but had never met him. She shook her head, smiling.

"Clay Dixon, meet Kasey Jacobs," Cole introduced them.

"I've heard of you," Clay remarked. "You sing."

"I've heard of you," Kasey retorted. "You sing too, and you have some eight-tracks out. I've heard a couple, and I really like them."

"I dabble in it," Clay said, "but maybe someday I'll be more serious about my music. Right now, I better ride the broncs while I can."

The waitress came and took her order. Breakfast was served all day, so Kasey opted for two eggs, hashbrowns, and bacon. The men were finished with their meal, and Kasey knew Cole would wait for her. She didn't want to hold him up.

Kasey studied the man across from her as she sat listening to their conversation. Clay Dixon was a bull rider and a good one. Some said he would win the title one of these days, and she'd seen him ride, so she believed that. He was a younger version of Cole. He was a good-looking man with the same easy cowboy grin. Clay had removed his hat and placed it on the bench beside him, and his hair was tousled by the hat.

Kasey's meal arrived and she wasted no time in getting started. She was surprised at how hungry she was and how good the food tasted. This was a run-down, out-of-the-way establishment, but the food was top-notch.

Just as Kasey finished, she heard the men at the next table laugh and call out to Cole. She glanced their way, noticing them for the first time. There were four of them, and they had to be the owners of the motor-cycles outside. They were in black leather and denim with beefy, tattooed arms. They were leaning back in their chairs, staring at Cole.

"Damn," one big burly man said sarcastically, "I sure like that hat. Bet that makes you a real cowboy."

Cole ignored them, glancing up at Clay across from him and continued their conversation.

"I should come over there and see how that hat fits me," another motorcycle gang member said. "Wonder if that would make me a real cowboy if I put it on?" He glanced at his companions, and they laughed.

Cole ignored them, but said to Clay, "You think those hombres are talking to me?" Cole gave Clay a slight smile.

"I think they just might be," Clay returned. Neither Cole nor Clay acknowledged the offensive men.

"I said," the first man repeated louder, "I should see how that hat fits me." He pushed back from his chair and stood, the rest following suit and turned toward Cole.

Kasey froze. This didn't seem good to her, but Cole just sat easy in the booth, ignoring the loudmouth. He and Clay never paused in their conversation. The motorcycle gang moved closer.

"I should just yank that hat right off your goddamn head," the first man growled, reaching the edge of the booth.

This is when Cole looked up at the man. Slowly, he took his hat off and considered it.

"This hat?" Cole asked calmly. "You want this hat? Mister, this hat is the same kind of hat my father wore. I've been trying to fit his boots for most of my life. And this hat has some special things on it. This feather was a gift from an Indian friend of mine, and the hatband is pure rattlesnake skin. And this," Cole pointed to the small Black Hills Gold bucking horse pin Kasey had given him for Christmas, "is a gift from a very special lady." Cole deliberately placed his hat back on his head and looked up at the big man standing in front of him.

"If you think you are going to touch this hat," now Cole's voice turned low and menacing, "You better think twice. You'd rope a tornado easier than get this hat from me, because if you think you are going take this hat, you are going to have to fight us all."

At Cole's words, Ben and the three men at the back table pushed their chairs back, scraping the floor, and stood up. The motorcycle gang stood there undecided. One of them reached forward and tapped his friend on the shoulder.

"Hell, Blake, quit making trouble. We got miles to go. Let's get out of here. It ain't worth it." He turned to go, and a second man left as well. The two loudmouths stood for a minute, staring at Cole, who met their gaze, but never wavered. Then they backed off, turned, and followed their companions outside. Ben and his friends grinned at Cole and sat back down, and Cole smiled at Clay.

"Guess they didn't want my hat that bad?"

Later, when Cole joined Kasey in her pickup and drove with her, Kasey asked, "Do you think it would have come down to a fight?"

"I think it was as close as it could get because I didn't care if I had backup or not, they weren't touching this hat."

"Well, I'm glad you had backup because I think those guys were too big for me to help much," Kasey grinned. "I suppose Clay would have jumped in there too?"

"Oh, hell, it would have been a free-for-all if those guys had started something," Cole grinned. "Now, it will be interesting to see if Clay does anything with it."

"What do you mean?" Kasey wondered.

"As we left, Clay told me that was a creative moment. I wouldn't be surprised to see a song about it sometime.

He's like that, taking an incident and turning it into a song." Cole laughed. "But sometimes the facts get changed."

***

The St. Onge rodeo was a sentimental favorite for Ben and Cole and had become the same for Kasey. They all converged on the little rodeo, camping in the back pasture. Kasey visited the grave of her old dog, finding it overgrown with grass in the year's time since the dog's death. She found that comforting. The earth had reclaimed one of its own.

The weekend went by quickly. Josie was home in Montana, so Ben and Cole had a motel room in town. They spent much of the day at the rodeo grounds, playing cards with other contestants or just visiting. St. Onge was a laid-back hometown rodeo. The weather was warm but not hot, and the South Dakota wind didn't blow. The only thing that made the weekend much better was that all three of them brought money home.

The big reason that Ben, Cole, and Kasey had hit St. Onge together, though, was that they were all going home to Cole and Ben's homes. Ben and Josie were getting married the following Saturday. They were taking the week off from rodeos. Cole was Ben's best man, and Kasey would sing at the wedding. Kasey intended to stay in her camper at the town rodeo ground, but Cole's folks would hear nothing of that, insisting she stay with them. So, it was almost like going home for Kasey too, as they pulled into the ranch.

***

Ben and Josie would get married in the yard at Pete and Anne's ranch. If the weather turned wet or windy, they could move the whole shindig into the indoor arena. Josie's parents and Anne planned a buffet lunch afterward and a local band would play for an afternoon dance. They decided to stay away from an evening wedding and dance to cut down on the drunks at the ranch. Kasey helped Anne bake batches of hamburger-sized buns for the meal, and Josie's family butchered a beef for hot beef sandwiches. With added salads, the meal was sumptuous.

The wedding went off without a hitch. Ben and Josie were married on the ranch house porch where the guests, seated in borrowed church folding chairs, could see them. Cole was the best man, and Josie's sister was the Maid of Honor. Josie looked beautiful in a white leather dress reminiscent of her Native American past. Kasey sang the Stevie Wonder song, "You Are the Sunshine of My Life," at the wedding, and Carol King's hit song, "I feel the Earth Move," for the first dance of the bride and groom. Then, the band took off with rock-and-roll and country songs for the rest of the afternoon.

It was a lovely wedding. Kasey enjoyed meeting Josie's parents. Other than Josie and Ben, Kasey had never had the opportunity to meet Native Americans. Josie's mother was a nurse and worked at the Indian Health Service hospital in the nearby town, and her father ranched. Quiet and shy, the couple had one more daughter and two sons, all younger than Josie. The rest of Josie's relatives were from the reservation and had various occupations. The few relatives from Ben's side were distant cousins, aunts, and uncles. None were very active in Ben's life and hadn't been there for Ben in his early years as he was passed among drunken relatives, foster homes, and his grandmother. But bring on a free feed, and they all showed up. Interspersed between these two factions of the tribe were ranching friends of Pete and Anne's, rodeo buddies of Ben's that were near enough to come to the wedding, and a few of Ben and Josie's high school friends. It was a cross-section of the West, and Kasey found all these people interesting.

It was late in the afternoon, and the dance was beginning to wind down. The elderly had started to wander off, and the young folk were the only ones still dancing. Kasey had danced the afternoon away with countless men from the area, as well as Cole and Pete. Finally, she took leave of her last partner and gratefully sank into an empty seat at a table by Pete and Anne.

"This has been a wonderful day, hasn't it?" Kasey remarked to Anne. "The weather couldn't have been better."

"You are right," Anne smiled. "We hoped for this kind of weather, but having the arena sort of took the stress out of the planning. We could have done this all in there, but it wouldn't have been this picturesque."

"I like Josie's family," Kasey continued. "You can see where Josie gets her drive to return to the reservation to live. They seem a real close family."

"They are very close and hardworking too," Pete contributed. "They are a whole lot different from the relatives on Ben's side. Ben was lucky to get away from them."

"Why is that?" Kasey asked. "Why are there such extremes on the reservation?"

Pete thought about that for a moment before answering. "Actually, it isn't that much different than any other place in this country, but on the reservation, you see the differences much easier because there are so few of us out here." He paused, then continued, "Go to a big city, and if you drive around enough, you will be in good neighborhoods, bad neighborhoods, and everything in between. But you drive into one area and out before you see the differences. Out here, the little villages are small, and the good, the bad, and everyone in between all live pretty much together. The ranchers, like Josie's family, have it a little easier to resist the bad influences, but no one is immune."

"It is such a vicious circle here too," Ann interjected. "Take Ben's family, for instance. His great-grandmother raised his mom because his mom's mom, Elsie, was a drunk. Then, as Elsie reached middle age with a pregnant daughter, Elsie finally got her head on straight, cleaned up, and raised her grandchild, Ben. But she's ruined her body with alcohol and fast living for so many years that she is in and out of the hospital, so Ben got thrust between relatives not fit to take care of him or with strangers in foster homes. Then, Elsie got out of the hospital and Ben had a stable home for a little bit until she got sick again. That is when Ben found us and started coming to the ranch."

"I remember when I took Ben home to his grandma one night, Elsie caught me at the door and wanted to talk," Pete took up the story. "She was feeling poorly again and was worried she'd go back into the hospital. One of these days, she knew she wouldn't be coming out. She worried about Ben, knew his mom wasn't able to take care of him, and knew if he stayed in town, he'd turn out like all the rest of his family." Pete stopped, surveying the thinning crowd, before continuing. "Elsie sent Ben inside, and she told me that she had straightened up too late to help her daughter, but she wanted to help Ben. She wanted us to take Ben if it came to that.

She had all the custody papers made up and asked me to sign. I was more than willing. It wasn't a week later that we got the call. Elsie had a heart attack and was back in the hospital. I went to town to get Ben. Elsie never came home again. She lived a couple of months in a nursing home. One of the last times I took Ben to see her, she reached out to me and said, 'Break the circle with Ben.' She didn't want him to be a drunk at twenty. We didn't either. Ben is a great young man. I'm proud to call him a son. I think he's broken the circle."

Kasey nodded. Ben had told her enough about his early life to know what it had been like for him growing up and how much he owed this ranch family. She watched Ben and Josie dancing to a slow tune. "I think Ben found the right girl to keep him on a good path too. Josie is really a dedicated young lady. They both want to come back to the reservation to live, and I know Josie wants to be a good role model to young kids. I think they will both be that."

The dance ended, and Ben and Josie took the microphone from the band and thanked everyone for coming. They thanked Josie's folks and Pete and Anne for all they did for them, not only raising them but also putting on this wedding. Then, they said they'd be leaving and asked the guests to gather for the throwing of the bride's bouquet.

"You better get in there," Pete said to Kasey. "Pretty nice bouquet."

Kasey just laughed, not making any move to get up. "Think I better get my life in order before I think about all a bride's bouquet represents," she said. "I am just starting to feel like a whole person again. I'm in no hurry for anything else."

***

The ranch yard was finally empty and quiet. The church chairs had been folded up and sent back to the church. The tables had been cleared off and cleaned, folded up, and put in the garage for some future need. Pete and Cole sat on the porch surveying the bags of trash piled in the yard, ready to be hauled away in the morning. The men could hear Kasey and Anne washing salad bowls and platters in the kitchen.

"After this afternoon, the quiet is even more peaceful than usual," Pete remarked.

Cole nodded. "It was a good day, though. But it was good to do this in the afternoon. I think I am getting too old for the late-night parties."

"You've just had too many all-night road trips," Pete smiled. "Gets to wear on you, doesn't it?"

"How long did you and Mom rodeo?" Cole asked.

"Not all that long," Pete answered. "We both had competed some before we got married, but after that, we went down the road a couple of years, is all. Your sister sort of came along and ended it for your mom, and this ranch opportunity came up, so we jumped on it, and here we are, still in the same place."

"Good place to be," Cole smiled at his dad. "I'm thinking it might be time after this season to stop. I'm riding good, drawing good, and staying healthy, but damn, that ground is harder now than it used to be." Cole took a breath and looked around the yard. "I find that when I drive in here now, I look forward to being here, and when I drive out, I don't really want to leave. Maybe that is the biggest clue that I will soon be ready to quit."

Pete didn't reply to that right away. The silence was comforting between them as they sat with their own thoughts. Finally, Pete began to talk.

"I have always wanted you to come back and take over this place. And I am getting to the age when I wouldn't mind stepping back a bit. There is nothing I'd like better than you coming home to stay, but it has to be when you are ready, not when I want it to happen."

"I want to finish this year out," Cole said. "Winning the bronc title last year was sort of a thrust to try harder this year, either to do that again or to make it in the bulls. But I don't think I have to prove anything anymore, not to myself or anyone else. Making the Finals as many years as I have is proof enough that I belong." Cole paused and thought for a minute. "But winning one more title would be something, and I am in a position to do it. I'll ride this year out and see where it goes."

The men heard the women laughing about something in the kitchen and paused their conversation to listen. Pete looked over at Cole.

"That Kasey girl is a treasure, isn't she?" he said.

Cole nodded, "She is that. For all that has happened to her in the last couple of years, she is a survivor."

"Anne even mentioned the other day that she sure wished Kasey could stick around more," Pete said quietly, watching Cole out of the corner of his eye.

A slow smile spread over Cole's face. He knew what his father was hinting at. "Well, that is good to know," Cole remarked evenly. "I'm hoping that maybe she'd want to come home with me next year." Cole turned to look at his father, his demeanor turning serious. "She's more than a treasure; she's real. She's who I want to spend my life with."

Pete couldn't hide his grin. "So, what does Kasey say about that?"

"Oh, Dad. I'm just at the hoping stage," Cole laughed. "Kasey needs this year to find herself before she thinks about any relationships. She's a smart girl and said something to me shortly after I first met her. She said she might date some guys, but she wasn't going to be serious about anybody for quite some time. She knew there was a chance she'd fall for someone just because she wanted a substitute for her lost family. She's right about that. And I know I don't want to be a substitute for her father or brother. I'll let her grow up this year. There's time."

CHAPTER 12

COMPLICATIONS

The summer run was in stride by the time Ben and Josie's wedding weekend was over. Ben and Josie only took the weekend for their brief honeymoon, and then they were home to repack and load the horses and head to North Platte, Nebraska, with Kasey and Cole. From North Platte, Cole flew off with Ted to compete at other rodeos, most notably Reno, Nevada. Kasey had a phenomenal week at North Platte, boosting her lead in the barrels by a wide margin. It seemed her horses couldn't put a foot wrong. Cole placed in the bulls at North Platte, but in Reno, Nevada, he won the bulls and placed second in the broncs. Ben had a good week at North Platte by placing fourth in the doggin', but he also went to Kingfisher, Oklahoma, and won the doggin' there. All three of them were in the standings and riding high on adrenaline.

Kasey, though, was feeling the effects of the days of travel. She had welcomed the week at Cole's ranch, thinking that was all she needed to get on her game again, but she found herself tired more than usual lately. She was grateful whenever Cole traveled the same way and would drive for her. She couldn't seem to get her energy back up to normal, and it took a toll on her on the road. She hadn't been to a doctor since the summer before her family was killed, so Kasey made an appointment with her family doctor in Denver for the end of July. Maybe she was iron deficient, and some iron pills would help.

***

Cole was riding with Ben, and they were heading toward Oklahoma City. They both were up that evening, but then Cole would catch a flight to Canada and hit Ponoka, Alberta. The payoff up there was huge. Cole had tried to talk Kasey into driving to Canada, but she wasn't feeling up to a 1600-mile one-way trip. He thought she was going to be in Oklahoma City that evening.

Cole was dozing in the passenger seat when Ben poked him awake.

"Hey, that isn't Kasey's outfit, is it?" Ben asked.

Cole sat up and looked up the road. "It appears to be from this angle," he said. "Slow down, and we can check."

As they got close, the men could see Kasey's big roan horse standing in the stock trailer. Ben eased the pickup and trailer to the side of the road and Cole made haste to get out and head to Kasey's pickup. It was a warm day but not hot, so the horses were comfortable in the shade of the trailer. As Cole approached the driver's side of the pickup, he noticed the windows were rolled down for ventilation. Reaching the door, he looked inside. Kasey lay on her side on the seat.

"Kasey!" Cole called, jerking the door open. "Kasey, are you all right?" He reached out to shake her.

Kasey came awake, startled, and sat up, blinking the sleep out of her eyes. "I'm okay," she said. "I got so tired I just had to stop for a nap."

"Shit, girl, you scared me," Cole complained. "Scoot over and let me drive. You can sleep the rest of the way." Cole looked over at Ben. "I'll meet you in Oklahoma City."

Kasey was quiet when Cole climbed in. "How long have you been this tired?" Cole asked her quietly.

"I just can't seem to get my energy up," Kasey explained. "I think after last year and the Finals, I have lost the adrenaline boost that kept me going. I think I am iron deficient or something. I'm going to my doctor for a physical later in July so maybe he can prescribe something for me. But I bought some vitamins yesterday, so hopefully, that will help too. It's not like we eat well on the road."

"Let's look at our schedules when we have time tonight." Cole looked over at Kasey. "If I can't drive with you, I'll see if I can find someone to ride with you and help you drive. Too bad Josie had to go home, or she could have helped you."

"I'll be all right," Kasey said. "I just need to get my rest. And with the Fourth of July rodeos coming up, it will be hectic."

"After the Fourth, I'll drive with you to Calgary," Cole told her. "That rodeo is over a week long, so if you aren't trading out anywhere else, you can get some real rest before coming back for the last half of July."

Cole looked over at Kasey. She hadn't slept enough, and he could see her eyes were drooping. "Here, lie down," he coaxed her. "You can use my leg as a pillow."

Kasey dropped gratefully to the seat and laid her head on his leg. It wasn't even a minute and her eyes closed. Cole looked down at her, sleeping peacefully and ran his fingers through her hair. *This is the way it should be,* he thought to himself, and after this year, he hoped that if she wanted to keep competing, he'd be driving her full-time.

***

Kasey did more sleeping in Calgary than anything else. There was a vast vendor fair attached to the rodeo, big-name entertainment, and parades, but for the most part Kasey stayed pretty close to the camper and the horses. Ben and Cole were entered up at Calgary, and their trailer with the horses was parked next to Kasey's. Many a night, they sat on easy chairs Kasey had stored in her trailer tack room and watched the contestants visiting back and forth. But Ben and Cole didn't stay at the rodeo grounds. They had a motel room they shared. Josie came for a couple of nights, but she had a part-time job at home, so she couldn't spend the whole rodeo with them. The nice thing for Kasey, when Cole and Ben were at the same rodeo and stayed in a motel, was that Kasey could shower in the men's room. Kasey took many showers in the men's room when they weren't there. Sometimes, Cole got an extra key and gave it to Kasey. She appreciated the use of the shower. Her homemade shower system in her camper was tight in her small space and required hauling water in and out. Driving to a motel and taking a nice hot shower with unlimited water was much easier.

The men's motel was not too far from the rodeo grounds. It was a one-story, mom-and-pop motel laid out in a U-shape with tables and chairs in the center. Ben loved to play poker, and many nights after the performances, a card game went on. It was one such night when Kasey drove in for a shower after a performance. Cole sat with some other cowboys visiting and hashing over the performance, and waved to Kasey as she went in.

"When the hell are those two going to shack up?" Bill Bose asked Ben as he dealt the cards. "They been doing this sharing of the motel for a year now."

"Huh?" Ben looked up. "Oh, Cole is just helping her out. She's pretty young, and he feels bad for her being alone."

"Shit, Ben," Bill retorted. "That man has been following that girl around all spring. And she's been right there waiting. Old Cole is missing his chance."

Ben looked quizzically toward the motel room where Kasey had disappeared. "She's just getting a shower," he said. "She's a great gal. She's not looking for anything else."

"She's just a successful buckle bunny looking to add to her collection. Cole's buckle is her next one," Bill laughed. "She's no different than the rest of the girls who chase around here."

Ben bristled at that. "Kasey has her own buckles, plenty of them. She doesn't need Cole's. They are just friends. Cole just took her under his wing. Doesn't mean a thing."

Bill studied Ben, thinking. "Tell you what," he said, "I'll bet you fifty they shack up before the end of summer."

"I don't want to bet on that," Ben said, uncomfortable with the conversation.

"Put your money where your mouth is," Bill taunted. "By Labor Day, those two will hook up. That girl is gonna get laid, and it's going to be Cole doing the laying."

Ben felt trapped, but he was also angry. He was too close to Cole, and maybe he was missing something between Kasey and Cole. Kasey was such a nice girl. She wasn't a tease, or fast, or anything but proper. But he was backed into a corner here.

"Fifty, you're on," Ben scowled. "Now, deal the damn cards."

***

Kasey sat in the waiting room nervously. Three days she had spent in Denver, and she wanted to leave. It was Deadwood this weekend, and she was up Friday. This was supposed to be a regular doctor's check-up, but her doctor had her go to the hospital yesterday for tests, and she was waiting now to see him about the results. Her first appointment had been on Tuesday, and it was Thursday already. She was up tomorrow afternoon in Deadwood, so she needed to make some miles today to get there on time. It was only one go-round this year in the barrels so the payout would be considerable. Deadwood was a favorite, so she didn't want to have to turn out. It was an added bonus to make her run on Friday afternoon and be able to relax and watch rest of the performances with no pressure of competing. But she was concerned. The doctor had not given her any indication of what he was seeing, but she could see he was troubled.

It was almost 1:30 when a nurse called her in. She wasn't taken to an exam room but rather to the doctor's office. Dr. Thompson was in a chair behind his desk, and he indicated a chair opposite for Kasey. He didn't make her wait long; he came right to the point.

"Kasey, I am not sure what I am seeing, but I do know this is serious. I've called the Mayo Clinic in Minnesota, and you are scheduled there for further tests and to see specialists at the end of August. I know that sounds like a long time to wait, but it takes time to get appointments scheduled. Plus, you need to get your affairs in order before going there. If this is what I think it is, you will be there for quite some time."

"Get my affairs in order?" Kasey asked, stunned.

"Honey, I know you are rodeoing. I know you are hauling horses. You need to find a place for them to go for an indefinite time." Dr. Thompson was serious. "If I am correct, this is something that is very rare. I don't even want to name it because I don't have the equipment here to do all the tests. But the doctors at Rochester will know. There are some experimental treatments. But there is no guarantee. I can't tell you what the outcome will be. You might want to contact your sister."

"But she's in Europe," Kasey stammered. "What will it help to have her know?"

"It might help you to have someone with you."

Kasey nodded slowly. "So, are you saying that this might kill me?"

Dr. Thompson hesitated before answering. "Yes, that is a possibility. If it is what I think it is, there has been some success lately, but it is spotty. Whatever the outcome, the road will be long. You will need to stay in or near the hospital for quite some time." Dr. Thompson said. "The doctors at Rochester will be able to give you more information after they do tests. And maybe I am all wrong. I am just a family practice physician and have never had experience with this. But I want you to be prepared. Find a place for your animals and get to the Mayo Clinic on time. My nurse has all the paperwork and the information." The doctor looked sternly at Kasey. "Don't blow this off. If I am right, your only chance is to get to Mayo's and see what they can do."

***

Kasey pulled over the mountain into Deadwood at eleven the next morning. She had picked up her horses and driven halfway after she left the doctor's office the day before. She was all cried out. She felt hollow inside. One part of her wanted to find Cole and tell him, but her rational side told her to keep quiet. There wasn't anything Cole could do. She knew what he would try to do. He would draw out of Deadwood and any other rodeos he had entered and would help her "get her affairs in order." But she didn't want him to do that. There was a limit to what one could ask of a friend. This was Cole's year. He was well up in the standings in both the bulls and broncs. She couldn't ask him to give that up.

Kasey had four hundred miles from Denver to Deadwood to think about this. When she concentrated on her situation, she knew where to take the horses. She would take them to her dad's former foreman and his family. They would keep the horses and ask no questions. Steve had been the foreman on the ranch when Kasey's father had bought it. Steve had stayed on, needing a steady job. He was a young man with a wife and three young children. They were barely making it on the foreman's pay the previous owner gave them, but they got the house and a few acres around it to live in for free. Steve broke horses on the side to supplement the family income. Kasey's dad had recognized the ability and drive of the young man. Not being a rancher himself, Mr. Jacobs handed the reins over to Steve entirely and raised his pay. The foreman's house was remodeled, and a bedroom was added to accommodate the growing family. The only extra work Mr. Jacobs had asked of Steve besides running the ranch was to help Kasey realize her dream of training and running a barrel horse. Steve and his wife had been instrumental in Kasey's life for the two years that Kasey lived on the ranch.

In the second year that Kasey's dad owned the ranch, Mr. Jacobs sold the foreman's home and 160 acres of the ranch to Steve. It had been a dream of the young family to have their own land, and Mr. Jacobs helped them realize it by helping Steve get the loan for the land. Steve stayed as the foreman for Kasey's dad, but could also train horses throughout the year. When the ranch was sold along with investment properties to pay off the failed resort, Steve and Peggy had their land to stay on. Kasey still kept in touch with the family. She knew that Steve still trained horses and did day labor as a cowboy for all the ranches in the area. All the children were in school now, so Peggy was a teacher's aide at the nearby school. Because Mr. Jacobs had helped them acquire the ranchette, they hadn't had to move when the rest of the ranch was sold. Kasey knew Steve and Peggy would be forever grateful to Kasey's dad for that. They were good people. Kasey could leave the horses with them and know the animals would be well cared for. She called them from a pay phone along the road and alerted them that she was coming for a visit.

As Kasey pulled into the Deadwood parking area and eased her outfit through the maze of trailers, she saw Cole standing near the Korkow Rodeo tack trailer. Cole was visiting with several other cowboys. He raised his hand to her in greeting, but didn't follow her as she found a place to park. Kasey was glad about that. She had to get her emotions under control before she talked to him. And she had the afternoon performance to get ready for. She'd decide by tonight how much she would tell Cole.

***

It was a hot afternoon at the rodeo. There was little wind, which seemed out of sorts for a South Dakota rodeo, and the sun had beat down on the arena and gravel lot around it. Kasey led the barrels after this performance by almost two-tenths of a second. She figured she would place, but that wasn't on her mind right now.

After the barrels were over, Kasey cooled off Roan by walking at the far end of the parking lot, near the end of the arena. She could watch the bull riding from there, although it was across the length of the arena. Still, she could see well enough to watch Cole. He had a National Finals-rated bull which was a good one. The announcer built up Cole's ride, mentioning that Cole was well in the lead in the standings. So often, when an announcer built up the cowboy, the contestant's ride seemed to go to hell. But it wasn't that way today.

The bull came out of the chute with a high leap, twisting in the air and coming down to a spin away from Cole's hand. The bull did not weaken, spinning and kicking high, but Cole didn't weaken either. The crowd was on its feet, cheering on Cole's stupendous ride. Kasey also wanted to shout, but didn't want to spook Roan. She just watched and was happy for Cole. This was Cole's year. Maybe his last year. And then she knew what she would do. She knew what she had to do.

***

Cole wandered over to Kasey's camper after the performance. He was still grinning from his ride.

"Great ride," Kasey smiled at him. "I don't think anyone is going to catch you."

"It felt good," Cole agreed. "But there are a lot of good cowboys here. I won't count on a win until it is over. You had just as good a run too. The week off didn't hurt ole Roan."

"He was raring to go," Kasey agreed.

"I'm going back to the motel to shower," Cole said. "You want to catch a bite to eat later? Maybe walk the midway?"

"I'd like a shower too," Kasey agreed. "Can I come over in an hour?"

"They won't give me extra keys, but I will wait in the room and let you in," Cole said. "Or if Ben is playing cards outside, I can leave my key with him."

"Actually, I wanted to ask you something," Kasey said. "Would you just wait for me to get there?"

"Sure," Cole replied, "but you want to ask me now?"

"No, if you aren't in a hurry to leave the motel, that would be fine. I'll be there as soon as I get the horses settled and get clean clothes laid out." Kasey turned away. "I'll give you time to shower first." She needed to talk to Cole later, not now. "See you later," she called, moving toward her horses.

***

The sun set earlier in the Deadwood gulch than the surrounding prairies because of the high mountains surrounding the town. The shadows were getting long outside the motel when Kasey arrived. Ben and several men were grouped around a picnic table, laughing as they played cards. Kasey waved to Ben, but went to Cole's room. Cole was wearing clean jeans and a T-shirt and watching television when Kasey arrived.

233

The room was unlocked, and he called out to her to enter.

"You look relaxed," Kasey teased. "And clean. That looks good after this dusty afternoon. Doesn't it ever rain in South Dakota? I thought the dust would choke me today."

Cole smiled. "Supposed to rain tomorrow. Probably rodeo in the mud next." He lay on the bed, propped up against the headboard. "You wanted to ask me something? Ask away, and I'll get out of here and let you use the room."

Kasey laughed at him. "I'm going to use the bathroom. There's a door on it, and I don't think you will break it down, so let me take a shower, and then I'll ask. You aren't in a hurry, are you?"

"No," Cole said, surprised, "I'm not in any hurry. Sure, knock yourself out. I'll wait until you get done."

There was a rerun of Bonanza on the television. Summer television was terrible–all reruns. But Cole had never been a big television fan, so Bonanza, even a rerun, was better than whatever else might be on. It wasn't like there was much choice as there were only two stations. Cole heard the shower running, then quiet, then the hair dryer. Finally, there was a click, and the bathroom door opened. The door was behind Cole, and he heard Kasey speak.

"You watching something really good?" she asked.

"A Bonanza rerun," Cole replied, not turning to look at her. "I probably catch less than half of that series in the winter, but I've seen this is one before. But there was nothing else on."

"You won't mind then if I turn it off?" Kasey asked, entering the room. She walked to the TV and turned it off.

Cole just stared. Kasey was wearing one of those terry cloth towel wraps. Callie had one of those way back in the day. It wrapped around the body and was secured with a button at the top. Pop the top button, and the whole thing would slide off. He'd enjoyed that when he and Callie were still a couple. Kasey's was the same, and like Callie's, it barely covered all the important parts, barely reaching over Kasey's rump.

Kasey moved to the bed and settled beside Cole. Cole was afraid to move. All he wanted was to pop the top button.

"I want to ask you something," Kasey said seriously.

"Um, you want to get clothes on first?" Cole managed, trying to sound casual.

"I want to stay with you tonight," Kasey said softly, watching for Cole's reaction.

"Here?" Cole was slow at processing her words or her meaning.

"Cole, I want you to make love to me," Kasey answered. "Here."

Cole sat up straighter and reached out to Kasey, touching her on the neck. She felt like silk and smelled of perfumed soap. "Are you sure?" he asked.

"I'm sure," Kasey replied. "I'm ready. I want this." She hesitated then added, "I want this with you." Then she popped the top button of the terry cloth wrap.

***

Ben was aware that Kasey had gone into his and Cole's room. There was nothing unusual about that, but it was unusual that Cole didn't leave then. *Maybe,* Ben thought, *there was a good show on TV.* But he watched the room as he played cards. He wasn't the only one watching.

"The television just turned off," Bill Bose said non-chalantly, studying his cards. "That flickering silver light shows through those flimsy curtains, and it ain't there anymore."

"Probably nothing good on," Ben said, measuring his words. "You going to raise?"

"No," Bill replied, "I got nothing."

The card game continued, but Bill was intent on the motel room. "The room light just went off. I'm feeling that fifty already."

Ben didn't reply. There was nothing to say. He willed Kasey or Cole to come out of the room, but by midnight, he handed his fifty over to Bill. He was going to have to look for another place to sleep, he guessed.

***

When Kasey woke, the clock read 3 a.m. Cole slept curled around her, his arm over her waist. She hated to move and hoped she wouldn't wake him. Her heart was already breaking, and she hadn't left yet.

The night had been almost magical. Cole had been so gentle with her the first time, knowing it was her first. They had rested then, talking about the performance that afternoon and about nothing important. It wasn't long before they made love for a second time. It was as if neither could get enough of the other. When Kasey lay exhausted in Cole's arms, Cole spoke.

"I love you . . ." he began.

Kasey put fingers to Cole's mouth, shushing him. "Not tonight," she whispered. "Don't say anything tonight."

"Won't change tomorrow," Cole tried again. But again, Kasey put her fingers to his mouth.

"Tonight, just hold me," she said. "Just hold me like you will never let me go."

And that is what Cole did. Neither was hungry, and Kasey was quick to drift off to sleep. Cole lay and watched her for a long time, until he, too, drifted off.

Now, at 3 a.m., Kasey quietly slid open the top dresser drawer and groped inside. Most motels had stationary there, and this motel was no different. Kasey took the paper and went into the bathroom. When she came out, she was dressed. She propped the note on the side table and quietly stole out of the room.

When Kasey opened the door of her pickup and threw her overnight bag into the passenger seat, she had tears running down her face.

"What?" Ben was startled and jerked awake when the bag hit him.

"Ben!" Kasey cried, surprised. "What are you doing in my pickup?"

"Wasn't sure if I was welcome in my motel room," Ben groused, blinking at her. "The bed in our topper is dirty. Neither of us has slept in it for weeks. I figured if you came out, I would know when I could have my bed back."

"Oh, Ben," Kasey said, trying to brush the tears off her face. "I am so sorry. I didn't think about you."

Ben looked at Kasey closely in the dim light of the pickup's interior light. "God, Kasey, you're crying! Cole didn't hurt. . ." He couldn't imagine Cole hurting Kasey and couldn't get out the words.

"Oh, Ben, no! Cole would never ever hurt me." Kasey understood what Ben couldn't say. "But I think . . . I hurt him." Kasey looked seriously at Ben as he climbed out of the cab. "I just didn't realize . . ." Kasey choked, then continued. "Take care of him, Ben. Please take care of him." Kasey got into the pickup, started it, and drove away. She couldn't look back, and she couldn't stop the tears, so she didn't see a stunned Ben staring after her.

***

Cole came awake when the sun streamed in through the flimsy motel curtains. The night came back to him, and he knew immediately that Kasey was not there. He saw Ben sleeping in the bed next to him. Cole got up and went into the bathroom. All of Kasey's things were gone. There was no hair dryer, no clothes, no remnant left behind. Cole wondered how long ago Kasey left. He hadn't heard a thing.

Ben was sitting up when Cole came back into the room.

"How long have you been here?" Cole asked, looking around the room. He reached down by the side of the bed and picked up the pale blue terry cloth wrap that Kasey had worn. It lay where it dropped the night before. Cole fingered the material, feeling the softness, remembering the night.

"Kasey left about three," Ben replied. "She was crying."

"Crying? Did she say why?" Cole was concerned.

"Tried to hide it from me, but she was." Ben pointed to the side table. "Looks like she left you a note."

Cole picked up the folded stationery sheet. His name was printed on the outside. Slowly, he opened the note and read it.

Cole, I am so sorry. I shouldn't have stayed last night. I am afraid I hurt you by staying. But just so you know, I love you too. I think I have for a long time but just didn't realize it. But I have to go away. I can't say why, just that I have no choice. Forget all about me and win those titles. Win for me. My heart is breaking. K

"What does she mean by 'she has to go away'?" Cole asked Ben, puzzled. He wasn't alarmed yet, but this note made no sense. There was nothing about the night that hurt him. He knew he loved this girl before last night but last night was a gift he didn't expect.

"Let's run out to the rodeo grounds," Cole said, looking for his clothes. "I have to see what she means by this."

But when the two men reached the rodeo grounds, Kasey's outfit was gone. No one had heard or seen her leave, but there were few people up and around in the wee hours of the morning. Cole stood surveying the parking lot. Now, he was getting alarmed.

***

Kasey took two days to get to Steve and Peggy's ranchette. She could have made the trip in a day, but she needed the time to get her emotions in check. She didn't want to pull into their place a sobbing wreck. She needed time to get herself under control.

The ranch couple welcomed Kasey warmly, and their three children were ecstatic to see her again. The oldest child, a daughter, was thirteen now. When Kasey lived down the road, Nan would follow Kasey around or would ride with Kasey into the hills on the ranch. When Kasey left for college, eleven-year-old Nan was already a good rider. Now, at thirteen, Nan was more than competent. She was gearing up for her first year of high school and was hoping to be able to compete in the spring in the high school rodeos. But Nan had an old horse that she had used in Little Britches Rodeos, and the old horse was slowing down. Steve had a young horse that he hoped would be ready for Nan in the spring, but it would be a horse that would still need a lot of training and might not be ready for serious competition for a couple of years. There needed to be more money in the young family's budget to buy a high-powered, trained barrel horse.

On the second day Kasey was there, she spoke to Steve and Peggy alone after the kids were in bed. "I need some time to get away. I have things I need to take care of, and I can't take my horses with me," Kasey began. "I was wondering if I could leave them with you. I will leave you board money for them."

"Kasey," Peggy was surprised. "You are leading the world in barrel racing. Aren't you going to finish the season?"

"Well, I hope this won't take long," Kasey lied. "But it is just something I have to take care of. Knowing my horses are being well taken care of would mean a lot to me."

"Of course, we will take care of your horses," Steve said. "And you don't have to leave money for them. They can stay as long as you need."

"Well, I have a few days I can stay too, if that is all right," Kasey told them. "I thought maybe Nan would like to try out Roan. I could spend a few days riding with her, getting Nan comfortable with the horse. She could maybe take him to some jackpots or even a rodeo this fall, if you agree. I could let her use Roan then for high school rodeos in the spring. I'd like JC to rest, though. She has been so super steady, but she is young. I think she will be a better horse if she can take it easy for a while."

And so, it was decided. Kasey and Nan spent a couple weeks riding the mountains. Kasey put her troubles out of her mind for a few days and just enjoyed being with this family and pretending that all was normal. Kasey tried to relax, tried to forget, and tried to be normal for these few weeks. But every night in bed, she knew her world was shattering, and she could do nothing about it.

CHAPTER 13

ALONE

For the first few weeks, Cole scanned every parking lot they pulled into, searching for Kasey's outfit. As the days passed, he grew quieter and quieter. People began to notice the change in him. He was moody, irritable, and distant. At first, friends would ask him where Kasey was, noticing her absence as well. But his curt, "No idea" answer would stop further discussion. Finally, most people just kept their distance.

Ben missed his mentor and friend the most. They still traveled the country together, but Cole had little to say. Ben watched him search fruitlessly at each rodeo for Kasey. At first, Cole would ask others if Kasey had competed at distant rodeos, but there was no word.

"Where the hell did she go?" Cole burst out one evening as they pulled into another rodeo without seeing her pickup. "And why?"

Ben could hear his friend's frustration and see the fear in Cole's eyes. But Ben didn't have the answers. He could only stick with Cole. Despite his prickliness, Ben would put up with Cole. He knew his friend needed him now more than ever. The tables were turned, and Ben needed to help Cole now if only to walk at his side.

***

Kasey lay in the hospital bed, exhausted even though she had done nothing all day. She had good days and bad days. This was an in-between day. She didn't hurt today. She was just tired. Some days she hurt, some days she was nauseated, some days were like a holiday, and she could get out of bed, play her guitar and sing. She loved going to the children's ward and singing silly songs to the kids. Seeing the children struggling to live made her realize how lucky she was. She realized how much of life she had already experienced. These little children were just starting out, yet here they were fighting for their lives.

Kasey had a lot of time to think; to remember. She had been at the Mayo Clinic for almost two months. The rodeo season was almost over for the year. Her last *Sports News* had arrived, and she had combed the issue, looking at the standings as well as at the placings at individual rodeos. Cole and Ben were still doing well. Cole was sitting first in the bull riding and second by a few hundred dollars in the bronc riding. He had also inched into first in the All-Around standings. There had been a couple of articles on him lately. The writers all agreed that this was Cole's year. Kasey was glad for Cole. If this was his last year, he was going out in style.

And in the barrel racing standings, she had dropped from first to eleventh. By the end of the month, she might be out of it altogether. She didn't let herself think about that. She didn't have time for rodeo anymore. She just wanted to live. And she had to live. She had to live six more months at least. She was carrying Cole's baby. She desperately wanted this little life to make it into this world. If she could make it six more months, she would send word to Cole. But she would wait because living for six more months was going to be a struggle.

She had been just short of one month pregnant when she entered the hospital. Of the barrage of tests they gave her, one was a pregnancy test. That surprised her. It never dawned on her what the complications of that one night with Cole might bring. But maybe carrying Cole's child was the impetus she needed to live. The doctors wanted her to abort the baby, but she refused. If she could live, she could bring a new life to this world. So, the doctors had to work around her condition. They had to try alternative medicine and alternative treatments. Some worked for a while, some didn't. When Kasey responded favorably, she had been released from the hospital several times, and as an outpatient, came in every day for treatment. During those times, Kasey bunked in her camper in the back of the hospital parking lot. The nurses would check on her, knowing she was there. Kasey had such caring nurses. When she relapsed, she was readmitted. It was a vicious cycle of good, bad, and in-between days.

It was well past bedtime for most patients, and the ward was quiet. As exhausted as Kasey was, she couldn't sleep. That was the price she paid for sleeping so much during the day. Kasey laid the *Sports News* on her bed, too tired to keep reading. She was lying there, staring at the wall, when her favorite nurse, Milly, bustled in to check on her.

"How we doing tonight, kiddo?" Millie asked cheerily. She noticed the folded newspaper by Kasey's side. "You want me to put that in your drawer?"

Kasey nodded gratefully.

"Say, I was reading the *TV Guide* this evening, and a local station is featuring some new cowboy singer. Want to watch it?" Millie asked.

"Sure," Kasey said. "Maybe some music will help lull me to sleep."

Millie turned on the TV and clicked around the stations until she found the one she wanted. The announcer had just announced the singer. Millie watched Kasey as the man came on the screen. She saw Kasey try to sit up straighter in the bed, and Millie hit the button to raise the head of the bed. Millie noticed Kasey's intensity as she watched.

The song was about a cowboy hat and an episode in a café with a bunch of bikers. As Kasey watched, her eyes filled with tears. The song told of the bikers threatening to take the cowboy's hat, and the cowboy removing his hat and contemplating it before he answered. In the song, the cowboy told of an Indian friend who gave him a feather for his hat. Then he sang of a special lady who gave him the hat pin. That stanza finished by saying he might never see that special lady again.

Millie heard Kasey gasp. "You know that man," Millie said to Kasey. She noticed Kasey's eyes filled with tears.

"I met him once, is all," Kasey whispered, trying to get her emotions under control. "But I was there." The song ended, and the segment went to something else. Kasey turned away from Millie. "I'm really tired," she said. "I think I can sleep now."

Millie studied Kasey for a moment, and then, she looked at the *Sports News* in her hand that she was going to put away. Tucking the newspaper in her deep pocket, she left the room. As she went through the door, she heard the muffled sobs coming from Kasey.

*****

Ben and Cole were both in Ridgeway, Colorado and up the same night. The season was winding down, but they still had a bit over a month to go. Cole pushed himself, trading out at as many rodeos as he could get to, hooking rides with any vehicle going his direction, or hopping a plane if he needed to get to more distant rodeos. Looking for Kasey but not expecting to see her haunted Cole. She had disappeared, leaving a hole a mile wide in Cole.

The barrel race was on. Ben had put his horses away and was heading back to the arena to watch the bull riding when a roan horse went by him, jigging toward the entry gate. The horse looked familiar. It was with a start that Ben recognized Roan, Kasey's Roan. He was sure it was Kasey's horse, but it wasn't Kasey riding him. Ben broke into a run, weaving through the crowd outside the back of the chutes.

"Cole," Ben called, seeing him putting on his bull spurs. "Cole, look!" Ben indicated the arena, where the roan horse was coming in on a flying run.

Cole looked up, studying the horse. He looked back at Ben and then back to the arena. "That's Roan," he said. Cole watched the horse turn the third barrel and race toward home. It was a closed gate run so the rider pulled the horse up at the gate and waited for it to be opened for her. Cole turned and headed toward the out gate.

"Hey, you there," Cole called out brusquely to the young girl riding Roan. "That is Kasey's horse." Cole lunged forward, grabbing the reins of the horse. "What are you doing with Kasey's horse?"

The girl paled, looking wildly around. Ben came up beside Cole. "Cole, you're frightening her. Let the reins go."

Just then, a man came striding up. "Daddy!" the girl on Roan cried out. Cole turned the horse loose and turned to meet the man.

"This is Kasey's horse!" Cole repeated, trying to sound calmer. "Where's Kasey? How did you get Roan?"

"We are friends of Kasey," Ben said, trying to sound soothing. "We haven't been able to find her. We are worried."

The man looked at Ben and Cole and then up to the girl. "Go put him up, Nan, and I'll talk to these gentlemen." The man turned to Ben and Cole. "My name is Steve, and I used to be the foreman on Kasey's folk's ranch. Kasey brought her horses to us in August. She needed a place to leave them. Stayed with us for a few days and helped Nan get comfortable on Roan and told her to take the horse to some jackpots or rodeos. Said maybe Nan could use him for some high school rodeos in the spring. Then she left."

"Where did she go?" Cole had to ask.

"I have no idea. She was pretty vague on where she was going or why," Steve said. "She wanted to leave some money for the horse's care, but I wouldn't take it. A couple of days after she left, I got an envelope with cash in it. A lot of cash. It was postmarked from the next town over. All she said in the note inside was she would contact me when she could. I haven't heard a word since."

Cole got out his wallet and pulled out a folded piece of paper. Tearing off a small corner of it, he wrote the phone number of his folks on it. "If you hear anything, anything at all, call this number," Cole said grimly. "It's my folks' phone. Let them know. And if you talk to Kasey, tell her to call."

CHAPTER 14

ANSWERS

The season was over, but there was a month before the Finals started. Ben thought Cole might go home and take a break before the Finals started, but instead, Cole was entering rodeos to fill the time.

"You sure you don't want to take a break?" Ben asked. "You've been pushing pretty hard."

"You stay home if you want," Cole answered shortly. "I need to be moving."

Ben understood. Cole was driven by a memory and a hope. He couldn't rest yet, and home was not a haven. So, Ben called Josie and told her he would be home later. Ben felt it was not the time to let Cole go off alone. Josie was in her first year of teaching, but she understood why Ben thought he had to stay on the road with Cole. She would meet Ben in Oklahoma City for the Finals. She would take the days off for that.

Ben pulled into the parking lot outside the St. Paul coliseum about an hour before the evening performance. Cole had been snoozing against the passenger door, but he was awake and surveying the area as they drove in. As they wove through the parked vehicles, Ben saw Bill Bose come out between some cars and wave him down. Ben let the pickup roll to a stop and wound down his window.

"Hey," Bill said casually, "I was wondering if you'd be here." Bill reached into his pocket and pulled out his wallet. "Here, this is yours," he said, handing a folded bill to Ben. "I, uh, just don't feel right about that bet." Without waiting, Bill abruptly turned and walked away.

Ben unfolded the greenback and looked at the fifty in his hand. He glanced at Cole but didn't say anything.

"What was that about?" Cole asked.

"Just a bet I had with Bill a long time ago," Ben replied. "But I have no idea what he meant." Ben shrugged and put the pickup in gear.

When they had the horses out of the trailer, Ben and Cole made their way to the rodeo secretary's office. It was the same big room in the coliseum where Cole and Kasey had eaten a Thanksgiving meal the year before. Remembering, Cole walked grimly inside. The office was crowded with contestants. Some stood around visiting, and some studied the draw sheets pegged up on the walls. No one was talking to the secretary, so Cole walked up to pay his fees and get his number. He knew this secretary. She worked many of the rodeos that the Korkows put on. As Cole approached, she looked up.

"Cole, I didn't expect you," she said in surprise.

"I'm entered here, aren't I?" Cole replied bluntly.

The woman studied Cole for a moment and then asked, "Have you seen the latest *Rodeo Sports News*?"

"We've been on the road," Cole said. "Haven't stopped anywhere to try to get one. Haven't called home either."

The secretary turned and reached behind her to a table. She picked up a *Sports News* and handed it to Cole. "Page three, letters to the editor," she directed.

Cole looked at her quizzically but opened the paper to page three, located the letters to the editor, and began to read. As he read, he wasn't aware of the silence that had fallen on the room as every eye was on him. Ben stepped up, trying to read over Cole's shoulder. The letter was the only one in this edition of the paper and read like this:

To whom it may concern,
We have a young woman here who I know is one of yours. I have seen her name in the standings. She has been steadily falling in those standings these last couple of months. We are a big hospital, but there aren't many here who don't know this girl already. She sings to the children when she's able or sits in hallways and sings to different wings. Everyone here loves her, and yet, we have just met her. But the whole time she has been here, she hasn't gotten one visitor. I've concluded it's because no one knows where she is. I've worked in a hospital so long that I know how easy it is to die if the patient is alone and if that person has no support group. So, maybe someone out there needs to know, wants to know. Because this girl is special.
Someone concerned at Mayo Clinic, Rochester, MN.

Cole's hands gripped the papers so tightly that the edges tore. When he finished reading, he dropped the paper in front of the secretary and said as he turned away, "Draw me out."

"I already did," the secretary whispered under her breath.

Ben reached down, finished the letter, and turned to follow Cole out. "What about you?" the secretary called out. "Are you drawing out?"

"I'll let you know," Ben called back to her, and then he was out the door also.

Ben caught up to Cole just as Cole reached the pickup and was unhooking the trailer. He looked up at Ben.

"I need the pickup," he said. "See if you can find someone to hook to the trailer and pull you home or part way
home. Call my dad if you have to, and he will come for
you and the horses. Call my folks and tell them I'm going to Rochester. Tell them we found Kasey."

***

Between the city driving, the traffic, and getting lost
twice, it was almost midnight before Cole reached the
hospital in Rochester. He didn't know what building he
needed to go to, so he opted for the main entrance. This
was the only entrance that was open at that hour of the
night anyway. The lobby was dim, but the receptionist's desk was well lit. Other than one woman behind
the desk, no one was in the lobby.

"I'm looking for Kasey Jacobs," Cole told the receptionist. "I think she's a patient here."

"I'm sorry, sir," the woman replied politely. "But I
can't give information about patients unless you're
a family member. It's also well past visiting hours."

Cole expected this. He had had plenty of time on the
drive to think through his response. He was calm but
firm. "Look, Kasey is important to me, and I just found
out that she is here. At least I think she's here . . . somewhere here. Right now, I need to know that . . . for sure."

The receptionist studied Cole for a moment and then
turned to her files. "Give me a minute."

The receptionist pulled out a notebook, thick with
lists.

She moved down the alphabet, searching for Jacobs.
Then her finger stopped moving, and she read. She
looked back up at Cole, "Would you take a seat over

there for a moment, and I will make a phone call." She indicated chairs in the lobby.

Cole moved away and took a seat but watched the woman. She dialed a number and waited. When she spoke into the phone, the woman lowered her voice so Cole couldn't hear her words.

"Is Millie working tonight?" the woman said quietly into the telephone receiver. "Yes, I'll wait."

It took several minutes before someone came on the line.

"Millie, someone is here to see Kasey Jacobs," the receptionist hesitated, listening. Then she continued, her voice dropping low, "He's a cowboy." She waited a minute more, and then she hung up.

"Someone will come and talk to you in a few minutes," the receptionist said.

It took fifteen minutes before anyone came to talk to Cole. It was hard to wait, not knowing what had been said. Why couldn't the receptionist just say yes to Kasey being here or . . . not?

Finally a nurse came to talk to Cole. The woman was in her mid-fifties, tall and slender, with a kind face.

"I understand you are asking about Kasey Jacobs," the nurse said. "I'm a nurse here. My name is Millie Johnson. How may I help you?"

"I want to see Kasey," Cole came right to the point.

"I'm sorry I can't take you up to see her at this time. Visiting hours start at eleven a.m. They have been over for many hours." The nurse sat down in a chair opposite Cole. "I can tell you she is resting comfortably tonight.

"Can you tell me what is wrong with her?"

"I can't. The doctor starts his rounds at about seven a.m. I could alert him that you are interested in seeing

Kasey." Millie looked curiously at Cole. "Do you mind if I ask you why you want to see Kasey?"

"Kasey disappeared several months ago, and I have been searching for her ever since," Cole looked solemnly at the nurse. "Frankly, I love her. I was going to ask her to marry me. And then she was gone."

"Why would she leave you without a word?"

"I can't answer that totally, but I have an idea," Cole said. He reached into his pocket and pulled out his battered wallet. Inside, he found the folded-up motel stationary, and unfolding it carefully, he handed it to Millie. "She left me this."

Cole watched the nurse's face as she read the short note. When she looked up at Cole, he continued, "These words: '*win those titles. Win for me*' give me a clue to her thoughts. This was going to be my last year on the circuit. So far, I couldn't put a foot wrong. Everything was lining up for not only my going to the National Finals again but to win the bulls, broncs, and all-around titles. And she was going to win the barrel race title. If she told me she was sick and coming here, I would have come here too. I think she knew that. She gave up her title because she had to, but she didn't want me to do the same. '*Win for me,*' Those were the keywords. And until this evening, I missed them completely."

Nurse Johnson nodded thoughtfully, carefully folding the note and handing it back to Cole.

"May I ask you how you knew to find Kasey here?"

"There was a letter to the editor in our rodeo newspaper. It didn't name Kasey by name, but she is the only one who fits the circumstances. I knew right away. Anyone who knew Kasey knew right away. I saw it tonight before the rodeo," Cole smiled sadly. "I just walked out of the rodeo office, got in my pickup, and came here.

Now, I'm waiting." Cole sat, watching the nurse sitting across from him, studying her hands. "Did I pass?" Cole asked softly.

Millie looked up at Cole. "This wasn't an interview, but yes, I think you passed," she smiled. "Look, I can't take you up to the ward. I couldn't hide that, and it could get me in trouble. You could get a motel and come back in the morning . . ."

"I'm not leaving here until I see Kasey," Cole interrupted her.

Millie thought about this. "Okay, there is a small waiting room on the third floor with couches. I'll take you to it. It is near the pediatric intensive care ward. You can stay there until morning. The doctor makes his rounds at seven a.m. I'll catch him and tell him you are here. He won't lose his job if he takes you in to see Kasey."

Cole rose. "That will do. But if I haven't seen a doctor by seven thirty, I'll search every floor."

"You do that, and you will probably get thrown out," Millie smiled. "But I'll get the doctor to see you. I promise you that."

Millie showed Cole to a dimly lit waiting room on the third floor. It had three couches and a couple of reclining chairs.

"There is a restroom across the hall," Millie told him. "Now I have to get back to work before I find myself in more hot water than usual." Millie smiled mischievously before asking, "That is a Black Hills Gold pin in your hat, isn't it? It's nice."

Cole took off his hat and looked at the pin. "Kasey gave me that," he said softly.

Milly nodded. "I'll get the doctor here in the morning. Be patient." She turned to leave.

"Thank you, Nurse Johnson, for writing that letter," Cole said softly before the woman reached the door. Millie turned toward him, scrutinizing him. Then she nodded and was gone.

***

The doctor found Cole at ten minutes after seven in the morning. Cole had been awake for an hour. He had dozed some during the night, but it was a fitful sleep. He knew he was close to Kasey, but that wasn't enough. He needed to see her. He needed to know more.

"I understand you are here to see Kasey Jacobs," the doctor began. "Nurse Johnson explained that you just heard where she was."

"I have been looking for her for months," Cole answered. "What can you tell me about her condition?"

"I can't tell you anything unless Kasey gives me permission to talk to you," the doctor replied. "Maybe we should go and see Kasey and ask her?" The doctor watched Cole's reaction.

Cole was already standing. "Yes," he replied anxiously. "Let's go."

The doctor led Cole up two flights of stairs rather than taking an elevator. On the fifth floor, they walked down a long hallway and stopped at a door. "Wait here," he told Cole. "I want to see that she is awake and willing to have a visitor."

Cole heard the doctor's voice drift out of the room. "Kasey, there is someone here to see you. May I bring him in?"

Cole didn't hear Kasey reply, but the doctor came to the door and nodded.

Cole entered the room. It was a small room with one hospital bed in it. Kasey lay on that bed, propped up with pillows. She was thinner than Cole remembered. Her arms in her hospital gown were more bone than flesh, her eyes sunken in her face. Her hair had been freshly brushed and lay long on her shoulders, and she looked toward the door curiously. When she saw Cole, her eyes filled with tears, and she reached her thin arms up to him. Cole didn't say a word. He just went to the bed and sat, drawing her to him. Kasey buried her head on Cole's chest and began to cry.

The doctor watched for a moment, then mumbling under his breath, "Welcome to the hospital," he backed out of the room and left the two alone. Kasey had her first visitor, and apparently, he was the right one.

***

"Don't ever do that to me again," Cole whispered into Kasey's ear as she relaxed against him, tears drying.

"What?" she asked.

"Go off and leave me without a word," Cole told her gently. "I can't go through that again."

"I'm sorry, Cole, I am," Kasey replied, "but I didn't want you to sit around my bedside, worrying, missing rodeos. It would be like putting you in a cage."

Cole leaned back, pushing Kasey away from him where he could see her face. "Silly girl, that is what people do for each other if they love each other."

"But . . ."

"No buts. I'm here, and I'm staying." Cole pulled her back to him again. "Furthermore, you are just going to have to marry me now. I don't intend to let you go again."

"Oh, Cole, no!" Kasey's eyes filled again with tears. "I don't know what the future holds. Who knows if I'll even get out of this place? What kind of a life would that be for you?"

"Let me worry about that. All you have to worry about is getting well." Cole pushed her away again. "So, are you telling me you don't want to marry me?" He smiled at her mischievously.

"No, I'm not saying that, but I . . ." her voice trailed off.

"What are you saying?"

"This disease, it could kill me. They keep trying new things, hoping something will be the answer. And, there is more," Kasey hesitated. "I'm pregnant."

"You're pregnant? Don't you think you should have shared that with me? We both know I'm the father." Cole was serious.

"I would have told you . . . planned to tell you. But I wanted to make sure I made it long enough to have the baby," Kasey explained. "I have a letter written, in case I were to, well, just in case. The letter would direct the hospital to notify you."

"All the more reason to marry you," Cole said firmly. "How about Friday? My folks would come. There must be a chapel in the hospital?"

Kasey regarded Cole before answering. She seemed to be more in control. "I'll marry you, but you have to promise me something. You have to promise me that you will go to the Finals, and you will win. Promise me that no matter what may come, you will go to the Finals and win for me."

***

It was decided. Kasey and Cole talked to the doctor, and he saw no reason they couldn't get married Friday afternoon after Kasey's treatment. They would have the weekend then before Kasey had any more procedures scheduled. If Kasey had a good week, the doctor would release her for the weekend so that she and Cole could spend a honeymoon of sorts away from the hospital.

While Kasey slept in the afternoon, Cole went through her dresser by the bed. He saw the envelope she had with his address on it and knew this was the letter she had referred to when they first talked. Cole also found Kasey's sister's contact information. Kelly was with a musical troupe in Europe, but there was an emergency phone number he could call and leave a message. Cole conferred with the nurse in charge and got the phone number to the nurse's station. Then he found a pay phone in the lobby and made the call.

***

Nurse Millie Johnson brought Kasey to the chapel in a wheelchair. Her sister, Kelly, walked beside Kasey, holding her hand. Kasey had on a simple white wedding dress, a gift from Anne. Anne brought it with her when she had flown in on Thursday. It had been Anne's wedding dress and Anne's mother's dress before her. Anne had offered to go to a bridal store and find Kasey a new dress, but Kasey loved the heirloom gown and chose to wear it. It was a little big on Kasey, but she didn't care. It was perfect.

As the pair rounded the corner, Kasey gave a quick gasp. People were lined up in the hall outside the chapel. She recognized nurses and doctors, but the many men and women from the rodeo circuit who stood smiling at her was a surprise.

"Oh, my," Kasey breathed to her sister, Kelly, "How did they know?"

"You don't think I am the only one who Cole called, do you?" Kelly smiled at her. "And I think these people are here because you are pretty special to them."

When Kasey approached the chapel door, Cole's father, Pete, signaled inside, and the sounds of the wedding march began to play. Kelly gave Kasey's arm a squeeze and left her, going down the aisle of the chapel. Pete came to Kasey and helped her up.

"You ready for this, honey?" he asked her.

Kasey looked up at Pete. "Only if you help me," she smiled. Then, with Pete as her escort, she entered the tiny chapel.

The tiny chapel was crowded to overflowing. As Kasey entered, the overflow of people in the hall crowded in behind her, taking their places along the wall. Cole stood in front waiting; Ben at his side as his best man. Cole had on a western sports jacket and freshly ironed jeans. He smiled widely when Kasey emerged in the doorway. Kelly reached her maid-of-honor spot and turned to watch Kasey walk slowly down the aisle on Pete's arm. When Pete and Kasey reached Cole, the minister began to speak.

"We are gathered here to witness the union between this man and woman," the minister said. "Who gives this woman in marriage?"

In a strong voice, Pete said, "All the friends and family who love her."

It was barely eight a.m., and Cole sat with his feet up on the porch rail, surveying the activity, or lack of it, in the yard below the house. The ranch had changed little in the last two decades since he and Kasey had returned to the ranch to begin their life together. Today, long tables were set out and covered with tablecloths, waiting for the food to be brought out. He could hear the activity in the kitchen on the other end of the porch, but he made no move to go and help. Cooking wasn't his expertise. What he should be doing is helping with chores. But he didn't feel like that either. The kids were taking care of the horses. The kids were adults now, or at least college kids and pretty darn responsible. He saw Gabe leaving the barn on the 4-wheeler, pulling the small manure spreader to the newly cut alfalfa fields in the distance. He knew KaLee was still cleaning stalls. She and Gabe would fill the little spreader at least one more time before they were finished. Cole didn't need to help them. They were more than capable.

There would be no horses to ride today. The kids turned all the stalled horses out to pasture for the day. The horses got a day off. The colts in the corrals would be fed and let out into their pasture. This was not a riding day. This was a burial day.

Cole knew his dad and some other menfolk were in the living room visiting to give Cole space. It wasn't like he had just lost Kasey. She had been gone over four months. But it was bitter winter then, and after a small family funeral, her body was sent off to be cremated. Today was her burial. They called it a "celebration of life." And it was going to be just that. A celebration of a life well lived, well loved.

As Cole sat, he saw the dust boil up from the gravel road. It was too early for guests to arrive. The burial was slated for eleven a.m. Here it was only eight a.m. But when the vehicle on the road came in sight, he saw it slow at the ranch drive and turn in. Cole didn't recognize the car. It was an older model Buick, big and boxy, covered by more dust and dirt than their gravel road would have put on it. Cole watched the car roll down the road and pull up to park in front of the house. He couldn't see the driver through the shine of the sun on the window shield. Cole stood and leaned on the corner post of the porch, waiting for the driver to climb out.

The car door opened slowly, and a lean man in a cowboy hat, jeans, and boots, stepped out. He was twenty years older than the last time Cole had seen Ted Langley, but he was the same bowlegged cowboy that Cole used to travel with.

"You lost?" Cole called out.

"Heard there was a free meal here," Ted answered back. "Thought I'd come up and see."

"Well, come up and take a load off," Cole smiled at his old friend. "Too early for food."

Cole met Ted at the porch steps, holding out his hand. Ted took it in his, and they shook. Ted looked up at Cole. "How you doing?" Ted asked softly.

"Oh, you know, learning how to live alone. You?"

"Well, I'm a long way from being alone," Ted laughed. "I'm still learning how to live with chaos."

The two men sat on porch chairs, and Cole put his feet up on the rail again.

"I heard about Kasey last February," Ted started, "but not until quite a bit later."

"We just had a small family funeral," Cole said. "Kids thought she'd like to be buried here on the ranch and in the springtime when the grass was green. I was all for it. I think Kasey would have liked this."

"I heard you had a little girl," Ted said. "You must have had more after that?"

"Doctors didn't want Kasey to have more. It was too hard on her. But we adopted a boy a couple years later. Gabe was almost two when we got him, so the two are about the same age. We used to joke that they were our twins." Cole smiled, then pointed toward the barn. "There they are, the two of them. Don't look much like twins, do they?"

Ted looked toward the barn. Gabe was carrying a couple of buckets, and KaLee was beside him. Gabe was tall and lean. KaLee was petite and shapely. Gabe was dark-skinned, clearly showing his Native American roots. KaLee was a miniature of her mother, with golden brown hair and fair skin. While the two men watched, KaLee said something to Gabe, and they both laughed.

"Kasey wanted more children, so we got to taking in foster kids. Gabe came to us at eighteen months. When the parental rights were terminated, we adopted him." Cole stopped talking, watching the two young people disappear into the indoor arena. "Those two are as different as they could be, yet they have been close, like twins all their lives."

"KaLee, that's a pretty name," Ted commented.

"Kasey liked the name. We used the first two letters of her name and the last two of my name to write it," Cole grinned at Ted. "Then we added an extra "e," so she wouldn't be called Kale, like the vegetable."

"Makes sense."

The men grew quiet then before Ted spoke again.

"It's been almost twenty-two years since you got married," Ted said. "You ever miss it, the rodeos and the travel?"

Cole surveyed the yard before answering. "I got everything I could out of rodeo. That last Finals was a fitting end. Two titles and the All-Around. It doesn't get much better than that. I walked out of that arena and knew I'd never go back. I had Kasey, our little girl was just coming then, and I had this ranch. There isn't a single thing I regret."

"What about Kasey? Did she ever run barrels again?"

"She hit some close weekend rodeos and jackpots just to keep JC in competitive form, but she didn't have any desire to go down the road again," Cole answered. "She never was entirely well. She got tired a lot, and she was smart about pacing herself. She might not have won a title, but everyone knew who she was after her one Finals. She knew that. And she was saving JC for KaLee. KaLee started out in the junior rodeos on JC. The old mare had slowed down some, but she gave KaLee a great start."

"What happened to the roan gelding?"

"Kasey left him with her friends in Colorado, and their high school girl rode him for years. He even took the girl to the college national finals. He had a good place there, so Kasey never brought him home." Cole looked down the road for a minute. "Those people are coming today, so you might meet them."

"You expect a lot of people?"

"If just the local people turn up, it will be a big enough gathering," Cole answered. "But then we have the relatives, my sister and her kids and their families, and Kasey's sister, Kelly, and her family. I expect we will have a couple dozen young people who came through our home as foster kids. A lot of them kept in touch with Kasey. And then there may be a renegade rodeo bum or two that turn up. You never know about these things."

"Rodeo bum, huh?" Ted grinned. "You gotta be one to know one."

"You had a couple kids when we were traveling together," Cole said, changing the subject. "You have any more?"

Ted laughed. "You could say that. When our eighth child was a month old, I started getting horny again, and my wife met me at the bedroom door with a knife," Ted chuckled at the memory. "Wasn't so funny then, but she told me I had a choice. She had made an appointment for me with a doctor. Either I could go under the knife of a doctor, or she'd cut the damn thing off. She pretty much meant it. I took the doctor."

"Eight kids. That is more than a basketball team!" Cole grinned at his friend. "You got any still at home?"

"Three in high school and one in junior high," Ted answered. "Why do you think I still drive an old clunker like that?" Ted pointed to his car. "Kids keep you broke. I wouldn't give any of them up, though."

Cole nodded.

"Dad," KaLee's voice broke into the men's thoughts. "You still have your shit-kicker boots on and an old shirt. You better go change soon."

Cole looked up at his daughter, who was coming onto the porch, Gabe beside her. "I'll do that, Daughter, in a few minutes. Come here and meet an old friend of your mom's and mine."

Cole introduced the two young people to Ted. "Ted was at our wedding. I used to travel a lot with Ted." Cole explained.

"I know that name," Gabe commented. "You rode barebacks back in the day. You went to the Finals many times."

"You must look at ancient rodeo history," Ted smiled.

"Bareback riding is my event too," Gabe told him. "Full ride to the University of Wyoming on a rodeo scholarship. Made the college finals every year so far."

"What year are you there?" Ted asked.

"Just finished my junior year. So, I have one more year, and I'm out."

"Gabe went to Laramie," Cole said, "and KaLee got a full rodeo scholarship to Colorado State University. So, they rodeo in the same region and at the same rodeos. Helps keep the travel down to go and watch them." Cole smiled at KaLee. "Especially when they both have made the college finals all three years."

"Dad, just watch the time," KaLee cautioned. "You need to spiff up some. Nice meeting you, Mr. Langley. Come on, Gabe. We still have to work on Mom's display."

As Gabe and KaLee moved off, Cole clarified, "They are putting together mementos of Kasey's in the barn entry. Scrapbooks, pictures, her buckles, things like that. They wanted to do it, so I said have at it. But I thought I'd just stay out of all these preparations. Glad you came early."

The two men fell silent. Finally, Cole spoke.

"She leaves a big hole," he said. "But we knew it was coming. We prepared, she and I and the kids. She made us all promise to go on living. So, we are doing that. We get through today, and we start to live again. But her memory will never leave any of us. She brought joy wherever she went. But for me, she left me a son and daughter and enough memories to keep me for the rest of my life. I had her for twenty-two years. I can't complain." Cole stood up and stretched, giving Ted a slap on the shoulder. "Come on in and see my dad. You remember him, I'm sure. Then I'd better go change before KaLee comes back. She can be some like her mother, you know." Cole looked out toward the barn and smiled. "She's actually a lot like her mom," he said softly, then turned and went into the house. "She's the best gift Kasey ever gave me."

AUTHOR'S NOTE

I met my husband at a Bob Barnes rodeo in Wisconsin in the summer of 1969. We were married in January of 1971. By this time, Jeff was a pick-up man for Korkow Rodeos, and our favorite rodeo was Deadwood, with St. Onge and Mobridge as close seconds. In the fall of 1970, I was still going to school at Colorado State University when Jeff called me and told me a young cowboy he knew from CSU was coming to Sioux Falls to the Flying Buckskins Rodeo that the Korkows were producing. Jeff wanted me to jump in with the CSU cowboys and come for the weekend. That was probably the most risqué thing I had ever done, but freshmen in college have no brains, so off I went to South Dakota. I remember there were three other college cowboys in the car. Our mutual friend, Marc Bluett, was a nice guy I met through the college rodeo club. I don't know how Jeff knew Marc, but when Jeff visited campus, he stayed with Marc. A young easterner was riding with us in the car who the guys had taken under their wings, so to speak. He wanted to cowboy. I do not know this young man's name, but everyone called him Vermont. I think he was from Vermont. The car had back seats that reclined backward so we could lay and sleep. Since we drove through the night, Vermont and I spent much of the night laying in the back, visiting and laughing. I don't remember who the third man was, but they were all great guys and treated me like a lady. I met a lot of nice guys while rodeoing and married one.

At the Flying Buckskin's rodeo, my fiancée won the bull riding and while not placing in the saddle bronc riding, he won the most money in two events and brought home the All-Around Saddle. I remember standing on the sidelines, thrilled that Jeff had won. I remember Erv Korkow standing nearby, a big grin on his face that one of his men was the All-Around winner. Special memories of special times.

So, if my readers haven't figured it out yet, those few episodes in this story regarding the unnamed young pick-up man and his girlfriend are actually Jeff and me. While maybe not exactly the same year as when this story takes place, near 1972 or 1973, it is close. There was a parking meter in Deadwood, South Dakota, outside the Franklin Motor Hotel that was crooked for decades, all compliments of me and my poor driving expertise. For years, the orange snake Jeff won for me in the carnival basketball game sat on a beam in the log cabin at my folks' mountain ranch. The rest of the stuffed animals were given away. Eventually, the snake was devoured by hungry rodents and thrown away. The barbecue outside of Deadwood was such fun, and my folks were there for it. Jeff and I did make out at the Spooner, Wisconsin rodeo in front of the pickup owned by the other pick-up man and his wife. I worked for the couple who ran a horsemanship school for youth in Wisconsin, and they hauled me with them to several rodeos. The announcer did announce that Jeff had just fallen in love right before the chute gate opened. I know he rode his bronc, but I have no idea if he placed.

Being part of the Korkow ranks was something I loved, hanging out by the tack truck, helping to make sandwiches, unsaddling horses, and carrying flags. There was a Thanksgiving dinner at the coliseum in St.

Paul put on by the rodeo secretary and the Korkows. I was a terribly shy girl then, and the Korkows all made me feel welcome. A heartfelt thank you to Jim Korkow who called me one night and gave me the details of the St. Paul Rodeo that I had forgotten. Jim did pull the stagecoach out of the arena, and Bunky did lay down in front of the bull, Hellcat. And I think it was at the rodeo at McCook, Nebraska that all the rodeo contestants camping on the rodeo grounds had ear corn boiled over a fire and hot dogs bought by Erv Korkow, so we didn't have to leave to eat and then pay to return to the grounds. After dark, we climbed the fence and went to watch the concert. I remember it was a woman country singer, but I don't remember who she was. Special memories.

I did run barrels at Deadwood for a couple of different years. What a thrill that was, but as I told the fictional Kasey in this story, I had an honest little mare, but she and I were not the caliber of the great girls and horses. Still, I don't regret a moment. Fun times, special people, the rodeo world. They live in my memory.

The scenes that depict Clay Dixon, are simply figments of my imagination and based on the Chris LeDoux song, "This Cowboy's Hat," written by Jake Brooks. The song, which included the words Kasey heard while in the hospital, is one of my favorites. It was the impetus for the café scene at Mule Creek Junction. I remember going to Denver once with my husband and a friend of his, and we stopped at the little run-down café at the junction there. Typical of so many little out of the way places, the food was good and plentiful, and the place was run down. In other years, I traveled that road many times, going back and forth to my parents' Colorado ranch. Several times, the parking lot of that little café was crowded with motorcycles, especially when the Sturgis Motorcycle Rally was going on. Somewhere along the way, my story was influenced by Chris' song.

I never got to meet Chris LeDoux. I remember the first time I heard of Chris LeDoux and heard a song of his. I was traveling from Colorado to South Dakota to meet Jeff's folks. We got engaged on that trip. We stopped at the Korkow Ranch and stayed a night with Jim and Carol. I was shy and pretty much stuck like a glove to Jeff's side. We were sitting in the living room, and Jim brought up that he had a song that Chris had recorded. I think he played it on an old 8-track player, either then or later. The rest all knew Chris, but I had no idea who he was then. It was the beginning of a life-long love affair of LeDoux music.

Chris traveled for a brief time with my husband before Jeff and I married. They were up at the rodeo at Kissimmee, Florida, and my folks, who wintered in Florida, knew that Jeff was there. My folks went to the rodeo to watch him. After the rodeo, Dad went behind the chutes and found Jeff, offering to take him out to supper. Jeff told Dad he would love to join them, but he was traveling with a couple of other guys, so he had better not. In customary fashion, Dad told Jeff to bring his friends, and he would buy them all a steak. One of the friends was Chris LeDoux. This was well before Chris won his title or had made a name in the music business. But my folks always remembered that. Jeff told me later that he and his friends felt like they hit the jackpot getting a free steak supper. They weren't much more than broke cowboys then. Until he died, Dad would tell that story and smile.

In the summer of my seventeenth year, I was working for Carolyn and Art Adams in Janesville, Wisconsin.

They had a horsemanship school for teenagers. I lived the whole summer with them. On some weekends, after our students were packed off to their homes, Carolyn and I would join Art at some rodeo. Art was a part-time pick-up man for Barnes Rodeo and also at some small local rodeos.

At one small rodeo, Carolyn and I arrived by Saturday noon, and we enjoyed a leisurely afternoon at the rodeo grounds. I didn't know anyone, but Art and Carolyn did, and I was introduced to several people. One person I met was a man probably ten or fifteen years my senior. I have no idea anymore what his function at the rodeo was, but I know he was there for a reason other than simply as a spectator. Looking back, I wonder if he supplied some of the stock. Before and during the rodeo, this cowboy, much my senior, visited with me along the fence as we watched the action. I don't remember his name. I don't remember being interested in him in any way other than he was friendly, and he was knowledgeable about rodeo and the contestants. He sought me out the second day also, and it was nice to have someone to stand with, ask questions, and feel like I belonged.

It is funny how our memory works, but I feel like Kasey in this story felt much this way about Cole, at least at first. But more than that, I think men and women of all ages can appreciate and enjoy the company of the opposite sex without always being infatuated by them. And if, as in my fictional story, love develops, sometimes it happens slowly without the fanfare of passion and intrigue. I wonder if that man was my inspiration for Cole. Sometimes I have no clue where the ideas come from. Thankfully, they just come.

I miss those rodeo days and the friends we made. The memories fade but are never truly forgotten. Today, I can watch rodeos every night on TV. My late husband, Jeff, would have loved that. But for me, I miss most the rodeo friends and being part of the rodeo world . . . the rodeo road.

ACKNOWLEDGEMENTS

I have to give a shout out to my sister-in-law Dayna Beckman for editing this manuscript for me before I sent it off to the publisher. As an author, I read a manuscript so many times that I usually read the words that are supposed to be there rather than what is actually on the paper. Dayna works tirelessly to try to get my manuscripts as clean as possible and for that I send her a huge thank you.

A big thank you to my horse and rodeo friends who read the manuscript and gave me feedback. From the horse side of things, thank you to Renee Toft, Kathy Triebel, and Jan Christensen, and from the horse and rodeo world, thank you to Judy Garon, Adele Enright, Steve Gander, and Jerry White.

A special thank you to Jim Korkow who returned my call with information about the St. Paul Rodeo that I had long since forgotten. If I got anything wrong, chalk it up to I am a fiction writer with poor long-term memory!

Thank you to JuLee Brand of W. Brand Publishing for believing in my stories and seeing them to fruition. I count the day I met you at the Tucson Festival of Books as one of the luckiest days of my writing career.

THE OVERNIGHT BUNS OF ANNE SANDERS

This recipe came from my mother-in-law who learned it from her mother by example. We called it Grandma Weber's Buns. When I asked for the recipe, Gram admitted she didn't have one. She had learned to make these buns before she was fourteen when her mother lay in bed dying of cancer. Her mother would give her directions and Gram would follow them. So, one day, Gram made buns and I followed her around, taking notes and insisting she use a measuring cup. It was this way I got the recipe. My family loves these buns, and both my daughter and daughter-in-law are proficient in making these for their families. Enjoy!

I start approximately midmorning to noonish, (So much of this depends on how warm your house is and how quick the dough rises . . . you will have to experiment to know what works in your place best.)

Boil together:
   4 cups water
   2 cups sugar for 5 minutes,

Remove from heat and add:
   1 cup Crisco (I like the butter flavored, but any
      will do . . . or even straight lard will work)
   1 Tablespoon Salt

Let cool to lukewarm (cool enough not to cook the eggs or kill the yeast when you add those)
Add to lukewarm sugar water:
    4 eggs
    1 package regular yeast

Mix with mixer (after years ruining small hand mixers, I finally bought a big stand mixer)

Begin adding flour, beating with mixer for as long as you can. If you have dough hooks, you can continue mixing in flour for as long as your mixer holds up!! You will use approximately 10 to 12 cups, but I never measure anymore . . . just go by feel. Not too stiff, not too sticky. To work with the dough, liberally grease hands with Crisco or lard. When ready, set the dough out to rise in a large bowl that is liberally greased.

Cover bowl with a towel and let raise to double. I usually aim at punching it down about 5 p.m. but dough has a mind of its own. Punch down and let raise to double again, usually around 8:30 p.m. (See Note Below.) After the second rise, make dough into bun or dinner roll size shapes, place on a greased cooking sheet and mash them down (squish them down with your hand). I usually get a dozen on a regular cookie sheet if I want them hamburger sized. Then let them rise overnight covered with a light towel. In the morning, bake at 350 degrees approximately 20 minutes or until tops are golden brown. I usually bake two cookie sheets of them at a time, changing the sheet on top shelf with the sheet on the bottom, etc., after 10 minutes.

Notes of Interest:
The original recipe said you set the dough out to raise the first time by two p.m., and it may be ready to punch down about six pm. Then the dough will raise again by ten p.m. enough to mix into buns. This was my mother-in-law's original instructions to me. Gram started making these back about 1940 or so before air conditioning. My buns seldom meet Gram's original schedule. Since I don't like late nights, I tend to start my buns earlier in the day and get them mixed out into buns earlier in the evening but then you could possibly be up at five a.m. to bake them (in the summer this happened when I didn't keep the air conditioning on high at night, but now I usually am up about seven a.m. to bake). Again, this depends on how warm or cool you keep your house.

This recipe just takes time to get to 'know' the dough and how it works for you in your home. I had no experience with bread making when I started making these, so while they sound complicated, if I can master them, anyone can. They are a crowd pleaser.

Good luck.

Johny Weber

Johny Weber is a retired assistant professor at Northern State University in Aberdeen, SD. Since childhood, her life has revolved around horses. Marrying a rodeo cowboy, she moved with him to the plains of South Dakota where they both competed in rodeos and then turned to a ranching lifestyle. Her career in education began by teaching first grade in 1975 and by retirement, she was teaching graduate courses to teachers in a state-funded program. Johny and her late husband raised a son and daughter on the prairies of the Cheyenne River Indian Reservation.

Also by Johny Weber
the *Mountain Series*

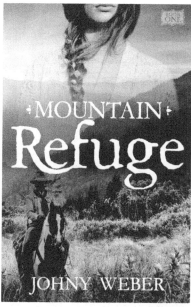

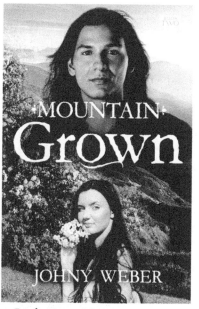

Book One, *Mountain Refuge*   Book Two, *Mountain Grown*

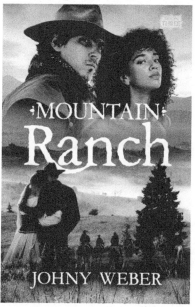

Book Three, *Mountain Ranch*

Made in the USA
Monee, IL
05 January 2025

73764671R00173